WOLFSBANE HALL

HAZEL ST. LEWIS

WOLFSBANE HALL

HAZEL ST. LEWIS

COPYRIGHT

Editing:

- Developmental Edit: Charlie Knight
- Line editing & Proofreading: Noah Sky
- Proofreading: Andrea Halland

Design and Art:

- Cover Design: © 2025 by Giulia F. Wille Art
- Character Chapter Headings: Graphic Soul Art

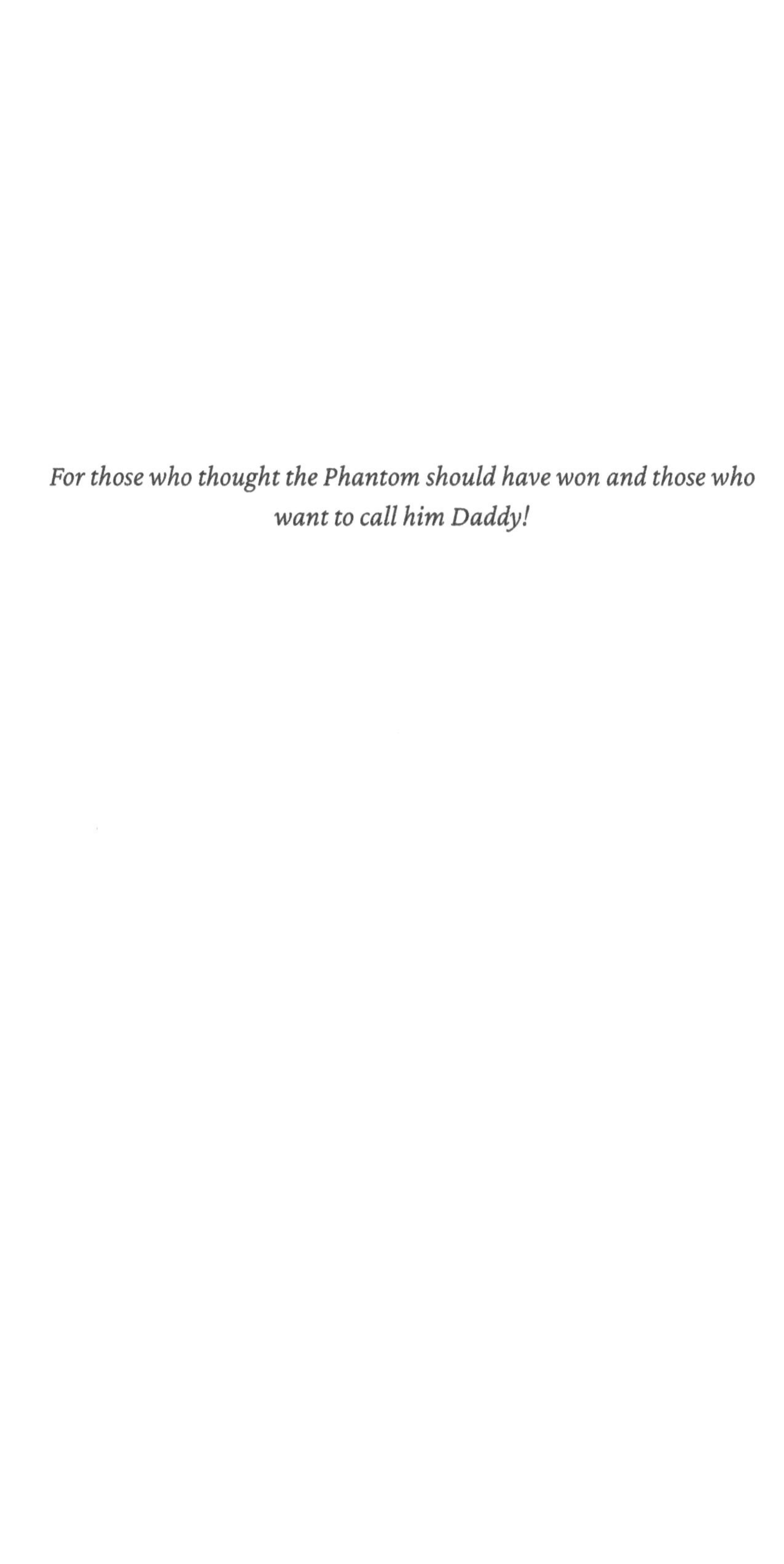

For those who thought the Phantom should have won and those who want to call him Daddy!

AUTHOR'S NOTE

Friday, November 3, 1939
Grand Ballroom
San Francisco, California

Celestine Sinclair hated being a murderer.

She hated blood dripping through her finger-tips and clumping in her hair. She hated watching poison devour a body, and the feeling of her hands stretching around a slender throat.

Everything about murder was ghastly.

But if Celestine had to choose, her favorite way to kill was suffocation. A pillow over the face while a person was drugged and unconscious. It was two and a half minutes of hell—hell she deserved—but at least it was quiet and didn't leave a mess.

Celestine loathed messes.

Unfortunately, the very nature of her profession required more...*theatrical* deaths. The audience didn't come to Wolfsbane Hall to watch, as they put it, "dull and tedious deaths." No, like vultures, the rich, pompous pricks wanted carnage.

They wanted a show.

So, Celestine Sinclair would give them one. That was her one objective as an actress at the infamous nightclub: *show above all else.*

Show above one's own sanity.

"You're wasting time," said a voice forged from darkness,

twisting from the room's shadows. Smoky sweet, like honeyed whiskey. Sugary, yet potent.

The Specter—the magical and mysterious owner of Wolfsbane Hall, the glittering palace at the edge of San Francisco, filled with as much mystery as magnificence. It was a place where patrons became a part of a murder mystery show. Glitter, grandeur, and witchcraft were laced through every inch of the manor, interwoven into a tapestry of entertainment.

"You must prepare for your next murder," the Specter whispered in her ear, darkness twirling and cloaking her from the patrons meandering into the Grand Ballroom—the club's showroom.

"I know, Specter," Celestine breathed. She wanted to call him something else, but she didn't know his true identity—no one did. People saw glimpses of him in the shadows and smoke, or as an animated, talking painting. He appeared silhouetted like a ghost in the reflections of the house's grand mirrors. But no one ever saw his face. He was a beautiful voice, singing grand arias and speaking through the walls and the calls of mockingbirds.

The Specter was everywhere in the house, and yet nowhere to be found.

Impossible to truly know. Impossible to hold. Impossible to keep.

"Open your character card, sweet Cellie," he said, the darkness vibrating around her.

Celestine flinched at the words. Opening the card would only confirm her as the night's killer, and she absolutely didn't want to do that. There would never be a day or a lifetime or even an eternity in which Celestine would get used to killing someone. And she'd certainly never enjoy it like some of the sick patrons of Wolfsbane Hall.

People came here to play out their fantasies of either

murdering or dying, and to Celestine, both options were equally disturbing.

At least the Specter had given her a heads-up this time. She was tonight's murderer, and that fact made her both furious and sad. She wanted to curse his name or punch him...but then, she didn't know his name.

Besides, she wouldn't harm him anyway. She couldn't.

He'd saved her life, and she'd given him her soul in return. Not literally, but he would forever own her and could forever have his way with her. And oh, she often wished he would take physical form to do just that. Fuck her. Hold her. Whisper dirty things into her ear.

Nine years of unbroken tension were far too much.

Her core grew wet. That's all it took, the mere thought of touching him.

"You have thirty minutes to open your card and perform the deed." His voice snapped her out of the fantasy.

"I know," she repeated with a huff as she nervously ran her willowy fingers through platinum-blonde curls. Celestine detested this role, but she would do anything for the Specter. He was her family, her home, her everything, and all she ever wanted was to make him proud. So, even though Celestine despised it, she would kill for him.

Always.

"Timeliness is next to godliness." The Specter spoke through the mouth of a Victorian painting, using the fanciful duchess's lips to form the words.

Celestine bit her lip, slightly smudging her bloodred lipstick. "Right."

With her crimson fingernails, she lifted the corner of the envelope housing her character card and sucked in a deep breath as she prepared for the onslaught. Pinching her eyes tight, she tore open the envelope as if ripping off a bandage.

The impact was immediate. Thoughts, feelings, a script, and a character background poured into Celestine's mind. She felt it like a physical blow, even needing to steady herself against the wall for a moment.

A character was transferred into her mind, teaching Celestine how to speak and behave during the game, while providing her with lines to say throughout the night. The role instructed her on whom to talk to, flirt with, and insult, as well as whom to avoid.

Every person at Wolfsbane Hall, from the patrons to the six cast members, received a card and played a part during the show, each becoming a new person. The only difference between the cast and a patron was that the cast helped the Specter progress the story along its desired path. Patrons tended to lose focus and meander, so they needed a push in the correct direction—sometimes physically.

There was only one rule at Wolfsbane Hall: *every murder must be solved.*

So, the cast became the Specter's hands during the show, ensuring it reached its conclusion. If a patron refused to be the murderer on any given night, the cast would step in for that, too—although typically, Everett or Babette preferred to take on that role.

Never Celestine.

She opened her eyes and officially became Dorothy Wolf, a movie star who had just signed a seven-year contract with a massive Hollywood studio.

A beautiful ingénue.

An object to be desired and a typical role for Celestine. She always played either the tempting seductress or the innocent ingénue. Beautiful, sweet, and all one's desires wrapped up in a tiny, busty package. It was a part designed for Celestine because she was the Specter's muse, and because she had considerable assets. Tits and ass, as the vulgar might put it.

"On with it," the Specter said as her shadow on the wall. "How do you plan to do it? And please, give me the short version. You can tell the longer story tonight in your rooms."

During the show, the Specter was often impatient and blunt, demanding that she be succinct. He disliked long, repetitive stories. Celestine put up with it because late at night, after the games, the Specter was kinder and warmer—even a friend. But show Specter was driven, consumed by the story and his genius.

"So?" the Specter asked when she waited too long to respond.

Knives, the character, Dorothy, whispered in Celestine's mind. While the characters Celestine played sometimes felt real, they never were. It wasn't like being possessed. The magic gave her a script to follow and a history to portray. Still, because Celestine proscribed to Stanislavski's and Strasberg's method acting techniques, her characters often felt real. She became her role for one night only.

However, there wasn't much to imagine at Wolfsbane Hall.

Much of it was *far too real.*

"Stabbing," Celestine finally said. Short and straightforward, just how he liked it.

The character, Dorothy Wolf, planned to kill her lover and director because he wouldn't cast her in his newest film. A film worthy of Oscar consideration.

A slight that caused a murderous rage.

The script gave many options for completing the murder, but the character favored knives and intimacy.

"Wonderfully horrific," the painting said as the shadows followed up with, "Knives will be intriguing." The Specter loved using multiple communication mediums, like a hovering voice, darkness, and animating objects. All at once. It was often disorienting for Celestine. "Now go."

The darkness receded, and Celestine was left alone in the nightclub of dreams—or, more accurately, the nightclub of nightmares. However, some people reveled in nightmares. Celestine only reveled in the stage. At least she could do that well.

Every detail of the grand mansion was unique and dripping with money. Even the wall sconces were formed from electrum, because gold or silver alone wasn't special enough for the Specter. The ballroom was no exception. It sparkled as she stepped onto the floor, with ten crystal-carved felt tables and two ruby-sculpted bars on either side.

Friday nights were casino nights. Anyone wealthy enough to pay the extravagant admittance fee could gamble and take part in the murder mystery, which meant all the usual patrons were here—the usual suspects.

Trying to avoid them and focus on her work, Celestine made a beeline for the bar. Liquid courage never hurt anyone. She ordered a rum cocktail and swiveled to survey the room for her target. He was nowhere to be found, and she was getting antsy. The script forced Celestine to be excited to murder one of her lovers. The character was a real Bonnie Parker, this one. Ruthless, devious, and exceedingly foolish.

Because Celestine truly became her character, she, too, took on that excitement, but it merged with Celestine's own feelings of dread. The result caused heart palpitations and a bead of sweat to roll down her back.

She just wanted to get on with the show. But no one was around to act with.

"The ingénue again. How very typical." The words jerked Celestine out of her pondering, and she looked up seconds before a cocktail waitress threw a glass of red wine in her face and down her emerald silk dress. "Ah, now you're a soggy mess. At least it'll match your personality."

Celestine sputtered as her lipstick streaked down her chin.

How dare she? Someone fire this wretched girl! Lines of the script screeched inside her mind. The magic was adaptive. If another character altered the story, the Specter's magic would modify the script in real-time. It was like reading off cue cards, but the cards existed inside her head.

But Celestine didn't say her lines; she just swallowed and squared her shoulders, holding her head high like a regal queen as confusion struck her stomach. The person who had accosted her was Babette Fontaine, a fellow Wolfsbane Hall cast member who frequently played the French maid or mistress roles. But Babette and Celestine's roles were not supposed to overlap much tonight. They didn't even share the same storyline.

Celestine barely had any dialogue with her character, meaning Babette was going rogue.

It was unsurprising; the girl was like a rose in full bloom, with thorns dipped in vinegar and laced with poison. Babette was a tiny thing that seemed entirely harmless, but her bite was deadly.

"What was that?" Celestine whispered, her eyes darting to the crowd now forming around them. "That wasn't a part of the show."

"No, but it felt good," Babette said in a low voice as she placed the empty wine glass on the bar and leaned closer. "I am sick of you stealing my parts. I was the ingénue long before you, and I will be again long after you're gone."

Celestine shivered at the threat, but also because the liquid now varnishing her dress had mixed with the cold air, causing goosebumps on her flesh. "I'm not stealing anything." Nor did she even want this role. Babette could have it; she could bask in its cruelty.

Babette grunted, unconvinced, but she pulled away, and her face changed, the mask of her role sliding over her features. Thick, wavy chestnut locks bounced around her powdered porcelain face. "I am so, so, so sorry," she said with a thick French accent. An accent that was as fake as the beauty mark painted beneath her left eye. "I didn't mean to, mistress." Turning her head so only Celestine could hear, the brunette breathed, "I hope you choke on poison tonight."

All around them, patrons stretched their necks to listen and get a better view, for the show had officially commenced. Technically, the show started when a single patron entered the building. There was no big announcement; the mystery was a part of the spectacle.

But the audience's attention was a clear sign. Celestine needed to take on her role and become Dorothy fully.

"Oh no, my dress is destroyed," Celestine whined in an over-the-top, rich, spoiled lilt, keeping with the persona. The true Celestine wanted to say nothing. She'd rather grin and bear it, but the character would never do that. So Celestine gritted her teeth and fanned herself dramatically while speaking her lines. "Oh, my night is ruined—ruined, I say!"

Celestine patted her soaked dress with a napkin she'd grabbed from the bartop and sighed hyperbolically, the hysterics on full display.

Babette rolled her eyes and sauntered away smugly like the wildcat she was.

"Sometimes I want to throw my wine on you, too," James Ashbrook said as he approached, his eyes sparking with mischief.

Excited shivers danced in Celestine's stomach at the sound of his rich baritone, and she sucked in a breath, taking him in.

His presence had a visceral effect. Some men were too handsome for their own good, like all the Ashbrooks. The three men, fellow cast members, were rich, too. James was the tallest and most refined. To Celestine's utter dismay, he was exceedingly charming and, oh, so good at tempting her into mistakes. It didn't help that he was blunt as a lead figurine, speaking in precise, concise, and sometimes cruel phrases. Unfortunately, she was drawn to bad boys who showed no emotion.

An added benefit was that they tended to have massive cocks and be great in the sack.

"No, you don't," Celestine finally responded.

He raised a midnight eyebrow as he chewed a piece of gum —the man loved chewing gum. It was like a tic. "Don't I?" When the sides of his lips drew up, she finally grasped his meaning. "It could be fun to lick off your smooth...folds."

Her center pulsed, wanting him to make good on that offer.

"James," she whispered and hit him with her fur scarf. "Don't be so vulgar."

He shrugged. "I can't help it."

"You very well could help it."

"Ah, but I don't want to." James stepped closer, and her back hit the bartop. "Nor would *you* want me to." With one more step, he pinned her, his arms snaking around her waist. "It seems like it's my lucky night. I get you all to myself, and my meddlesome cousins are nowhere in sight."

Celestine's eyes snaked through the room, not seeing the twins either, but they had to be somewhere. Despite being as rich as Croesus, they were in the cast, and the cast never missed a show.

James leaned in and placed a chaste kiss on Celestine's lips. The gesture wasn't new. Outside of the shows, they were sometimes lovers. Mostly when he was bored, or she was desperate for a human touch. James Ashbrook wasn't capable of true love or connection, and she would never ask it of him—or at least, that was the lie she always told herself. Because if she ever truly cared for him, he would break her.

James was a psychopath. He reveled in the murder—enjoyed both killing and dying. It was why he worked at the club. Only those who were truly desperate or fucked up worked here. James was no exception. He bathed in the carnage.

But he was good to her, and even more importantly, what they did together gave her a chance to numb herself. To fall entirely into pleasure and forget everything else.

A moment of respite.

Celestine pulled away from the kiss. "The show, James."

"Tonight, our little kisses fit into the show."

"Perhaps, but save some room for imagination."

He wasn't wrong. Dorothy had many lovers, and James's character was one of them. But the story required that piece of information to come out a bit later. Or, at the very least, be more obscured. So Celestine stopped him from making a spectacle by placing a hand on his well-manicured suit. Everything about James Ashbrook—including his clothing—was clear and measured. Studied like a scientist. And he always played characters like himself.

The Specter was far more accommodating to him than he ever was to her.

James's eyes examined her. "Fine," he sighed. "Perhaps not before the murder."

Celestine flinched at the reminder, and her eyes tracked to the clock. Seven twenty-five.

Shit. Celestine had only minutes to complete her task. So she leaned close to James and whispered into the shell of his ear, "Meet me in the Red Parlor in ten minutes, and then you can do whatever you want to me."

His lips curved further up. "I'll take you up on that." His eyes twinkled with domination and the promise of the depraved things he'd do to her later.

"Sorry, love, I must leave you," she said loud enough for the room to hear. "I need to change."

James leaned in and caught her hand before she could run off. "I have a beautiful dress in my room if you need it."

All three Ashbrooks had rooms in the East Wing. The Specter only allowed cast members to stay the night at Wolfsbane.

"Oh, thank you, but I have my own."

With that, she dashed out of the ballroom and stopped in her dressing room to prepare for her task. Rifling through her bag, she searched for the lipstick, the tool she needed. But as she grasped them, she braced her makeup table with her hand tightly, and she sucked in a pained breath. All the excitement and running had overexerted her, and she needed a minute to breathe.

Celestine's heart shuddered in her chest, beating asynchronously.

No...not now.

Get yourself together. She didn't have time for her body to melt down. She needed to get changed and prepare. So she slid her fingers along the grooves in the wall, grounding herself and communing with Wolfsbane, sending it her intentions.

Wolfsbane, please fix my makeup and enchant my lips. Help me to complete this killing.

Every night, Celestine drank the Specter's elixir, a potion that allowed her to use his magic to further the show. It allowed her to interact with the house and ask it to do her bidding—create a musical ambiance, manipulate the audience's emotions, or even morph the setting and her clothing. The only way to use the magic was to physically connect with the house; the walls and floors were the most accessible connection points.

Sometimes, the house listened; sometimes, it didn't. Other times, it twisted the request so much, Celestine wished she'd never asked to begin with.

So tonight, Celestine asked for help with the murder…and to fix her makeup. She didn't bother asking to change her dress because it would get stained soon enough anyway; Babette didn't realize the gift she'd given with the wine-throwing stunt. It gave Celestine an excuse to announce she'd changed her clothing publicly.

An alibi.

The house complied. A rush of wind circled through the dressing room, and magic poured over her face, tingling. The enchantment the house placed there burned her lips.

Thank you. She patted the wall, but her face soured as she remembered what came next.

"You look like the wind's gone out of your sails and took all the sunshine with it, my sweet dame," came the Specter's voice from a shadow in the mirror. The Specter and his idioms. "Cheer up. It's going to be fun."

Celestine swallowed. "Death is never fun."

"Perhaps…" the Specter trailed off as a grandfather clock chimed.

Celestine cursed under her breath. She needed to get moving. She had a murder to complete. At least tonight's victim was a regular to this type of debauchery. He'd been murdered and done the murdering before. He wasn't new, which was a significant relief. Sometimes, the attendees didn't know what they were coming to. They were blissfully ignorant of Wolfsbane Hall's true nature.

A monster house.

The Specter loved to play with newcomers and render a horror show where everything felt real until the end.

Because everything *was real* until the end.

The killer physically murdered their victims, and every moment of the show was, in fact, not an illusion. But new guests assumed it was all fake, that Specter fashioned expansive fantasies to make the bodies feel and look deceased.

The Specter's true magic was in resurrection—although he could cast illusions and play with emotions, too.

The one rule of Wolfsbane Hall was: *every murder must be solved; then, and only then, would the body resurrect.*

Celestine stood in the Red Parlor, waiting for her prey. One minute until he was supposed to arrive, and James Ashbrook was always on time, even as his characters. He believed it was never appropriate to keep someone waiting.

As her character, Celestine raised her lips with feline delight and leaned against the side of a lounge like a seductress draped in silk and jewels, waiting for a midnight assignation.

James stormed into the room like a cowboy in a Western film about to rescue his damsel in distress. He walked with purpose, and, without hesitation, he cupped the back of Celestine's neck and kissed her fiercely.

The kiss was beastly and consumed by unfiltered vigor. Almost as if they didn't do this every week. But that was the nature of their relationship. They were a wildfire that burned until it would eventually flame out and die.

James was not for keeping.

No rich man was. A lesson she'd learned long ago. Poor girls don't end up with "the man," even if they desperately want to.

James was for fucking and, tonight, killing.

Celestine's back slammed against the wall as their mouths devoured each other, his hands stroking up her legs and bunching the fabric of her dress up to her core with their movement.

"You taste of champagne," he whispered, his lips on her neck and his fingers digging into the curves of her thighs, their rhythm like magic. "And is that a hint of raspberry?"

The elixir. It tasted like champagne and raspberries tonight. But Celestine didn't mention it. She had a murder to complete, and too much conversation wouldn't do, so she pulled James's lips to hers again.

Kisses made such useful distractions, so she deepened their passion until he jerked, his hands stilling.

James pulled away, his eyes widening with betrayal.

"I'm sorry," Celestine breathed into his hair as his limbs went limp. "You're the Specter's victim tonight."

Celestine had poisoned her lips with a tranquilizer strong enough to sedate a horse. Only a thin layer of plastic and Specter's magic kept the lipstick from incapacitating her.

"How are you going to do it?" James croaked as his head lolled to the side.

"Stabbing." She caught him as his body slid to the floor.

"Ah...I've never been stabbed before." James smiled, lopsided and bright. A sick part of him enjoyed dying over and over again. He once said it made him feel alive every time he died in Wolfsbane Hall. He enjoyed it so much that he often volunteered as a victim, choosing to die every other week.

Although he enjoyed it, killing still made Celestine's stomach churn and her arms quiver.

"I'll see you after." And while he was still conscious, she gripped an ornamental knife from above her head, rolled her hand into the stabbing position, and thrust down.

"Thank you," he said, blood bubbling from his mouth as he stared gleefully down at his wound. She knew he thanked her for starting while he was still awake to experience it. He wanted to see and feel the knife as it slid in.

James had a terrible trauma in his past, which he refused to speak about. It caused him to enjoy pain and victimhood—to feast on it. But who was she to judge? She had her own crooked, scarred history.

Celestine pulled out the knife, then slammed it in again and again and again. It was a crime of passion, after all. Her character was overcome by rage and vengeful lust. But all of it made vomit snake up Celestine's esophagus. She continued her job regardless. Celestine Sinclair was loyal—the perfect employee for her Specter.

Loyal to a fault and to the detriment of her sanity.

2

The room tasted like iron and misery. A flavor that matched Celestine's mood.

She stumbled backward and caught herself on the couch, leaving a bloody handprint in her wake as she slid —nearly fell—to the floor. Rivulets of blood dripped down her face and streaked her skin, blossoming across her silk dress. Blood was everywhere, dusting the room in her shame.

She sucked in a rattling breath as the knife slipped through her fingers and clinked against the hardwood.

Clink, clink, clink.

The sound haunted her soul and clung to the back regions of her mind.

Celestine broke into full-body shakes as her eyes latched onto James's glassy, lifeless stare. The shakes were accompanied by quick, shallow, panicked breaths and a burning esophagus, which caused a coughing fit.

She didn't have a handkerchief, so she clumsily clutched for anything to stifle them, but all she found was a white throw blanket. It would have to do, because thick red mucus escaped her lips as she hacked. Celestine's body didn't respond well to murder or the lull as adrenaline slid out of her system.

Regulars and cast members at Wolfsbane Hall never reacted like this; they didn't break down mid-show. Probably because they were psychopaths. They basked in the excitement and torture, but she always cracked—because she was weak. She couldn't forgive herself for being a murderer, despite the resurrections. Every night, if the game was solved—and she always ensured it was, confessing if need be—her victims would return to life. But none of that mattered to Celestine. She was still a monster. A pathetic girl who would do anything for the one she loved. And, unfortunately, the one she loved was far more monstrous than she.

"You have to get moving, Celine." A gentle voice floated on a manufactured breeze, humming through the red curtains coating the walls. The voice moved like physical matter, knocking things over and caressing her face like a concerned paramour. It was the Specter being kind. "You have to get up."

He was rarely empathetic during a show, reserving that for later.

"You need to stash the knife, wash, and change." This time, he puppeteered the bust adorning an end table. "You only have ten minutes," he said, adding the vibrating shadows gripping the walls.

The Specter was a showboat, always talking with as much flair as his personality. Or, at least, as much as his feigned stage persona.

Grab the knife, you fool, the magic character card whispered in Celestine's head. It was less of a whisper and more of a dialogue line floating inside her mind. A cue card telling her what to do.

The magic was getting restless. It wanted a show. Seeing that it was an extension of the Specter, this wasn't a surprise. He always wanted a show.

A crashing sound pierced into Celestine's consciousness, and her head cocked toward the hallway.

Footsteps and debauchery. The club was in full swing. Drinking and gambling governed the place, but soon, people would fancy the *real* entertainment, and they would go in search of a dead body.

Celestine rubbed her thigh to settle herself, and she repeated the Specter's words in her head. *Stash the knife, wash, and change.* Half of it, the Specter's magic would aid with, but the other half she must do alone. Creating a "good" show took effort.

"Move, Cellie," the Specter demanded as the shadows. "You only have—"

The door handle rattled. "It's locked."

The patrons had found her.

Locked? Celestine hadn't done that. So it was either the Specter or Wolfsbane helping her out. Or, possibly, James had locked it before he'd died.

"It must mean this is the room we need to enter," an excited person called out, and the whole door shook like someone had thrown themselves into it.

Celestine's pulse hammered. The percussion was that of an angry war drum, and every muscle in her back grew taut.

This was a disaster.

She pinched her eyes closed and dug the bases of her palms into them. If she got caught, the show would end immediately, and the Specter would be furious.

She couldn't let that happen.

All she wanted was to be chosen by him, seen by him, his attention like a purifying fire. It made her feel whole, like everything would be fine. He was her safety net and confidant, and the sad truth was that Celestine would do anything for a moment of praise and affection from him.

The alternative was horrifying. Celestine never wanted to let him down.

A loud bang echoed again through the Red Parlor, and the door shook, the hinges sounding like they'd crack at any moment.

Shit. Move, Celine. Move. Celestine sucked in a hoarse breath and pulled herself to her knees.

"Distract them?" Celestine asked in a voice lower than a whisper.

The shadows wrapped around her arm in answer, trying to pull her into the fireplace, but she couldn't let it yet.

"No," she breathed before dipping her hand into the blood pooling under James's body. She smeared the blood over her handprint on the couch to obscure the true size of her hand. It was possible that she still left fingerprints, but no matter.

It wasn't like most patrons knew how to pull prints or check them.

Once she had effectively covered her tracks, to the best of her ability, with no time, she allowed the Specter's shadows to guide her into the fireplace, and with his push, she knew what to do. She placed both palms on the bricks and connected to the house.

Please, please work. She held her breath, waiting, hoping.

As the door to the Red Parlor opened, a barrier like a two-way mirror slid up in front of her, blocking the intruders' sight but allowing her to see them.

Her toes curled in relief, and her head fell against the bricks as she let out a low sigh.

But she only had a moment.

A scream tore through the night like a tidal wave, drowning everything in its path. A crowd collected in the room, their faces lit with horror, but their eyes were bright with excitement. It was all the sign she needed to get moving.

Wolfsbane? She ran her fingers along the cracks between the bricks. *Please, help!*

It took what felt like an eternity for the house to respond. But it eventually did.

The bricks crackled, sliding apart and opening to a secret passageway. Without hesitation—there was no time to waste —Celestine ducked into the tunnel and crawled until she reached the end: the floor-length mirror inside her dressing room. Celestine tested it to see if it was solid. The mirrors in the house were enchanted, bending and moving under the command of the Specter. Sometimes they were solid, but just as often, they were portals or doorways. Her fingers grazed the silver surface and sank through into rippling liquid metal.

Strange. Wolfsbane was utterly compliant tonight. An unsettling fact. The house never did exactly what she wanted.

Swallowing, Celestine pushed forward. The manor wouldn't hurt her.

Probably.

Celestine held her breath and stepped through the mirror portal. It was cold but not uncomfortable. It was like a bath after months lost in the wilderness, cleansing and rejuvenating. The liquid slid over her body like milk water, and her face tingled, her skin blazing, but it wasn't painful; rather, it was pleasant, like a moonlit stroll on a beach.

Celestine released her breath and stepped onto her carpeted floor, allowing herself to get her bearings. As she did, she noticed an absence of blood.

Completely gone.

The mirror had rigorously cleansed and reclothed her, including changing her lipstick. She now wore a dress spun from deep red spider silk and hand-stitched embroidery with an elaborate peacock design. Wolfsbane had removed most traces of the murder, but not everything.

The tips of her hair were wet, indicating that she'd taken a shower recently, and her blood-stained emerald dress was rolled into a ball at her feet, because the show needed evidence. She needed to give the patrons a way to uncover the truth. She had to stash the dress somewhere hard to find, yet not impossible.

The goal was to get caught, but not too soon. An elaborate display to make the Specter proud. He loved to see what she would do as the murderer—how she would hide her tracks. He was a puppet master, pulling her strings, but often held her with a loose grip to see how she would respond.

So if she were forced to play the murderer, she would do it well; despite her foolish emotions getting in the way of her job.

Celestine needed a rock-solid alibi, not just Babette ruining her clothing. She needed to do what she did best. Seduce someone and make them believe she was *with* them the whole time. But that wouldn't be enough; she would then steal something from them and plant the evidence near James's body.

Her job was to get an alibi, plant evidence, frame someone else...but don't do too good of a job. The murder needed to be solved. That last bit was the hardest, because Celestine had become a brilliant killer. Okay, fine, not brilliant—she didn't have the temperament for that—but she had become quite accomplished at the cover up.

It was a great plan, but she first needed to stash the evidence.

Celestine combed through her options. The Library, Conservatory, Billiard Room, and even the bedroom suites in the East Wing were contenders. Still, if she was going to be a suspect from the beginning—and she would be, by the very nature of her relationship with the victim—those options were too easy.

So she settled on the Smoking Room, because women were

forbidden from entering it and it would take longer to get discovered. But unfortunately, she didn't have much time to stash the dress and find her next victim.

At least it was the best time to sneak into the room. Everyone was busy with the body.

So Celestine removed her high heels and tiptoed through the halls with a bag stuffed to the brim with the bloody dress and knife. Quickly entering the Smoking Room, she hid the evidence and put her shoes back on before quietly making her way to the door.

Almost done.

All she had left to do was to get out without any noise.

Easier said than done.

Anxiety snaked up her body, climbing the rungs of her ribs. Celestine sucked in a breath and held it, begging for a bit of luck from God or whatever entity existed up in the sky. Slowly —miserably slowly—she clicked the door shut.

She'd done it! *Thank heavens.* Now, all she had to do was find her next victim. Celestine had three options to choose from—thank God Dorothy was as amorous as she was—and she would choose the first one she stumbled upon.

She headed in the direction of the commotion.

Celestine turned the corner and was about to reach her destination when a tall, haunting figure appeared inches before her as if conjured. As if he were a predator seeking his prey.

Fuck.

She jolted and clutched a hand to her chest, a small squeak escaping her lips. She didn't respond well to surprises, and it took her a moment to process who, or what, was before her. It could have been a ghost. They lurked on the edges of the manor. The Specter *could* summon creatures from the great beyond.

But this man was no ghost.

"Oh, you gave me a fright," she said, flattening out a wrinkle in her dress to hide her nerves.

Silhouetted by a darkness that seemed to stick to his clothing, like parasites feasting on human flesh, was Dean Ashbrook—the man who made brooding an art form. He was James's cousin and one half of a set of identical twins. The twins had black hair, blue eyes, and pale skin. Many considered them the ideal gentlemen, looking like a modern-day Adonis. And boy, were they indeed mouth-watering.

"Are you going to say anything?" Celestine twisted the straps of her bag awkwardly and waited for him to do something...anything, but all he did was glower, and his stare was like obsession, like possession. His eyes traced her like the chalk outlining a corpse, catching first on her new red dress, then moving on to the wet tips of her red hair, and finally landing on a spot behind her ear.

"You have something—" Dean ended his sentence by pulling out his pocket square and using it to point to her neck. He held it out by a corner, making sure to hold the cloth at an angle to avoid touching her.

Dean Ashbrook hated Celestine and always had. From the moment they first met, Dean was obsidian, unknowable and as cold as mountain rock. But regrettably, that's what excited her about him. The hatred fascinated her, and she spent countless hours trying to figure out what she'd done to offend him. Alas, she'd never discovered it.

But perhaps one day she would.

Celestine grabbed the cloth and dabbed it against her neck, holding his glare the entire time. Electric tension stormed between them, and her traitorous heart leaped into her throat, her stomach tying itself into knots. It happened every time Dean was near. He was a poison designed solely for her.

Celestine bit her lip and glanced down at the fabric—a drop of red coated the sea of white.

Well, fuck.

He lifted one manicured eyebrow. The gesture said, *I assume you weren't gallivanting with vampires.*

Anxiety twisted her gut and burned her lungs. Dean had to know she was the night's murderer, but if he said anything, it would ruin the Specter's show. And it was far too soon to unmask the killer.

Celestine gulped and steadied her hand against the wall, glancing at her surroundings. She'd never been caught out this early.

No one was around. Could she murder him and get away with it?

No, it was far too risky.

But Dean noticed far too much, including her fear. The side of his mouth curled up as he drank in her current state. He slid his hands into his suit pants pockets, and his eyes sparkled with mirth. Oh, he enjoyed torturing her, having her at his mercy.

The man always delighted in having something over her.

"Please don't say anything yet. It'll rui—"

"Sometimes you should let the show be ruined instead of suffering through something you loathe," Dean interrupted, his voice like a velvet noose circling her slender neck. "Leave your Specter and get far away from this den of sins. Go down to Hollywood and leave us be."

Celestine jerked back as if slapped. Did he really hate her so much that he wanted her gone immediately? Dean normally wasn't this direct. Usually, he barely spoke to her, let alone said, what was that, twenty words? It was the most he'd ever spoken to her at once, and he used it to tell her to leave. The valves in Celestine's heart clenched.

He wanted her gone. And that hurt more than Celestine cared to admit.

A manufactured breeze stroked her neck, and the hair on her arms rose.

"You must truly hate me."

Dean's chin slightly dipped into a nod, his jaw tightening, but his lips remained shut. He'd used up his allotted word count for the moment and refused to say anymore. Instead, he rotated on his heel and strolled away, as if completely unaffected by the interaction. Done engaging altogether.

Fury stroked through her. He was so...frustrating, and worse, condescending. But she couldn't focus on that now. She needed to find a target. Thankfully, luck was on her side tonight, because just as Dean made to turn out of her sight, one of Dorothy's many lovers turned the corner and nearly ran into him.

Richard Monroth.

Dean scowled at the other man. They hated each other. Richard was a regular at Wolfsbane Hall who enjoyed fucking and murdering—he got off on both. Often at the same time. He had long desired a night with Celestine, but there had never been a show that would satisfy that desire.

Not until tonight.

And Celestine had no qualms about fucking him, especially not if it would anger Dean Ashbrook.

A bright smile appeared on her lips, and she said, "Ah, Lord Mountdrake, I have been looking everywhere for you." She bounced on her toes and ran toward him, hoping he would accept her affections and catch her.

He did, and she jumped into his arms, her legs wrapping around his waist and her lips touching his. He met her with a hunger that far outmatched hers. His tongue jutted inside her mouth, greedy and demanding.

Celestine met his ferocity, but eventually, she pulled away to breathe. She'd expected Dean to have left, but he merely leaned against the wall and glared at her. Celestine's nostrils flared, and she met his glare with one of her own. Dark and provoking.

His lips curled slowly and sharply into a smile that seemed to be carved from dark warnings.

Celestine gulped and turned her gaze back to the man holding her up by her ass cheeks. "Would you like to go somewhere more private?"

"I thought you'd never ask," he said in a smooth voice, but he didn't put her down as expected. Instead, he held her tighter to his chest and walked her to the closest room.

The Downstairs Study.

As the door closed, Celestine looked once more out into the hallway, where her eyes again found Dean's. He gave nothing away on his face, but every muscle in his body was stiff.

Celestine swallowed but turned her attention back to her next victim.

It didn't take long for Richard to have her dress up around her waist and his dick pounding inside of her as she was perched on the desktop. There was no foreplay, no seeing if she was ready, and no attending to her needs.

His sex was all about him.

She didn't mind. Sometimes, she just wanted it rough. Sometimes, she enjoyed the pain. Celestine didn't have to fuck Richard—she never had to fuck any patron. She could have stopped with a few kisses; usually, she would. But it was a murder night, and on a murder night, she would take any distraction, any drug.

And for the moment, her drug of choice was his dick.

The slight pain, the pounding, and the lack of care fueled

her in a way. She was using him just as much. Sex for her wasn't about love. It was a transaction. She usually got pleasure with James, but with others, she got something different.

As he pounded into her, she used the distraction to rip one of his cufflinks off and hide it in a marble jar that shook with their movements.

At some point during the encounter, Richard pulled out and flipped her, smashing her head into the desk as he took her from behind. Her eyes focused on the marbles rattling in the glass. It wasn't that she felt no pleasure at all, his penis stroking her velvet did feel good, it just wasn't great.

It simply *was*.

A slightly gratifying means to an end.

He roared as his hot seed filled her, and he convulsed, his weight resting on top and pinning her further into the desk. "Oh, that was so good," he growled, panting into her hair.

She stifled a sigh. At least it was for one of them. She gritted her teeth, waiting for him to climb off her and remove his below-average dick. When he did, she turned around, meeting his sex-soaked, satisfied gaze. At least she was of service to someone.

Cum rolled down her leg. As he saw it, he said, "What a good little cum hole you are," and slapped her cheek softly in the most condescending of ways. Then he cupped her chin and pulled her into him, taking another kiss, his cock hardening again. Eventually, he released her lips. "On your knees. I want to fill both of your holes with my seed."

Celestine swallowed past the lump in her throat. Men were so predictable. Channeling her character Dorothy, Celestine said, "As truly tempting as that suggestion is, I'd rather not. I've gotten my use out of you." She tapped his cheek like he had done to her before she reached into the jar, took a handful of marbles—including the cufflink—and twirled on her heels, walking away, treating him like trash the same way he would have treated her.

"Well, that was fun," she said, clicking the door closed and leaving him alone with his seething thoughts.

elestine wanted a bath more than anything, but she didn't have time for that. So she made her way to the bathroom and used a cloth to wash between her legs and breasts, trying to get the smell of sex off her.

She wasn't worried about catching any diseases or getting pregnant. After the first time she'd fucked a patron, the Specter had given her a magical protection against both.

Celestine twirled the cufflink, feeling it against the balls of her fingertips. *Men.* She sighed. According to the world and the culture, she was a loose woman, undesirable—yet paradoxically, she was also an object to be desired and possessed.

The world was a place of contradictions, but then so was she. As a character, she could do anything. As herself, she'd fall apart. She knew she should never want a man like an Ashbrook, but at the same time, it was what she wanted most. To be chosen and cherished by a powerful man.

She was a lost, sad girl.

But alas, it didn't matter, because she had a job to do. She had to plant the cufflink and join the spectacle.

So, Celestine adjusted her dress and made her way back to the crowd, still hovering over the dead body. Everett—Dean's twin—was at the center, inspecting James's dead body, playing the stumbling, lovable fool of a detective. The Quirky Detective. A Poirot-style mustache kissed his face and was complemented by thick, over-the-top glasses. He looked ridiculous, yet still wickedly handsome.

Celestine watched as anxiety snaked up her ribcage. Trying to deal with the rotten energy settling in her core, she tapped her toes within her shoes and fidgeted with her dress.

This was the worst part of being the murderer—besides the actual killing— was waiting to get caught.

Time always seemed to move horrifically slowly.

Inching closer to the crime scene, Celestine twirled the cufflink in her fingers. When she got close enough to the body, she dropped it to the floor, making sure to do so on the carpet to minimize the sound. At the exact moment, she let out a horrified scream, covering up the sound even further.

"No, Andrew! Not my Andrew!" Celestine screamed and ran to the body, flinging herself onto him. She did this for a multitude of reasons. One reason was to establish the relationship with him for the audience, but also to cover up any remaining evidence she might have left on the scene.

Because now there was a reason for her hair or fingerprints to be there.

"Miss Dorothy"—Everett patted her on the back, cautiously trying to calm her down—"you must not grab the body. You're messing with the crime scene."

"But...my Andrew." Celestine was hysterically cradling the body and rocking back and forth, letting out her own pent-up emotions as she did it.

After a long, dramatic moment, Frances, another cast member who was often referred to as the Mother Hen, calmed Celestine—Dorothy—down, so the act could continue.

The show must go on.

Celestine was still sitting next to the dead body, rocking back and forth with both Everett and Frances beside her. But now, it was just for show. She had to keep up the act. However, sitting next to James's body made her stomach churn.

Everett whispered under his breath for only her to hear. "I could use your help here, Celestine. Where were you?"

Celestine lifted her head and met his eyes. The two shared a poignant moment. Almost as if Celestine were asking him for help instead. After a long pause, Celestine averted her gaze, and focused instead on the body and the investigation.

Everett almost always played the Quirky Detective—but wasn't very good at it. Often, he was far too drunk and missed obvious evidence, and other times, he was just too clumsy. Occasionally, when he got stuck or was simply bored, he asked Celestine for help. Celestine saw life in a series of patterns, and putting together a murder investigation was relatively easy for her—easier still, when she was the murderer.

"Have you not spoken to your brother?" Celestine asked, just as quietly. She had expected Dean to turn her in, if not to everyone, then at least to his twin.

"No, he's disappeared somewhere."

Hmm. Dean wasn't going to turn her in right away. Interesting. Utterly unlike him.

"Where should I go from here?" Everett asked, his gaze stroking across the body.

Celestine didn't know what he had already done or said, so she just reviewed the basics. "He has been stabbed multiple times. If I had to guess, at least seventeen. That indicates a crime of passion or a lot of rage."

Everett nodded and waited for her to continue.

"All the wounds are centered on his torso, and there is no sign of him fighting back."

"How do you know that?"

Celestine's eyes traced the body once more. "There are no wounds on his hands or arms. No blood or skin under his fingernails?"

Everett cocked his head, checking the fingernails. "What does that indicate?"

"Drugged, most likely."

"Anything else?"

"The room was locked from the inside, and there is no sign of forced entry. You should look for an escape route."

"Suspects?"

Celestine closed her eyes and searched through her character card and what she knew about this setup. "I would start with his lover, newest lead actress, rival movie director, jealous sister, and business partner. They would seem to have the most passion and motive for the crime."

"Righto." Everett began to stand to act out a scene, but she cleared her throat.

"Oh, and that." Celestine pointed to the cufflink that she had dropped on the floor next to the body.

Everett smiled and nodded his appreciation, then he stood and put on a long, showy monologue, going through the evidence and pointing out the obvious. He adopted his over-the-top Australian accent. He wanted to be like Poirot so much, but he couldn't manage a French—or more accurately, Belgian —accent. So, ridiculously, he chose an Australian accent instead.

The current evidence was the knife Celestine had dropped and the cufflink found next to the body. He ended his speech with, "Now, for the main suspects. We have the Scorned Lover" —he pointed at Celestine—"The Rival Film Director"—he pointed at Richard—"The Jealous Sister"—he motioned to Vivian, James's actual biological sister, who apparently was also playing his sister tonight—"his newest Leading Lady"—

Everett waved at a young female patron with a soft, beautiful face and luscious curves—"and lastly, the Business Partner." Everett pointed at his twin, who had slowly strolled into the Red Parlor, his hands in his pockets. "You were all the closest to Andrew, so let us begin the questioning."

Everett asked them all to follow him to the Grand Ballroom, where he commandeered a table and forced them to sit in a circle. He then interrogated them one by one in front of the audience.

"Let's start with you, Mr. Mountdrake."

"It's *Lord* Mountdrake."

"Righto, well then, Lord Mountdrake, where were you when the murder was committed?"

A sick grin climbed Richard's face as he answered. "I was fucking Dorothy Wolf in the Downstairs Study."

A sea of gasps lit up the room.

Everett raised an eyebrow at her. "Can you corroborate that?"

Celestine gulped. "Yes." The gasps got louder, with poisonous whispers breaking out across the room. Anger bubbled in Celestine's chest. Her character would not have stood for such treatment, so she decided to be even more shocking. "We got up to a bit of mischief on the study desk."

Richard let out a self-satisfied sound. Dean grunted, and Everett chuckled.

"Well, then." Everett shook his head in amusement, not judgment. "So, you both have an alibi."

Everett continued his questioning, turning next to the New Leading Lady. In the meantime, Celestine leaned into Vivian Ashbrook. "So, you're playing James's sister tonight?"

The girls got along quite swimmingly. In fact, Vivian was probably her closest friend at Wolfsbane Hall, with the exception, maybe, of Everett.

"Yes, how utterly tedious." Vivian crossed her arms. "I wish I could play a hussy like you occasionally. But no, just a jealous sister. Seeing that is simply my life on any given day, I am unaccountably bored."

Celestine bit her lip. Vivian loved insulting her. It was a game they played, and Celestine always grinned and bore it.

Vivian was a bright, burning star. A source of pure joy, excitement, and warmth. She was charismatic and mesmerizing. One couldn't help but want to be near her. And like a star, she would consume anyone who got too close. That was precisely why Celestine let the other girl insult her. She had no interest in becoming the object of her ire. Plus, she was drawn to Vivian's histrionic nature, because Celestine liked fire. She liked danger, and maybe she even liked the excitement of it all. But most of all, she liked that she never had to take the lead when Vivian was around. Celestine could be the dutiful follower and fade into the background.

Celestine might be an actress and the center of attention, but she was also inscrutably shy. So, having Vivian around was a relief.

Vivian was also the town gossip, and she would always update Celestine on the newest dramas in San Francisco.

"Anything new and fun happening in the city?" Celestine asked.

"Not particularly, unless you count my mother trying to marry me off once again." Vivian clicked her tongue. "The woman can't accept that I don't want anything to do with her plans."

The conversation was cut off, because Everett had made his way over to question Vivian. Her alibi was poker, and about fifteen witnesses could corroborate that. So, finally, Everett's gaze locked on his twin. "Where have you been?"

"Here and there."

"Is that all you plan on saying?"

"Yes." The side of his lips ticked up. "And this." He held up both of his arms, showing off his intact cufflinks.

"Ah, that's an excellent point. Lord Mountdrake, show me your jacket."

Richard let out a long sigh, because everyone could see that he was no longer wearing his jacket. "I took it off to fuck the actress."

It wasn't true, but Celestine wasn't going to correct him.

"Ah, righto. Well then, I think it's time for a little scavenger hunt, don't you all?" Everett stood quickly and addressed the entire room dramatically. "We shall all hunt through the house for his jacket, and the clothing the murderer changed out of as well." When the entire audience remained stationary, Everett waved them out of the room. "On with you; it's your time to be involved in the show."

When most of them left, he sighed and sank into his chair again. "Murder is exhausting."

Celestine couldn't agree more.

Everett looked directly at Celestine and mouthed, "You want to meet me on the Upstairs Study Balcony?"

"Yes, very much so."

"Say, how ya doing, darling?" Everett asked, leaning over the railing and looking out at the newly built Golden Gate Bridge, lit up in the darkness.

It was a sight to behold at night—a modern marvel. Celestine was glad Everett was merely looking at the bridge instead of drunkenly walking on it again. Celestine had once had to pull him off the railing. He had climbed up in a drunken stupor and balanced on it quite impressively—but it was unclear what his true intentions were.

The man was reckless.

"Fine." She smiled with her teeth.

"You seem it." Everett raised an unconvinced raven-black eyebrow and took a drag from his blunt. "Of all people, you can level with me. You stabbed James seventeen times, doll. *You* don't walk away from a murder like that saying you're fine."

Celestine blinked twice, reeling. Everett rarely solved the crimes on his own. "When did you figure it out?"

"The first time you met my gaze."

Celestine bit her lip and reached for the blunt, and when he handed it over, she took a long hit.

"It wasn't the evidence that tipped me off. It was you." He

waved at her. "You might be able to pull the wool over everyone else's eyes, but not mine. You're coming undone, Celestial. And let's get one thing straight: only one of us gets to fall apart tonight, and it's not you."

Everett had three nicknames for her that he cycled through. This one he only used when he was being affectionate.

Celestine let out a long breath. "Ah, so that's why you offered me the smoke."

"Oh doll, I never need an excuse to take you to cloud nine." He winked. "But yes, I am the Ashbrook of distractions, and since you're currently in an amorous relationship with my cousin, we will have to settle for drugs and not sex."

"Everett." Celestine playfully hit his arm. But he wasn't wrong. He was her favorite Ashbrook because he was the fun one, but he was also gently blunt and honest, which she appreciated. Unlike James, who callously spoke his mind without hesitation.

He was also her favorite because he was the most open with her. Now, that didn't mean he told her everything, far from it. All Ashbrooks kept secrets in a crypt with no name or discernible location. Nearly impossible to uncover. Everett was no exception, but at least he wasn't cagey—like the other three.

He only kept one secret from her, and it was a dark one from his past. It haunted him so deeply that he used alcohol, drugs, and fake jubilation to cover it up.

The closest Celestine got to uncovering it was that infamous night on the Golden Gate Bridge. He rumbled, mostly incoherently, but he repeated a girl's name over and over again. Unfortunately, it was so slurred that Celestine couldn't make out the name. But it was something like Margaret or Meagan—something starting with M.

But as soon as she broached the subject again, he shut down harshly and withdrew, not talking to her for three months. She never brought it up again, because it wasn't worth losing their friendship.

And Celestine needed Everett to survive at Wolfsbane Hall.

Celestine brought the joint back to her mouth and inhaled slowly, holding the smoke in her lungs for a moment before exhaling. The smoke hung between them, catching in the silver light of the moon. Then she handed the blunt back to Everett.

"So, where did you hide the evidence?" he asked, taking out another match to relight the joint, cupping it and protecting the end from the wind as he did it.

"I am not sure I should tell you that."

"Cece, I am lit like a Christmas tree. I ain't exactly in the mood to go on a scavenger hunt."

"You have a whole house of aides looking for evidence right now for you."

"All fools, the lot of them."

Celestine closed her eyes, letting the comfort of the high hit her. "If I tell you, are you going to end the show right away?"

"Of course not."

"Show above all else?"

"Show above all else," he repeated.

Celestine nodded. "I hid my bloody dress in the Smoking Room."

"Clever." He brought the blunt to his lips and savored the last drag. "I assume you are framing Richard."

Everett was putting it all together. He wasn't a good detective simply because he didn't have the patience, but the man was brilliant. All the Ashbrooks were, in their own ways.

James was a scientist who enjoyed tinkering with metal and

inventing new devices. Dean was observant and clever, while Everett was the book-smart gentleman. He read everything from physics to romance novels, nearly as much as Celestine.

"Yes."

"Tell me the truth, did you really shack up with him tonight?"

Celestine inhaled sharply, staring at the circles of silver smoke lingering between them. "Yes."

He chuckled. "You're almost as bad as I am. You'll partake in anything when you're the murderer."

She tipped her chin in agreement. There was no arguing with that.

"Alas, our respite has come to an end. We need to get back to our little play." Everett looked nearly as frustrated with that fact as Celestine felt.

Neither was particularly in the mood to continue. Everett was probably feeling too inebriated and unsteady, while Celestine simply hated waiting.

Waiting to be discovered for murder was its own torture. And tonight was no different.

After they returned inside the house, Celestine watched the show unfold over the three hours, moving like honey dripping from a jar. Thick, sticky, and utterly uncomfortable. Celestine played her part, acting shocked and flabbergasted as she was repeatedly questioned. Despite Dean and Everett already having the answer, the show continued.

Yet, anticipation and its resulting anxiety still twisted her stomach. Waiting to be discovered was its own form of purgatory. Dean should've ended the game hours ago, but he didn't, and she didn't understand why. And that lack of understanding caused her to fret more, the worry eating away at her body.

"You need to eat." A voice pulled her out of a dazed state. It was Frances Deere, the sixth member of the cast.

"I'm fine." Celestine couldn't eat, not with angst stirring her stomach.

"Like hell you are. You look like a ghostly child coming back to haunt the room," Frances said. Freckles and wrinkles lined her face, neck, and hands, and her voice cracked from a lifetime of overuse on the world's grand stages. At Wolfsbane, she typically played roles like the concerned grandmother or the overly invested housekeeper—the Specter liked to give people parts that matched their personalities. It was also why Celestine always referred to her as the Mother Hen, because she coddled everyone she met. Celestine appreciated the gesture. She needed a family, even if it were a makeshift one held together by scraps and the Specter's generosity.

"Eat up." Frances handed Celestine a plate with a peanut butter and jam sandwich diced into little square bites, as if the older woman thought it would be too straining for Celestine to have a whole sandwich. Celestine pursed her lips. Everyone treated her like a highly breakable porcelain doll.

It was so frustrating. She was fine, but she had to admit in this case, Frances was right. Celestine needed food, so she took a bite as Dean appeared at her side. She jumped, rattled by his quick appearance—possibly a magical one. Dean also had the Specter's elixir swimming in his veins. He was also able to manipulate the house and cast spells. Spells like invisibility.

Celestine shuddered. The man was like a vampire.

"Are you ready to be put out of your misery?" Dean asked.

Ten words.

"Please," Celestine breathed.

Dean stepped toward the center of the ballroom, but Frances caught his sleeve. "Wait, boy. What did you mean by that?" She glared between the Brooding Bad Boy and the

Blonde Ingénue. "No," Frances gasped. "The Specter made you the murderer...again?"

"Yes." Celestine wrung her hands.

"I thought you were going to tell him never to do that again." Fury danced on Frances's face.

Celestine chewed on her cheeks. "I was but—"

"But what?"

"I couldn't."

Dean watched the exchange silently, a dark amusement coloring his features.

"Why not?" Frances asked.

Because I love him. "Because I owe him everything. He saved me." Celestine's voice wobbled. "I'd be starving on the streets if it weren't for him." *I'd be dead.*

"We all owe him, but you don't owe him your life or sanity, Celeste." Frances rubbed Celestine's back in soft circles. Everyone at Wolfsbane Hall called her something different. "You're too fragile to continue having nights like this. They're making you sick."

Celestine knew it, but what could be done about it? She couldn't anger the Specter. He might throw her out. At the thought, a shudder coursed through Celestine's skin like a termite eating its way through wood. The murders *were* making her sick, but what could she do?

Nothing.

"Child," Frances's voice softened, "you can't go on like this."

"I know." A soft sob escaped Celestine's lips. "I'm sorry."

"Don't be sorry, darling." Frances stroked Celestine's blonde locks. "Emotion is not weakness."

No, weakness was weakness, and Celestine was carved of it. She didn't have a strong bone in her body; from her pathetic heart to her frail muscles to her fragile mind, she was made of straw like that silly little pig's house from the nursery rhyme.

"Shall I end the show, then?" Dean directed the question at Frances.

"Yes." The older woman nodded and clutched Celestine's fingers within hers.

As Dean walked to the center of the room, soft music began to play from hidden speakers. Violin strings plucked out a twisted yet thrilling song. Setting the stage for Dean's show-ending monologue—setting the stage for an entertaining climax.

Celestine didn't understand why he had waited the entire night, and only acted with fifteen minutes left to go. He could've claimed the honor of being the fastest person to unmask a Specter mystery—ever. A prestigious title. But still, he chose not to.

Why?

Dean Ashbrook wasn't chivalrous. He wasn't good. He was a nightmare dressed as a man. He was a riddle not meant to be unraveled.

The show was over.

Thank God.

Once Celestine had been tied up and paraded out as the murderer, James was resurrected. He woke covered in blood, with knife-sized holes in his dove-gray suit.

Then the incessant questioning came.

As was tradition, the murder victim and murderer held something akin to a press conference for the attendees to ask their sick questions. Questions about how it felt to kill, how it felt to die.

James chewed on minty gum the whole time, using it to avoid answering questions he didn't want to. Although he enjoyed this part far more than Celestine, his answers were short and clipped, and when he'd had enough, he walked away without another word.

The man did as he pleased, when he pleased.

And he left Celestine to the hyenas.

After fielding another volley of questions, Celestine also bowed out and went in search of James.

It wasn't hard to find him; he always did the same thing

every time he was murdered. And she always, without fail, followed him.

Metal and glass parts clinked together as James troubleshooted his newest invention. He was trying to build a color television and was currently tinkering with his Cathode Ray Tube. Celestine hadn't known any of this, but James had already explained it to her multiple times because he was close to getting it to work. But something was off, and he couldn't quite figure it out.

However, if he had any chance of finding the solution, it would be after being the victim. He said that the adrenaline of death helped him focus, and it was when he got his best ideas.

Celestine knew all this, but it didn't help her feel better. She knew stabbing him was helpful, but she still hated it. She still felt the need to apologize every time.

She cleared her throat as she stepped into his room—or more like his train museum and workshop. Every inch of it was covered in photographs documenting the advancements in trains and railways, from horse-drawn wagonways to the first steam engine to passenger trains and the transcontinental railroad. Every moment of train history was documented on his walls. James even insisted on having a long twin bed instead of a queen in the corner so he would have more time to work on his current projects.

His every gesture, every habit, exuded science. Exuded engineering. Which was precisely why Celestine affectionately referred to him as the Obsessed Scientist.

"I'm sorry for killing you." There was no good way of saying it, so Celestine just laid it out.

"Ah, Stella, it's you," James called her by his favorite nickname while barely taking his eyes off his project, chewing his gum the whole time. "Come over here, pet." He patted his thigh.

Celestine complied. Mainly because, like the Specter, she'd do nearly anything for James. When she reached his side, without even taking his gaze from his device, he pulled her into his lap, causing her dress to rise on her hips as she straddled him.

Instantly she felt his cock stiffen against her.

"Hello, pet." His lips touched her neck, but his eyes were still focused on his work.

Only he would try to seduce her and work at the same time. But he was that good, because Celestine melted when anyone touched her neck. "James, you just died."

"Yes, I did." His breath was hot on her neck. "I was rather hoping you might have waited for my cock to be deep inside of you before stabbing me. It would have been rather fascinating to study."

"James," Celestine reprimanded, but her protest was cut off by a sigh as his tongue caressed her neck. After a long moment of indulgence—the man was truly talented—she placed her hands on his chest and pushed herself away. "James, we can't." The words came out far too wanton, but she was determined to stand her ground.

Something she rarely did with the men at Wolfsbane Hall.

But she didn't have time to play around with James. She had to get back to her rooms. After every show, she had a nightly ritual. And she couldn't—wouldn't—miss it.

"Ah, yes, your all-important meeting with the Specter. I wouldn't dream of keeping you from it." His tone was biting. "And you can't miss your nightly visit with Dean."

"Is that feeling I detect?" Her lips twitched as she watched him closely.

"If it is a feeling, which we have established many times that I do not possess, then it would be one of frustration. I don't like sharing."

Afer painfully extracting herself from James, she returned to her rooms.

Unfortunately, as soon as she made it under her sheets, the weight of the night hit her, and her body reacted.

Horrifically.

Celestine trembled uncontrollably, curling up into her covers, the sheets pulled up to her chin. Her eyes were pinched shut. If she ran away from the reality of what she had done, if she pretended it didn't exist, she would be okay... right? But despite all her efforts, the darkness still seeped into her soul.

This reaction wasn't nearly as severe as the moment right after she'd killed James, but it wasn't much better either. Anytime she killed, it required days for her to recover. But if Celestine closed her eyes, tucked into a ball, breathed through her nose, and begged the world to disappear, she'd usually manage to get through it faster.

Bang. Bang. Bang.

Celestine's door rattled as her head popped out of the covers, and her eyes met those of a drunken Everett Ashbrook —who had just forced said door open. He poured into her room like a waterfall down a canyon. Loud, destructive, and beautiful.

She let out a loud sigh. Well, there went her recovery.

Everett was highly inebriated, with four ladies dripping off his arms like diamonds. Two on each side. One of whom was Babette, who seemed to be equally as intoxicated as him.

That bred disaster.

The two had what could only be described as an interesting, if volatile, relationship.

"Come party with us, Celestial," Everett said, a lilting slur to his voice. When she didn't respond, he added, "Come on, Cece, let the good times roll!"

Everett ran a hand through the hair of one of his ladies as he stared Celestine down, tempting her into his debauchery. He was a playboy made manifest, fabricated from pure passion. Sometimes, Celestine enjoyed the distractions and pleasures he could bring. But not right now.

She didn't want to be around anyone except the Specter.

"Drink away all your cares, Teetee." Everett hiccupped as he said the nickname he knew she hated, trying to provoke her.

Celestine fought the urge to roll her eyes. He typically called her Teetee when he was being excessively irritating or dramatic. He was the most hyperbolic person she'd ever met. And he enjoyed provoking emotions—any emotion, which was why he loved Wolfsbane Hall.

While James enjoyed the physical pain of dying over and over again, Everett enjoyed the drama of the shows. He worked for the Specter because he loved plucking people's strings. He liked seeing what they would do when they were cornered.

Which was precisely why he enjoyed tempting Celestine into anger—or at least trying. He wanted her to yell at him. He wanted his words to wound her, for passion to spill from her like blood.

But it wouldn't work.

This was the side of Everett she didn't particularly enjoy. At least it only came out on rare occasions.

"Cece, come play with us."

"I truly shouldn't." She tried to smile brightly, but she was slightly off-kilter and struggled to hide her emotions. Celestine sucked in a breath and grasped the blankets tight, her knuckles growing white. She needed to ground herself enough to conceal her panic from the man. But it wasn't working. "I must wait."

"Ah, yes." Everett made a theatrical motion with his arms. "It's your private time with the Specter. Time to debrief?" He suggestively pinched his nose, his eyebrows raising with the gesture.

Everett knew there'd never been a physical relationship between her and the Specter—especially since he never took physical form—but he still teased her relentlessly about it. Besides, Celestine's only sexual relationship outside the show was with James. Precisely why he had wanted her to join him in *his festivities*. He wanted to fuck her hard until she screamed his name. But as much as she enjoyed that particular activity— as much as she tried to forget about everything—her body wasn't up for it. Her heart was too weak. It could give out at any minute.

"Leave her alone," Dean said, cutting a path through his twin and ladies.

"Ah, I forgot you were her bodyguard." Everett slurred his words and stumbled a little as Babette held him up.

"I make sure the cast is safe and comfortable after the show, brother." Dean flashed a false smile—all teeth. "Perhaps I wouldn't have to, if people like yourself didn't bother them so much."

The twins couldn't be more different. While Everett was fashioned from energy and charisma, Dean was forged from mystery, dark temptation, and pure protectiveness—or possessiveness. He was also heartbreak in human form. One was light, and one was dark, but both were equally fucked up.

"She's my friend, Dean. Lighten up." Everett rolled his eyes.

"Friend, right..." Dean glanced at him, completely unconvinced. "Yet she asked you to leave."

She hadn't. Not in those words, but Celestine wouldn't correct him because she did want all of them gone. The Specter didn't appear when guests were near, and he was the only person who could calm her down after a murder night. And although she was angry with the Specter, she wanted his comfort more. She wanted the after-show version of him—the warm, almost loving one.

"Alright, fine," Everett said. "But join us if you get bored with this brooding flat tire." He motioned to his twin as he fell out of the doorway, Babette and his other girls trying to keep him upright as they walked—stumbled—away.

A stilted silence swarmed the room. All the jubilant energy was sucked out by their exit, leaving only the king of brooding behind, radiating a sweetly-toxic energy like belladonna. The berries were heavenly in their poison. A kiss of death, and so was Dean.

He held a single red rose in his gloved hands.

A gift.

This was his routine. Nightly, he visited her and silently placed a rose on the bedside table, their eyes meeting in the mirror on her wall, the tension crackling between them like embers escaping a fireplace. Hot but dangerous, if they landed in the wrong spot. Tonight was no different.

Celestine sucked in a breath. It was utterly unfortunate

that she always wanted men who would never want her back. Dean was only the messenger. The rose was the Specter's gift, but sometimes Celestine liked to pretend Dean-the-Brooding-Bad-Boy wanted to give it himself.

But that would never happen.

Celestine's eyes traced the rose petals as she tried to maintain her composure. Her one goal with men was never to show them how much they affected her. It gave them too much power. And Dean always conjured unwanted feelings within her—a mixture of excitement, fear, and utter frustration.

"You know, one of these days, you'll speak to me when you check in on me." Celestine clutched her hands in her lap with a sugar-bright smile dusting her face.

Dean lifted an eyebrow, which said, *Now, where would the fun be in that?*

Every night, they played this game. He refused to speak, and she tried to coax him into breaking—to give her at least one word.

"You don't have to look so pained when you visit me." She motioned with her head to the flower and was met with another irritating brow lift, which seemed to say *yes and no.*

Right.

Dean always won this game.

Every muscle in her body tensed as he patted the comforter inches from her knee, his hands still gloved. It was unclear whether the gesture was intended to be comforting or just a means of saying goodnight. Either way, Dean exited without another word.

Celestine cupped her head in her hands, hating the feelings stirring in her belly. Poor, broken girls did not get rich, powerful men, and she needed to remind herself of that.

Yet, as she lifted her eyes to the rose, her core tightened, and stillness stroked through the empty room. She bit her lip, and it took her a moment to realize she was no longer shaking. Despite his silence, Dean was also part of her cure. Anxiety no longer clung to her back, at least not now. The man's mere irritating presence was the boon she needed.

Strange...

Celestine released a staggering breath, thinking about those implications, and her eyes locked on the book that lay next to the rose. *Murder on the Orient Express* by Agatha Christie. Her favorite.

She liked the twist—that everyone was responsible. What did that say about her?

Surrounding Celestine's bed was a trove of books. Her entire room was more of a small library than a bedroom. The walls were covered with tomes. Even her armchair and bed frame formed bookshelves.

Above all else, Celestine loved reading. She enjoyed getting lost in stories and daydreaming about different worlds and lives. While she cherished all books, mysteries were her favorites. She owned Agatha Christie's complete collection— all first editions, all leather-bound. The Specter spared no expense for her hobby; if she desired a book, it would appear bound in brown paper on her bed.

"Are you here?" Celestine asked the emptiness.

"Yes." His voice was soft and smooth like liquid fire, and it came from a spot at the end of her bed as if a ghost lingered there.

After the show, the Specter dispensed with all his theatrics, almost as if he wanted to be a true genuine person. No façade or masks.

Just him.

Celestine's gaze narrowed on the small table between her

wall and the bed. On it rested a half-played chess game—the pieces formed from blue sapphires. The Specter took every opportunity to impress.

Even when no one else would see.

"Knight to F5," she said without hesitation. The move had been planned for days. Every night after a show, they each took a move, but only one.

"Bishop to F1." His words were nearly a whisper in her ear.

The pieces moved on the winds of magic, settling into their new positions.

Celestine cocked her head and rubbed her face. It was a sacrifice play. The Specter put his knight directly in the kill zone of her queen.

What are you up to? He was filled with tricks. Tricks on tricks on tricks. But sometimes, Celestine thought she could match him. In this, at least, because she was a brilliant strategist.

But he would always be more powerful—always more clever.

Her eyes tracked to the cabinet filled with corked bottles of the Specter's extra elixir—the source of his magic. Every night, she drank some of that power, but he also gave her an additional bottle, which she placed in her cabinet for later use.

The Specter *let* her have his power.

She often needed it to live in the house, but it was still touching that he gave it to her so freely. Celestine had hundreds of vials because she used them very rarely.

"I wish you would stand up for yourself and tell Babette off. For that matter, all the patrons, too." His voice was rich and dark, sweet yet bitter. "You don't deserve that treatment."

Celestine had no response. There was no value in standing up for herself. It wouldn't change anything. It would only make the situation far worse. Whenever Celestine tried, it only ended in more pain and abuse. It was far better to fawn, withstand, and not rock the boat.

The only times she was truly able to stand up for herself were when she played a character. Dorothy could tell off Richard and the audience at Wolfsbane, but Celestine never could.

Not as herself.

"Fortune favors the bold," the Specter said.

"As does misfortune."

"Celine… " He pulled out the word in an exasperated sigh. "Don't let her treat you that poorly. At this point, she could knock you over with a fender."

It was a malapropism. He meant feather, but he often misspoke. The Specter was brilliant, but sometimes he struggled with words. Using words that were very close but oh so subtly off.

"Anyone could knock me over with a feather." Celestine hated the truth in that.

"Celine…"

His Celine. She loved that nickname, because he was the only one who used it. And only when they were alone in her rooms. Their little secret, and it warmed her soul. The Specter called her by many nicknames, but this was by far her favorite.

She liked it so much that she began to refer to herself by this nickname.

"Celine…" he said again. The Specter didn't like the lack of response. He was impatient, but not as impatient as he was during the shows.

In as soft a tone as she could muster—because she'd learned that negative feedback could only be given in a biddable fashion—Celestine said, "If you want me to stand up to her, shouldn't you also want me to stand up to you, Specter? You force—"

"Don't call me that. Not right now," he interrupted, but the words weren't harsh. The words were a caress. It was like a plea to see him differently—to see him not as the monster who played with her emotions during every show. "I'm sorry about tonight. I don't like it when you're the murderer, either."

Celestine swallowed. What he meant to say was, *I don't like it when I make you the murderer.* But she wouldn't correct him. Forgiveness was not in the cards for the night, but she softened. He'd saved her life, and she repaid that debt with murder and obedience.

"I no longer want you to call me the Specter at night. It's too..."

Too what?

But Celestine would never find out, because the Specter never let anyone into his deep feelings.

"Will you tell me your name, so I don't have to call you the Specter?" It was an appeal. *Tell me something profound. Tell me something real, please.*

Please.

He said nothing.

"What would you like me to call you?" Celestine stared at her ceiling and pulled her covers ever so slightly up, as if defending against the inevitable rejection.

The Specter may not tell her anything tangible, but he showed his thoughts in the rustling of the curtains, the whispered hum of the electricity, and the oh-so-slight rattling of the shadows. The room twisted with his emotions, but Celestine wasn't scared. It sometimes shifted with hers, too, but only after she'd drunk the elixir.

"For now, call me Winter." His voice echoed through the

pages of the books strewn throughout her room, even causing some of them to flip.

A muscle in her cheek twitched, unprepared for an actual answer.

"Winter," she whispered back, testing the name on her tongue.

"Yes, like your favorite season."

Celestine gulped, and her face burned with unwanted emotion. Emotion she couldn't let him see. But his response meant far too much.

And that was dangerous.

"Wolfsbane was incredibly helpful tonight," Celestine said. "It did everything I asked."

"Ah, yes." The air sparkled as he spoke. "I made sure of it. It was the least I could do after…" *After I forced you to murder again.* He didn't need to finish, and never would. He changed the subject instead. "If you could have anything, what would it be?"

He never talked shop in her rooms. He only asked about her life, books, and their common interests. They had comfort and camaraderie in her chambers, but never work. Never. Except to sometimes reprimand her for being too lenient with people, like Babette.

She rolled her fingers into her blanket and propped herself up. "Including impossible things?"

"Yes, of course."

"A family."

"Children?"

"No, children are not in my future." Celestine swallowed. "I mean siblings, parents…people to infuriate and love me. *Family.* I desire nothing more than to have people who will be there for me no matter what. People to be by my side through thick and thin." She was forced to stop, because her throat grew too dry to continue. So she swallowed several times in order to finish what she truly wanted to say. "Someone to mourn me when I am gone."

"You already have that." He didn't say *with me*, but it was implied. Tears leaked from her eyes, and the Specter reached out with his shadows to stroke them away. "I will mourn you when you're gone."

He said it like it was a foregone conclusion that she would die before him—which it was. With his magic, he would outlive her. It was inevitable.

Celestine sucked in a breath, and her eyes burned from withholding more tears. She was frail. It was the one thing everyone knew about her, but just because it was true didn't mean she had to display her weakness for the world to see—and especially not him.

But inevitably, she feared they already saw everything anyway, despite her attempts at hiding it.

She cleared her throat. "So, a book or piano tonight?"

Every night, they fell asleep with either her reading to him or him playing the piano for her.

"Your choice," he said. "Always your choice."

Celestine reached out and touched the wall as if he were there on the other side. "I'll read to you. Would you like to reread *And Then There Were None* or start *Death on the Nile*?"

The Specter didn't like reading; he found the practice difficult, so she always read them their favorites, which were always Agatha Christie.

"*Death on the Nile*. We've read *And Then There Were None* too many times."

Celestine nodded, leaned down to the bookshelf holding up her bed, plucked out the book, opened it, and began to read.

She read to him for what seemed like hours, time blurring

together like a Picasso painting, lines swirling with the abstract art.

Eventually, her eyes fluttered shut, too weary to read anymore, and as sleep nearly claimed her, she whispered, "One day, I would like to know all of you." Celestine's eyes closed, and she barely heard his final response as sleep claimed her.

"Perhaps someday soon you will."

EIGHT DAYS LATER

Celestine was late.

One hour before the show, the cast drank the Specter's elixir. On the hour, on time...always. For the Specter, timeliness was truly next to godliness; which, of course, meant Celestine was highly ungodly. For her, time was a blur that tangled into itself like an unwindable ball of yarn.

Impossible to track.

The cast was supposed to be in the Green Parlor ten minutes before six. But it was at three minutes till the hour when Celestine burst in, her damp blonde locks spilling over her shoulders in clumps.

Everyone else was on time, and they were lounging on the couches, waiting for her. Embarrassment stroked across her cheeks.

"Apologies, apologies," Celestine whispered, averting her gaze and taking her place around the center table.

The Green Parlor was the "backstage" and the only room outside of the North Wing, where patrons couldn't enter during the show—named the Green Parlor because it was a confection of green. Everything was coated in a spectrum of seafoam, evergreen, and even salamander, from the velvet curtains to the couches and wallpaper. Like St. Patrick's Day had spewed all over the place.

"Thanks for showing up," Babette said sarcastically from Everett's lap, playing with his green dress shirt—apparently, he wanted to match the room. Babette desperately wanted to be one of *his* girls, and Everett was more than happy to oblige by running his fingers through her long brunette curls. "At least we can start now, since the Specter would've never let us without you."

Celestine swallowed, and instead of getting upset at the other woman's ungracious words, her stomach twisted. As much as she hated the brunette, she felt for her. Babette was rude, but her heart was in store for a heartbreak. Everett would eat her up and toss her out. She was like willow branches swaying in the wind, trying to capture a butterfly. The butterfly might grace it with its presence for a while, but it would always fly off.

Everett could make a girl's heart soar with the weight of his attention, but his love and affection were as fleeting as the butterfly.

The Ashbrook men were uncatchable. It was a rule every woman understood, yet time and time again, they all tried to tame them.

Even Celestine was no exception. But at least she knew she wasn't a monster trainer.

She knew better than to get attached to an Ashbrook. Precisely why, while she fucked James, she vowed never to love him. He wasn't capable of loving her back. Sex was a fun distraction—that was it. Despite the fact that it sometimes made her heart sick. Because deep down, as much as she promised herself she wouldn't fall for an Ashbrook, she knew she had already fallen for all three of them in different ways.

And they would one day destroy her, just like they would Babette.

The difference was that Celestine knew it.

Because wealthy men weren't for keeping.

Nor was Celestine. She was for breaking.

"Well, I am glad you're here." James's arms circled Celestine's waist as his lips stroked her neck, tickling her.

"James." Celestine giggled. It was impossible not to love the man's ministrations. He was just as much a butterfly as Everett, but Celestine tried not to care. She'd adore every moment she got with him and let him fly away when the time came.

Even though it would break her already fragile heart.

Dean cleared his throat, unapproving glare fixed on his cousin's lips as they slid along Celestine's flesh. "It's time."

Dean strolled over to the round table at the center of the room. Six character envelopes graced its edges, along with twelve bottles of elixir—the supplies the cast needed for the night's private dinner party.

Two bottles of elixir each, because one wasn't always enough.

The manor had a distinct personality of its own, and it often locked people out of rooms or completely altered the orientation of the halls. It was, in essence, a magical maze animated through the Specter's spells, which was precisely why the cast needed an extra elixir after the show. If the house decided to shift, someone with elixir could change Wolfsbane back, or at least try to convince it to.

A grandfather clock struck six, and like a synchronized dance, Frances, Babette, and Celestine took their places around the table, brought the elixir to their lips, and drank.

But as the liquid touched Celestine's tongue, a shiver ran through her bones, and her brow furrowed. It felt like lightning ripping apart the lining of her throat, worse than heartburn.

Something was terribly off.

The potion typically tasted of cherry wine, figs, and chocolate, and on rare occasions, a different wine. Tonight, it tasted like orange liqueur and coconut, with a hint of something Celestine couldn't quite put her finger on.

"Welcome, or should I say unwelcome, to tonight's adventure." A booming voice shook the room. The frequency of the sound licked at Celestine's flesh, and her poor little heart jumped, breaking its rhythm as the hairs at the nape of her neck rose.

The Specter sounded...his voice, it wasn't *his*. It wasn't liquid chocolate and smooth liquor. It was rotten ash and spiced whiskey. Close, but oh so wrong. An impersonation.

And it was a floating voice. *Floating*. The Specter only used that in her presence, and usually only in her rooms.

It was *their* special thing.

Now, he'd used it in a room of six people. The Specter would never betray her like that. Never.

This—whoever it was—was not *her Specter*. Of this, she was certain.

With gentle fingers, Celestine turned the shot glass, inspecting it. Nothing about the container was different, but she brought it to her nose and instantly shuddered. It smelled the way the voice sounded. Distorted.

"Ah, yes, our beautiful little seductress has sensed it." The false Specter's words stroked her spine like a knife. "Tonight, I'm not your Specter; I am the Phantom." His deep and sordid laugh coated the walls like clotting paint. "You are all his favorite, loyal toys—too loyal for my liking. Tonight, I'm going to play a little game with you. Tonight, *you are mine*."

Light drained from every bulb in the room like a slow
death. Celestine sucked in a breath, and gooseflesh rose on her
arms. Then rows and rows of beeswax candles burst into high,
unnatural flames, outlining everyone in an anxious, flickering
light. The green fabric coating the furniture began to refashion
itself into black, as if it had been dipped in ink.

Celestine's throat closed up, and fire scratched at her vocal
cords, cutting them off from use. Her gaze shot first to Frances,
who was equally confused, and then to Babette, who was shiv-
ering, though she tried to cover it up with a clenched jaw.

They instinctively knew this was bad and could feel it in
their bones, too.

But when Celestine's gaze stopped on the men, she realized none of them seemed surprised at all.

She knew they had already betrayed her; she just didn't yet
know the depths of their depravity, nor did she know how.
"Tonight's game is simple," the Phantom said, cutting into her
thoughts and starting an eerie rhyme. "Your Specter will in
attendance be; find him first, and you will be free. Fail, and
death will be the only thing you see."

Find the Specter? What did that even mean? Did he mean
for the cast to unveil the Specter's true identity?

That was an impossible task.

No one had ever unmasked the owner of Wolfsbane Hall.
Ever. Not in over a hundred years, since the palace first
appeared in New York in 1833.

Celestine's heart thundered, and her limbs grew weak.
Placing a hand on the table for balance, she tipped her chin up
to catch James's gaze. He shrugged, not so baffled by the situation. But he reached out and clutched her waist tightly,
drawing her into the curve of his side. She burrowed into his
protection, even though she knew she shouldn't.

It was moments like these when she wished she could keep

him forever, but that was as impossible as unmaking the Specter.

"Ah, the rhyme doesn't fit, does it?" the Phantom asked, and the inky blackness spilled from the couches and across the floor, slithering like snakes. "Let me explain more simply. I have poisoned your elixir, and you have until the end of the show—give or take five hours—to let me know which of the rich assholes in attendance tonight is your Specter." He let the words sink in before continuing. "Your options include the three fine male specimens standing before you. I'm sure you've noticed by now they didn't drink their elixir."

Her eyes dropped to each man's full, untouched bottles.

What? The question rang in Celestine's head, and her gaze touched each of theirs in turn, but it was Babette who vocalized the question.

Celestine was too stunned to process the word *poison* or even the concept that one of her friends could also be her Specter.

"Haven't you wondered why these three are cast members, despite being as rich as King Midas?" The voice vibrated with glee. "Perhaps it's because they're related to the Specter...or perhaps because they *are* him."

"Tell me it's not true." Babette faced Everett, her expression glistening with hurt. "Please, Ev."

Everett pinched his lips together and refused to speak, but his eyes spoke volumes. Saying things like, *I'm sorry. It's true, the Specter is a member of my family. A member I know intimately.*

Celestine didn't have a moment to process the exchange, because the Phantom cut in. "To solve my riddle and make a guess, all you must do is speak the Specter's name into existence. Don't worry, I'll hear you—for I will also be in attendance."

A fog traveled through the room on the wings of magic, the

Phantom making his point utterly clear. He was evil, and the cast members were his marionettes on strings. Celestine sucked in a tight breath as soft violin music underscored the point even further, but the notes were sharp, like the strings had been tightened just a little too much.

The Phantom was just as much of a showboat as his counterpart. "Unmask the Specter and live; guess incorrectly, and you will die. Forever. This time, there will be no resurrection."

8

Saturday, November 11, 1939
Green Room

This time, there will be no resurrection.

The Phantom's wicked voice lingered in Celestine's mind long after he had disappeared from the room, leaving her reeling. The cast spoke to each other in soft, confused tones, but Celestine was a limestone statue. Frozen forever in a state of horror.

There was no way to process what had just happened.

Poison. A phantom figure. A true death if they guessed the Specter's name wrong, with no Specter to rescue or resurrect her. It was all too much.

A tear rolled down her face, and she somehow made her way to the green chaise lounge and nearly fell onto it. She wasn't strong like her peers. She didn't want to process or deal with anything that had just happened. She wanted to curl into a ball in her bed and give up. For now, the lounge would have to do, because her legs were too wobbly and useless to make it all the way to her bed.

Babette didn't have the same sensibilities. She was all fight, the kind of girl Celestine so longed to be. "Wait, don't leave!" Babette yelled at the ceiling. "I have questions." She drew her lips into a flat line, waiting for a response that didn't come. She turned on Everett, rage sparking in her irises. "Where's the Specter? He's just letting this happen?"

Everett stepped back, throwing his hands up in surrender. "I don't know."

Babette shook her head. "If you don't know, why didn't you drink your elixir?" She raised a furious eyebrow. "You were always a terrible liar, Everett."

Babette stomped out of the room in a fury, and Frances followed her, trying to calm her down.

Celestine agreed with Babette, but none of it mattered. The world fell into a haze, and she barely listened as she pulled her knees into her chest, staring vacantly out into the room. She knew the Specter better than anyone else, which meant she knew how useless this task was. They were dead women walking. Souls stuck in decaying vessels. No one had ever successfully unmasked the Specter. She'd tried to figure it out for the last nine years, ever since her first day at Wolfsbane Hall. But there was nothing to find. The magic wouldn't allow it.

It was an impossible riddle with an impossible answer.

Celestine's death was inevitable. It would just take five hours to become official. What was the point of fighting? She already felt it settling into her. The poison in her veins was a physical force, like hungry acid. She felt it eating away at her already sickly body.

Time slipped away, and she completely lost track of her surroundings. The voices in the room were merging into eerie music—or possibly the Phantom was simply pumping the music into the room. It didn't matter. Celestine clutched her chest, feeling her traitorous, broken heart, and begged it to end quickly.

Just finally give out and let me be.

She didn't mind death; she just wanted it to be quick and painless.

But, of course, that was never in her cards. Her life was shaped by pain, and it had been ever since she was ten years old hearing her family brutally murdered. Listening as her mother and older sister died, screams coating their tongues. Only her father was spared, because he had already abandoned them long before that night.

If Celestine died, at least she could finally join her family in heaven—or hell. For her, probably hell, with how many times she'd murdered.

"I think you broke her," one of the Ashbrooks said, but Celestine couldn't decipher which one. They had similar tones. Plus, her brain was too engulfed by fear to hear properly.

The men continued to speak, but she didn't let her eyes focus.

"You mean *we* broke her."

"This place broke her."

One of them touched her face.

"Cellie, can you hear me?"

"Let me try. Celine? Darling, look at me."

The Specter? Only the Specter called her Celine. Maybe it was him, but she still couldn't get herself to care. Betrayal tore her insides apart. Her Specter was allowing this to happen. He had just let the Phantom take over this show, and so had these men. It was a betrayal—by all of them. And it was that bit that was too painful.

"You have to snap out of it and play the game."

She blinked, but her eyes didn't focus, and she refused to look at them. Willfully avoiding them.

"You're the only one who can win, Celine."

"No, go away. I will stay here and die in peace," Celestine said, her voice cracking.

One of the men grasped her hand. Probably James. He

never could keep his hands off her. Celestine used to like it, but now his touch only felt like treachery.

"You have to fight, Celine; this isn't how you die," the man with the velvet voice said. "You must fight."

No. The heartbreak would kill her anyways; the poison was simply speeding it up. The Ashbrooks didn't understand. What the Phantom did was bad, but it was the Specter's betrayal that truly hurt her. She had expected him to keep her safe, and now their deal was broken. She would be a victim or the murderer—playing his stupid games—as long as resurrections were in play. But now, they were completely off the table. No resurrections, and an impossible puzzle.

So what was the point of fighting? In trying? There was none, not when she barely had life left anyway.

"Fight, Celine..."

"No, I can't," Celestine whispered.

"If you don't play for yourself, play for Frances. She's like a mother to you."

Now that was just dirty.

Whichever man said it, he knew Celestine down to her core. Because there was one thing above all else that she cared for. Her family. And the cast—even Babette—was her family.

As fucked up as that family was.

Celestine hugged her knees tightly to her chest. Frances was her greatest motivation.

"What is it that you suggest I do?" Celestine blinked a couple of times, and the world finally drew back into focus. Her eyes caught first on Dean, who was standing directly in front of her, then James, who clutched her right hand, and finally Everett, who was on the other side.

"Play the game. You're the best at solving the shows," James said, chewing on a piece of gum. Except when he was kissing her, he always seemed to have a piece of gum.

"The show will help you discover the answers." Dean leaned slightly away, as if he'd just realized how close he was standing. Too close.

"And how do you know that?" Celestine once again hugged her knees, a surge of frustration stewing in her stomach.

"Because it's the Phantom," Dean said as if it were the most obvious thing in the world.

"Right, and you know who the Phantom is?"

Dean shrugged and brushed a piece of nonexistent lint off his suit coat.

"Then perhaps you could simply tell me who the Specter and the Phantom are so I can win this futile game and punch him in the face." Celestine would never, even if she could, but the sentiment felt good. It felt like milk chocolate and salted caramel. Glorious and fulfilling.

"Which him are you going to punch?" Everett asked, playing with the cufflink of his disheveled shirt. "You weren't clear on that part."

"*Everett*," Dean and James both reprimanded at once.

Everett raised his arms in a what-gives gesture. "Seemed like a fair question."

"Both." Celestine glared at all three men in turn. It was apparent none of them were taking her impending death seriously. She never expected seriousness out of Everett—he didn't have a serious bone in his body—but she expected it out of the other two. But more irritating than their lack of seriousness was that they tried to dodge her questions. "Everett, you're avoiding the question."

"Even if we did know the answer, we couldn't tell you."

"Why?"

They shared a look between them. A look that meant understanding, secrecy, and unbreakable promises. They were vaults, and she wouldn't ever get anything out of them. But now she knew all three of them were aware of the identities of the Specter and the Phantom. It was the only logical conclusion. One of them had warned the others not to drink the poison.

Warned them.

Yet, all three of them let her drink it.

Betrayal's claws ripped at her spine, and she wanted to scream.

"I don't know," Everett finally responded. "I don't know who the Specter or the Phantom is. It just felt like the right thing to say."

Lies.

Celestine inhaled sharply.

So many fucking lies.

This house and the Ashbrook family were built on them. She shouldn't have been surprised.

"Then how did you know not to drink the elixir?"

Dean answered. "We all got a note, from who I now have to assume is the Phantom, warning us not to drink it."

"Right," she said. It was just more lies. Lies on lies on lies. It was what rich men did. "And you couldn't possibly know who sent it." Sarcasm spilled from her crimson lips.

"Even if they knew, the magic wouldn't allow them to say it." The hairs on Celestine's arms had rose seconds before the booming voice of the Phantom returned.

Shadows leaked down the walls, covering the sconces in darkness and setting her head ablaze. The Phantom was so liberal with his use of magic, like his very essence—his very breath—was varnished in spells. So different from the Specter.

The Specter was a showboat, but he rarely used his magic before the guests arrived or after they left. He didn't show off to his cast. But the Phantom used magic as a tool of communication to set the tone and get under one's skin.

"Magic is a fickle thing, little Celine—"

"Don't call me that," Celestine interrupted.

He ignored her completely, and continued. "If someone reveals the source of the magic—reveals the identity of the Specter—then the magic stops working for the person receiving the information," the Phantom said. "These precious men would never ruin that for you."

Celestine watched the faces of the men in question while the Phantom spoke, measuring them and trying to find micro-expressions. Nothing. They were granite. Hard and sharp.

Maybe none of them were the Phantom, but Celestine had a feeling, a deep, instinctual feeling, that he was in the room.

Because of what they had said earlier.

You broke her.

No, we *broke her.*

An admission.

Probably.

Oh, it was so convoluted and messed up. She didn't know what to fucking think or believe.

"Magic is fickle," the Phantom repeated.

"What does that mean?"

"If any of us gave away the answer, you'd no longer be able to see the illusions or interact with the house. But most impor-tantly, you would never be able to be resurrected."

Wasn't that the threat he'd already made? Why would he care? The Phantom didn't want her resurrected. If he did, he wouldn't have given her an impossible puzzle.

"The only way you can learn our identities is to discover them yourself." The Phantom's voice touched the back of her neck.

Celestine bit her lip. There had to be a loophole, some other way to get information. If no one could tell her the identity outright, she might be able to gather it by asking questions.

If the men and the Phantom played along.

"I can ask about how the magic works?"

"Yes."

"Fine, can you project your voice through your mind?"

"Meaning?"

Celestine grounded herself by rubbing her fingers through a tassel on the throw pillow next to her. "Could you be standing next to me right now?"

He chuckled. "Perhaps."

Her skin grew taut, from the flesh of her stomach to her tingling scalp. And as if the Phantom were mocking her, the shadows currently burrowed into the walls, and the hollows of the fireplace and beneath the chairs froze, petrified like ice sculptures formed from dripping ink. The room was now filled with a maze of them.

"Stop playing with her." James slid onto the couch and pulled her into his lap like a weightless doll.

The Phantom scoffed—if a floating voice could scoff. "But is that not what you do?"

What did that mean? As the Specter? Or did the Phantom mean James's stolen kisses?

"Hilarious," James said, his lips on Celestine's hair. "Why don't you go and bother someone else? I'm sure my family will be starting to show up soon."

As if on cue, the sinister sounds of a theremin scratched at the door. The music was a beast that desperately wanted in. "Perhaps I shall leave for now." He disappeared, and Celestine's entire countenance turned gray with sorrow.

These men had betrayed her in one way or another. "If you didn't drink the elixir, how will you interact with the house tonight?"

"It would seem that the Phantom wants us only to

observe," Dean said. "Perhaps that's how he plans to play with us tonight."

Celestine scoffed and turned her head into James's chest. Dean said it like their fate was worse than poison. "You're letting this happen," she cursed into James's shirt. "All three of you. You're allowing the Phantom to torture and possibly kill me."

James kissed the top of her head, trying to be comforting. "You're not going to die. I know you'll figure it out—"

"Your faith in me is supposed to make me feel better?" she interrupted.

"Yes," Everett said. "You've never met a riddle you couldn't solve. I mean, you help me every time I play the detective. I love the part, but we all know I'm shit at it."

"This isn't a game, Everett. This is my life."

Everett shuffled his feet. "It is a game. This is Wolfsbane Hall. It's always a game."

"Even my life?" Her voice shook, and her chin quivered with anger or fear. Maybe both. "Are you hearing yourselves?"

James and Everett shared a concerned look, but Dean smiled. Amused by her pain, as usual. "Finally, a genuine reaction."

"What is that supposed to mean?" Celestine snapped.

"I've never seen you get angry with anyone." Dean slid his fingers into his pockets. "You simply accept the way people treat you. Which is terrible, in case you were wondering."

Celestine inhaled sharply and ignored the comment. "Twenty-nine."

"What?"

"Words." She bit the inside of her cheek. "In case you were counting."

"*Celestine...*" Dean pulled her name out like he was trying to savor a delicious chocolate while at the same time reprimanding her.

"Your sweetness is a problem, love." James stroked his fingers along her waist, and she batted them away.

For the first time in possibly all her life, she didn't want to appease people. Fury was stoked in her stomach. At that moment, she hated every one of them and their manipulative ways, but she still wasn't brave enough to speak it aloud. There was too much at risk.

Her life philosophy was: *suck it up and move on.* It had worked, thus far.

So instead, she excavated herself from James's lap—as painful as it was, because she did want the oblivion of a good fuck right about now.

He tried to grasp her wrists as she went, but she quickly pulled out of his grip and ran out of the room.

9

Saturday, November 11, 1939
Hallway

Celestine rested her head against the wall and pinched her eyes tight. The hallway smelled of elderberry and freshly cooked pie. It was soothing and homey, but the antithesis of her current emotions. Although the sharp edges of the gilded decor scraped against her cheeks, it helped to set the proper tone.

She hadn't made it very far. The men's voices still reached her from within the room.

"It seems she's figured out we're all rotten and not to be trusted." Dean's voice was husky with amusement.

"You don't have to sound so happy about it," Everett said.

Celestine listened for scraps of information. She knew they'd never make this game easy, and they wouldn't give her anything for free, but it was still worth a shot. Although Celestine still didn't want to play this game at all. What was the point? Death was waiting for her, no matter what.

James's voice cut through her thoughts. "Someone should go after her."

"I don't think she'll want it to be you." The timbre of Everett's voice was deep and smooth, with a knowing quality.

"Why?"

Dean let out a wolfish chuckle. "You're a scientist, but you can't figure this out? Being complicit in any way will make her hate you. Especially when you fuck her at any chance you get. You're the one she trusts the most."

"Oh…"

"I'll go," Everett offered but was quickly shut down by his brother.

"No. You are incapable of being serious or sober. I'll go."

"She hates you."

"Precisely why he's perfect for the job." James chortled in his professorial way, which drove Celestine mad.

The creak of wooden chair legs was enough warning to get Celestine moving. The last thing she needed was for *him* —Dean—to catch her listening. She tiptoed away and tried not to make a sound, her heels softly sliding against the redwood floor. Not like her sneaking mattered. If any of them were the Specter…or the Phantom, they'd already know. The walls were their eyes.

No secrets existed in Wolfsbane Hall…at least not from the Specter.

It stood to reason that the Phantom was no different.

Well, *fuck*.

Celestine glanced around at her surroundings. She'd gone north, deeper into the labyrinthine house, and she didn't know what to do. She'd gotten away, but it didn't change anything about her situation.

Poison stroked through her veins, and her limbs were already weakening. Celestine had a sickly body on a good day, but this was something different. It was like she could feel the sinister magic coursing through her blood.

Her heart was frustratingly irregular, even normally. It was either speeding up so fast she might faint, or crawling to a halt and making her lightheaded.

Sickly. She was sickly. Always.

And now she was poisoned.

Celestine steadied herself against the wall and began devising a plan. The men were right; if Frances and Babette were going to live through the night, they needed Celestine's help. Her body might be a gorgeous, useless vessel, but her mind was a sword—sharp and deadly. To her knowledge, she was the only person who could beat the Specter in chess, and she usually solved his riddles hours before the rest of the guests but remained silent to allow the show to play out. In another life, she would have been a scholar.

In another life, she would have been Sherlock Holmes.

But that life wasn't for her. She wasn't lucky enough to be born into the right family, nor was she lucky enough to be born a man. Modern women in 1939 had made waves in the last twenty years, gaining the vote and challenging restrictive dress codes, but men still owned the world.

And the Ashbrooks owned San Francisco, and to them, she was a lowly whore. The mere fact that she wasn't chaste made her untouchable by the elite society.

No, the life of a scholar wasn't for her. So, her job was to be a masterly maneuvered puppet with a pretty face and big tits. But tonight's job was to survive, even if it was just one night.

One day at a time.

But where to start? Only one option immediately sprang to mind—one terrible option. If the game was about uncovering the Specter's identity, then the logical location for her to search was his rooms. Under normal circumstances, Celestine wouldn't dare enter his forbidden chambers in the North Wing, but tonight, she was tempted.

She bit the inside of her cheek. Oh, she hated everything about this night. She couldn't violate Specter's privacy.

The mere idea caused the hairs on her arms to rise, but her life was on the line—and more importantly, Frances's life was on the line. The only mother figure she'd known since she was ten years old.

Celestine bit her lip and rubbed her hands down her face before stepping toward the North Wing.

Oh, this is so reckless, so, so foolish, Celine, she thought.

It didn't matter. Frances mattered, and Celestine would ask forgiveness from the Specter tomorrow if her frail body lasted the night.

Unfortunately, nothing was ever easy in the ever-moving, ever-knowing house. She wanted to rip open its secrets like it was a body in an autopsy, crack open its ribs and poke through its darkest and most hidden parts. So, of course, the house actively worked against her. The halls to the North Wing coiled like snakes, shifting and moving so that it was nearly impossible for her to walk through.

The process of navigating the halls made her feel like she had ingested seven cocktails.

Still she tried.

Wolfsbane was in a rather obstructive mood, but it was unclear if it was the work of the Specter, the Phantom, or simply the house itself. Celestine never knew how much of the house was her immortal lord pulling the strings, or if the house had a personality of its own.

Given that she was hunting down the Specter's secrets, it seemed more plausible that he was coaxing the house. But if that were true, it infuriated her. It would mean he was here, allowing this.

But none of that mattered right now. She had a plan to

complete. And if the path was treacherous, so be it. The house still allowed her movement until—

Marionette dolls dropped from the ceiling, flanking the walls. Celestine froze in her tracks, her breath hitching as spiders climbed the rungs of her ribcage. The dolls hung down, floating like corpses, standing at attention like palace guards on duty. To say it was eerie would be an understatement. It didn't bode well for what lay ahead throughout the rest of the night.

The Phantom's disposition was sinister—nothing like the Specter's glittering jubilance. The house never tried to scare her on a normal night. It would rather lure her into subservience with glamour and decadence.

Celestine sucked in a breath, her gaze locked on the closest doll. Its eyes sparked with excitement, staring—no, glaring—back at her. Its porcelain face was carved and painted with a delicate hand. The details nearly looked real but fell just short enough to send shivers of fear through her bones. And the thing stared at her...waiting...for something she didn't know.

A bead of sweat clung to her temple as she picked up her foot. It might be foolish to walk into the dolls. Theoretically, they could do anything from spitting venom out of their mouths to catapulting arrows from their eye sockets to whispering sleeping spells.

But Celestine would reach her destination, and the only way forward was to go through. So foolishly, she continued, her pulse hammering in her ears.

As the soles of her shoes touched the red embroidered carpet, the dolls opened their mouths in unsettling unison. Celestine ducked, preparing for projectiles, but she was met only with song.

A children's rhyme repeating over and over and over again. It sounded like nails on a chalkboard mixed with the tones of a mezzo-soprano jazz singer. Soothing and horrifying all at the same time. It didn't help that violins were playing under the song, mostly in key.

It took a moment to decipher the rhyme. It was well-known, written over two hundred years ago about a young woman's suicide.

Celestine's stomach churned, and she wanted to clasp her hands to her ears, but instead, she chose to run and not stop until reaching the Specter's chamber doors.

As her fingertips touched the ebony handle, the chorus of voices stopped, but the dolls, in unison, turned their heads to watch her more closely.

Celestine twisted the door handle frantically. She didn't expect it to open. Luck was never on her side, but one could hope.

And, of course, it didn't open. Not after that display in the hallway.

The rosewood door stood at attention, menacing and tall. A winged lion was etched into its center, and Celestine slid a finger along its smooth edges. *Wolfsbane, darling, will you open the door for me?*

The paintings along the halls viciously rattled in response.

A "no," then.

Alright. Celestine huffed. She'd have to do it the hard way. Her hair always had a pin for a reason. She pulled one out and bent it into a lockpick. Being a starving orphan had some advantages. Stealing might be a sin, but it had kept her alive, and she'd perfected her lock-picking skills at a young age. Seven years on the streets did that to a kid.

Desperation did that.

The pin slid around the gears of the lock. The sound of the metal scraping against metal and clicking into place was beautiful. It was seductive—a song of success, a promise of food for an empty stomach. A shiver of pride skated through her veins as the tantalizing sound rang into her ears.

But it was short-lived. As she moved to turn the pin, it disintegrated between her fingertips.

"Fuck, fuck, fuck." Her hands fell to her sides, and she gritted her teeth. There was no way in. Not if Wolfbane was this determined to thwart her attempts.

"That's going well." Dean chuckled, and she jerked back, goosebumps rising on her skin.

Where the hell had he come from? He leaned against the wall behind her, his arms crossed and a lethal smile gracing his too-perfect lips. The man moved like smoke and secrets. And it was just as discomposing as the Phantom's dolls.

"You could assist." She grunted, kicking the door and immediately regretting it because her feet were already swollen; she didn't need to add more pain.

"Does the kicking help?"

She flashed a glare. "It seems as helpful as you are."

His smile widened, and the act should've been illegal, because when Dean Ashbrook smiled, he glowed like he was Apollo in human form.

It was utterly unfair.

"What makes you think I would know how to open that door?" He arched one eyebrow as if it were a competition. "That magical door…"

"Because apparently you either are related to the Specter, or you are the Specter."

Dean wiggled a brow at this as if saying, *Am I?*

She turned her back on him. His disgusting perfection was too much to look at. "And that was fifteen."

"Fifteen? What do you keep counting?"

"It's the number of words you manage to say to me at once." She returned to ignoring him, biting the inside of her cheek, and examined the door again. Specifically, the hinges. She cocked her head sideways. With enough upward force, she might be able to get the door off its hinges.

But she wasn't strong enough for that.

"Well, here are eighteen more: You should try asking the Phantom for help breaking down the door. He seems to hate the Specter."

"Twenty-two words," she corrected. "Or you, as the Specter's relation, can open it for me."

He slid his hands into his pockets in direct defiance. "So demanding, Celine. You're never like this with anyone else."

Don't use that name. Only the Specter called her that, and now both the Phantom and Dean had. It wasn't a name for them. It was for her Specter.

Celestine scrunched her nose. But she had to admit, Dean was right. She wasn't demanding. Dean did something to her, causing fire to lick the inside of her veins and allowing the carefully hidden frustration to float to the surface. It was so...irritating.

"Why *are* you talking to me? Aren't you breaking your number one rule: Never speak to Celestine?"

He loosed a half-grunt, half-chuckle—a grunkle? *Heavens, Celine, never think something so foolish again.* "Do you truly think the Specter would leave something lying around in his rooms for anyone to find?"

No, she didn't. But Celestine knew the Specter better than anyone. Something might help.

"Dean Ashbrook"—she waved at the door—"show me your magic."

She asked because she wanted to trick him into showing her the truth.

"I don't have magic. Not without the elixir."

Liar. All Ashbrooks were such liars.

Celestine had lived in Wolfsbane long enough to notice when things were off, and there was always something off with those men. If the Specter was related to Dean, then didn't it stand to reason that Dean would have magic, too? Even without the elixir. And if he did, did it mean he was the Specter...or the Phantom?

"I know you have magic," she said. "So show it to me."

"Why?"

"Because I asked you to."

"And why would I ever do anything for you?"

Celestine shook her head. He wouldn't, because he hated her. It was the one true thing standing between them.

She huffed. This was a useless task. Even if Celestine managed to get the door off its hinges, the Specter would put up barrier, after barrier, after barrier. Plus, there was only so much of Dean she could stand. So she pivoted on her toes and walked off.

"Wait."

Celestine paused her footfalls and twirled on her heel, her arms crossed.

"I'll help," he said, touching the door. "But only because I am fascinated."

By what?

As she stepped back up to him, the door clicked and swung open, the creak of the aged wood rattling through her ears.

Celestine's jaw slackened, and she physically recoiled from Dean and the Specter's quarters. The temperature in the hall dropped, and the sound of rain pounded against the house's windowpanes, banging like her heart inside her chest.

"You are magic." It came out as a breath.

She wrapped her arms around her center as if she could protect herself, because this meant one of three things. One, he was the Specter; two, he was the Phantom; or three, all the

Ashbrooks possessed magic. And Celestine didn't know which scenario was scarier. It made sense for Dean to be the Phantom because he'd always hated her, but if he were the Specter…

She wouldn't know what to do.

A teardrop of sweat rolled down her temple. If Dean was the Specter, then it meant nothing between her and him was real. Nothing. And that was the worst feeling imaginable.

"But the elixir." She finally got her tongue to form more words.

"I don't need it," he admitted. "I never have."

Celestine gulped and wrapped her arms tighter. "Why would you simply show me that?" *Why now?*

"Because I can."

Thunder boomed outside her, scoring the unease that cut through her bones. Processing all the new information seemed impossible. Poison, magic, and devious men—men she thought were her friends.

But people didn't treat their friends this way.

Celestine chose not to process any of it, because if she did, she would totally unravel. Instead, she locked it away for future inspection.

The door creaked again as Dean pushed it further open, his eyes sharp on her, examining all her flaws.

He stepped into a massive antechamber, and she followed. The room had no furniture, but it was decorative and led to three ancient red oak doors.

The room didn't need furniture, because it was laced with sorcery, the walls looking like they had been formed from the fingertips of gods. Every surface vibrated with life. One wall moved like a breathing, living thing, and a mural of a tranquil waterfall, surrounded by a periwinkle garden, rested on its surface. Across from it was a wall with a glittering mirror. It was formed from swirling silver liquid, and both walls looked like they could have been portals into another world. On the final wall hung a massive family portrait of the Ashbrooks, but it seemed to have been painted ages ago. All the women wore rococo dresses, and the men wore exuberant wigs.

The hairs on Celestine's arms rose. It was either an original painting or just a mock-up designed to resemble the 1760s. Her gaze flickered to Dean and burned through him. Wolfsbane Hall had been in operation for 104 years, first established in New York and later relocated to San Francisco during the Gold Rush. If the painting was original, then was Dean immortal? Was his entire family? Or was Wolfsbane passed down from son to son like a dukedom?

"Unsettling, isn't it?" Dean asked, his eyes catching on a doppelgänger of himself.

Unsettling was an understatement.

Immortals weren't real, right? Vampires and other creatures of the night didn't exist. They were creatures of storybooks and nightmares, not reality. The painting was just a painting, showing the Ashbrooks as if they were nearly 300 years old. Except if all of that were true, then where had Dean's magic come from? If magic were real, so too could immortals be.

"And for the first time, you are speechless in my presence." Dean slid his hands into his pockets and leaned against the wall, knocking the frame of the mirror.

It took everything within her not to ask if he was immortal. The words would sound foolish, escaping her lips. Wouldn't they?

But the Ashbrooks couldn't be. They were new money, like the Vanderbilts of New York City. Upstarts, clout chasers, and everyone knew they had gotten rich off their railroads.

Celestine inhaled sharply. The painting didn't matter.

There were bigger missions at play. Find evidence of the Specter's identity in order to save Frances's life.

So, by pure feeling, she chose one of the three doors. To her relief, it opened with a simple twist of the door handle. Inside was a bedroom suite featuring a bathroom, a small study, and a dressing area.

The study was bursting with cabinets, shelves carved into the walls, piles upon piles of papers, stacks of boxes, and all manner of elaborate decorations. Even a snow globe, which looked to be filled with rose gold glitter, adorned the desk at the center of the room.

Not wasting time, Celestine focused on the study and ransacked the drawers. All unlocked.

Dean followed close behind, sometimes accidentally blocking her rampage—and it *was* a rampage. All the anger building inside of her poured out onto the Specter's belongings.

Celestine tore through useless papers discussing taxes, boring vendor deals, food for the kitchens, florals for the halls, and paint for the walls. All normal housekeeping stuff. The only bizarre part was that Wolfsbane Hall wouldn't even need it to begin with. And unfortunately, all the documents were conveniently missing identifying information.

Because luck was never on her side.

Throughout most of her "inspection," Dean stood, silently observing, occasionally sidestepping out of her way. Lord forbid he touch her. He had been letting her have her way with the stuff. Perhaps a positive sign. She couldn't imagine the Specter standing by and watching as she destroyed his things.

Celestine turned violently, wanting to rip through another cabinet, but a wall of lean muscle blocked her. She instinctively jerked away, her back hitting a filing cabinet, the sharp edge of it leaving a bruise that would blossom later. She stepped toward Dean, figuring it was a mistake and that he would move, but he didn't. Instead, he'd placed himself inches from her, his chiseled chest nearly touching her.

Celestine's breath hitched. The energy surging between them was electric. Powerful, but deadly to the touch. Her heart screamed in her ears. But Dean didn't move. Instead, he stared down at her, arms crossed and eyes sparkling with an emotion she couldn't decipher.

A warm stroke of his breath caressed her neck, and shivers danced down her spine. Celestine swallowed hard, begging the man to move, because she absolutely wouldn't touch him.

She *wouldn't*.

He would hate it, and she would...like it?

Oh, she was in a terrible state. All she wanted was to tame the man who hated her. To be worthy of a powerful, rich, possibly immortal man's attention. She wanted to be seen and known by him.

But she never would be. She was too poor and too garish.

"Dean." Her voice was breathy. She swallowed and curled her nails into her palms, leaving indents. "You should get out of my way."

He eyed her, the corner of his lip lifting, moving his hands firmly into his pockets—he loved his pockets. Or he loved the fact that he couldn't touch her if there were a barrier between them.

Life was a series of unfair events. For as much as he longed not to touch her, she longed just as much to touch him.

"I think those might be of use to you." He pointed to papers that had fallen from a book during her tirade, and then he stepped aside to let her reach them.

There was a series of old newspaper articles dating back over two hundred years. Obituaries and gossip sheets about a noble family and a girl's deaths. Article after article. All rumors. All personal sources, except a few newspaper sources, were relaying big events of the day.

Celestine turned through them.

One article was dated 1760 and read, *The Duke of Breython's maid found on Christmas Eve, dead of an apparent suicide. The Marquess and his brother are heartbroken by Miss Marguerite's death.*

Celestine flipped the papers and continued reading headline after headline.

1893: *Business tycoon embroiled in scandal at the railroads. Should he be charged with murder in the train crash?*

1758: *Another fiancée of the Beast of Winter, Marquess Winterly, mysteriously disappears.*

1761: *The Duke of Breython and his family were mysteriously poisoned during the annual house party on Christmas Eve. Thought to be dead, the family made a miraculous recovery and are all in good health and spirits. It is still unclear who might be responsible for the poisonings, but some believe Marguerite's vengeful spirit came back to haunt the family, as it has been precisely one year since her demise.*

1810: *Young Lady Breython is caught scandalously with a dead man in her bed.*

And so on and so forth. Piles of newspaper clippings about rich, powerful families doing bad, bad things. Then there was a pile of love letters. One started: *My Dearest M, it feels like ages since we've been together...*

Sappy, terrible stuff.

While Celestine read, Dean hovered behind her and grunted, judging the letters the same way.

"What are they supposed to mean?" Celestine asked, looking up at him.

Dean shrugged.

"They were hidden away in a book, so they must be important, right?"

He shrugged again. Frustrating. The man was utterly maddening and unhelpful, like all men, really.

Celestine sucked in a breath and decided to do something brazen. "So, Dean Ashbrook, are these your rooms? Are you the Specter?"

Dean raised a single, manicured eyebrow as if it were a sport.

"Oh, I know you won't say." She stood and took a step toward him, cornering him like a doe in headlights, intentionally getting close enough to make him uncomfortable. Celestine wasn't brazen, but she had played enough characters in her time at Wolfsbane to fake it. "I wanted to see how you would respond."

"And?" he asked, standing his ground.

She inched closer, her gaze raking over his form. Frustratingly, he didn't give anything away. But he never had. The man was talented with his masks, wearing them like a crown of indifference and loathing. Always.

"You couldn't possibly be."

"Oh." The corner of his lips drew up.

"You're more likely to be the Phantom."

"Hmm..." His eyes pinned her in place, and he closed the distance between them, daring her to retreat and calling her bluff. "An interesting conclusion."

Every muscle in her body shook, and she gulped. "You hate me just enough to poison me."

"Do I?" He flashed a dimple, and desire trickled down her spine.

Dimples surely should be outlawed.

Warmth spread over her body, and red painted her cheeks as the articles slipped through her fingers. Proximity to devils was always dangerous, especially this one, because he caused unwanted, terrible sensations in her body.

And she was so hot. Too hot, painfully hot. The hairs on her arms were singed, and her lungs were filling with toxic smoke.

She shook her head, coughing.

It wasn't just runaway lust. The room was literally on fire.

10

Saturday, November 11, 1939
The North Wing

Flames licked up Celestine's spine, and the air filled with thick black smoke. She coughed, drawing the top of her dress up to filter the air, but she couldn't leave just yet. She had to scour the floor for the articles. They were important. She knew it in her bones, and if she were to save Frances's life and hers, Celestine needed to get them.

So she fell to her knees, frantically trying to gather the lost ones. A letter burst into flames as her fingers touched it. Intentionally destroying itself. The house? Or the Specter? Or the Phantom?

It had to be the Specter, because the house was actively impeding all her efforts to discover more about the Ashbrooks. The Specter impeding *her...her specter...*hurting *her.*

It shouldn't have been surprising, yet it was. A part of her believed the Specter wanted to aid her—the part of him that cared for her. And if she were being honest, she wanted him to love her enough to save her.

But it was all foolishness.

No one would ever love her that much.

Embers popped as she managed to read the beginning of another letter before it, too, burned away in her hands, the paper flaking into charred pieces. *Brother, I really must protest your plan...*

Brother.

The word triggered a memory. *It was after a show, and Celestine was tucked into bed, her covers up to her chin. She was always cold, due to the unreasonable slowness of her heartbeat at rest.*

"It's more complicated than simply getting along with her. Babette is confrontational and often adversarial, but she—"

"She reminds you of your sister?" the Specter asked. He knew Celestine far too well, and she barely knew him. It was utterly frustrating. But it was life.

"Yes."

"Understandable. My brother can be quite adversarial as well. Sometimes I want to kill him, but he's family."

Brother. The Specter had a brother! So the Specter was one of the twins. James didn't have a brother—only a sister. Unless...the cloaked owner of Wolfsbane was one of the Ashbrooks' other male relations. Their fathers?

It was the only other option. The Ashbrooks were infamous, and their antics were published in all the San Francisco gossip rags. So everyone in the city knew that the twins' father was also a twin. Walter and Archibald. The only other male member of the Ashbrook clan was James's maternal uncle Jon, but he didn't have a brother.

So the Specter was a twin. But which generation, and which man?

And more importantly, which one did she want it to be? Everett? Dean? Her gaze tracked to the handsome devil, his muscular body silhouetted against the flames.

Celestine swallowed smoke and coughed.

It was a riddle made just for her. No one else would have that level of personal information about the Specter. Perhaps

James was right, and would she be the first person to uncover the Specter's identity in over 100 years?

Doubtful.

But possible?

Celestine coughed, the world coming back into focus. How had she wholly forgotten she was in a burning room? Her hands drew up to her forehead, and she clutched her face. Her eyes stung, watering. Heat clung to her face, and smoke filled all her pores.

Yet even knowing she was seconds away from passing out from the smoke inhalation, Celestine wouldn't leave the room.

I can't leave yet.

She needed answers. It was the only thing that might keep her alive for one more day.

She *was* truly a fool.

But the fire meant she was getting close.

"Celestine, we have to go." Dean shook her shoulders. "Celine, the fire. Come on."

"No, there has to be something else."

"The only thing here now is your death," Dean said. "You have to leave."

She sucked in a breath, the smoke caking her lungs. A cough ripped from her burning throat. She *was* going to die. A red haze covered her eyes, but it didn't matter; there was a mission to complete.

"You have to leave." Dean's voice was husky and dark.

"No." Her fingers caught more articles and letters as blood dripped from her nose and her eyelids drooped. If she didn't get out of the room soon, she would die, and there were no resurrections tonight. Celestine had died more times than she could count, but she always came back to life.

"For the record, you're forcing me to do this," Dean growled, scooping her into his arms and throwing her over his shoulder as if she were a weightless doll. His touch sent a current of electricity through her veins. It was utterly inappropriate to find it so enticing...yet she did. She truly, truly did, even when facing death.

Celestine's eyes fluttered shut, and in her smoke-addled condition, she nestled into the warmth of his body, as content as a cat sunbathing.

His rosewood, musk, and citrus scent wafted into her nostrils, the smell of pure *man*. He smelled like oranges and carnal desires. But she didn't have time to appreciate it, because darkness clawed at her mind and ripped her consciousness away.

"You're a fool."

Celestine blinked, confused by the words and the voice that had to belong to Dean Ashbrook.

"I, what?" she said, rubbing her stinging eyes.

"You're a fool," he repeated. "You could have died from the smoke intalation." He said the word wrong. That was... interesting. "Do you have a death wish?"

"Would it matter? I am already dying." Celestine's words were thick and chalky.

"You're poisoned, not dying."

"And what is poison, Dean?" Defiance seeped from her tongue, and she sat up, blinking again. The room came into focus. It was the Red Salon, and she was strewn across the couch like a throw blanket. Dean kneeled on the floor as if nursing her back to health. A task she was sure he hated.

"If you die in the game, you die. You won't be able to guess the Specter's true name if you spend the night dead." Which was why even magically controlled fire was so dangerous. It might not take her life on a typical night, but there was nothing typical about this night.

"What happened?" she asked, voice strained.

"You mean the fire?" Dean furrowed his brow and braced the cushions next to her—always keeping space between them.

Celestine nodded, resting her sore vocal cords.

"The Phantom or the Specter wanted to keep you from discovering the room's secrets, and they set it on fire."

"I know that part. I am not stupid." Celestine's lips fell into a flat line as her fingers fiddled with the fringe of a red throw pillow. She, too, wanted distance from the man, but she also needed something to do with her hands. "After I passed out."

"The fire stopped as soon as we left the wing. It was a warning." He shifted uncomfortably on the wooden floor, yet he still avoided her, which was impressive because keeping any amount of distance from her in his position was nearly an impossible task.

"Why won't you touch me?"

"I just touched you, unless you don't recall how I threw you over my shoulder like a bratty child and saved your life." His words were rude, but they were also fermented by concern. His eyebrows creased as he lifted himself to view her eyes better. His gaze probed hers, checking her pupils for dilation. It was as if he wanted to make sure she didn't have a concussion.

The dimple in his cheek flashed, soaking with a mixture of exasperation and genuine fear.

Celestine didn't know how to handle the weight of his attention, so she said, "I remember." She shook her head and immediately regretted it. Dizziness stroked the edges of her cerebellum, and she placed a hand on her head.

So weak.

Dean's reaction was instant. Quickly, he grasped her face with his strong, steadying hands. Celestine blinked and stared at him. Her breath hitched, but this time not from the fire. The feel of his flesh on hers devoured all her resistance, ripping through her like a tidal wave.

Celestine's ribcage tightened in on her, and she felt like she was suffocating as time froze.

Dean Ashbrook was touching her. *Actively* touching. And it was so bewildering. Celestine's heart could have stopped from the shock. The touch must have pained him, because he winced—actually *winced*.

One thing was true. Celestine might have been poisoned, but she was his poison. That was how much he hated her.

11

The grandfather clock chimed seven o'clock. The official start time for the Ashbrook show. Celestine stood in the ballroom, her head resting against the golden ballroom wall. As soon as she could stand on her own, she got as far away from Dean as she could manage.

The night glowed with enchantment, but it rotted like long left-out fruit—once beautiful and life-giving sustenance, now just a waste of space. The room smelled of roses and aged brandy. Sweet yet pungent. It was a night of contradictions.

None of the guests had arrived yet, so Celestine rested, holding her character card, once again refusing to open it. Apparently, this was becoming a thing. But she didn't want to open it, because if she did, everything would be too real.

So, like a child, she refused. Celestine was becoming rather defiant. It wasn't one of her usual traits, and it surprised her.

But in this case, avoidance was the best practice...wasn't it?

It had to be.

Celestine's simple red dress shifted around her shoulders as she watched Wolfsbane Hall. The club sparkled and gleamed like a far-off star. Brilliant yet untouchable. Jazz music floated through the halls, calling to the depths of her soul. Ghost-like illusions danced the jive, emanating laughter and excitement. They were like dolls from a music box, given life and one magical night to live like Cinderella. The light shining through the stained-glass ceiling painted them in hues of purple and magenta, and they looked like a whisper in a dream. Glimmering, beautiful, but ethereal.

The only real people in the room were the cast.

Dean stood off to the side, taking everything in like a brooding prince on the edge of a battlefield, yet he wore modern attire, a cobalt-blue suit jacket, vest, and tie.

James, Everette, Frances, and Babette played a hand of poker at a round dinner table, set off to the side of the dance floor, a ghost dealer handing them cards and telling them scandalous tales.

The ghosts were such terrible gossips. So much so that Celestine sometimes had a hard time believing they weren't real—the actual dead appearing for a night of terror and debauchery.

At a closer glance, Babette sat on an unopened briefcase, as if guarding it. She kept it away from the rest of the cast, hoarding it like a dragon's treasure. Per usual, Babette was stingy with her clues. She always refused to help anyone else.

Celestine couldn't relate. She didn't see Wolfsbane as a competition. It was an experience—one that could be far more enjoyable with cooperation and friendship.

But they were fundamentally different in this way.

Celestine's eyes tracked to Everett. He wore a moss-green jacket with a matching vest and tie, while James wore shades of dove gray and ash. All three men looked like a kaleidoscope of bad ideas. Charming, gorgeous, and bound to destroy one's reputation. Celestine had already fallen prey to that indecency too often—especially with James. He was a tempting disaster, and far too good of a fuck for his own good...and hers.

"You look absolutely atrocious tonight," a sweet, saccharine voice said from Celestine's left, and she jolted, clutching her already erratic heart.

"Vivian," Celestine said, "you scared me."

"Jumpy tonight?" Vivian Ashbrook, James's younger sister, asked with a twinkle in her eye. "Does it have anything to do with your sickly complexion and general sad sack demeanor?" Vivian pulled Celestine into a hug and held her tightly. "I am not sure why you look so atrocious, but clearly, you need this."

Celestine allowed herself a moment of comfort.

Vivian was a life raft in a sea of betrayal. She was both Celestine's best friend and eternal adversary. They could read each other's moods down to the smallest microexpression, which was both wonderful and horrible. It was great to be known so deeply by someone, but it also meant she was left vulnerable. Because Vivian saw everything. Worse, Vivian didn't always handle their closeness well. She had two sides, an angel or a demon. It depended on the day and the moment. She could make you feel so safe and loved, but she could also rip you to shreds. She was one of those rich girls with mommy issues and deep emotional instability. Not that Celestine was much better as the sad little orphan girl with abandonment issues.

"You didn't answer me." Vivian pouted.

Because what did one say to *you look atrocious*?

"Do you know about the Phantom?"

"Phantom?" Vivian questioned, smoothing out her sleek black dress spun from spider silk. She wore a platinum-blonde wig with a full face of makeup—her real hair color was dark brown. Pearls laced her neck, and rubies draped from her ears. Everything about the girl screamed old money. Except she never wore furs, as an act of rebellion.

"Well, the Specter isn't—"

"Wait." Vivian held up a hand. "Don't tell me. It will ruin the show, won't it?"

Would it? Celestine wasn't sure.

"Well, I got this." Vivian handed over an envelope. "It's my invitation."

The letter was written on parchment, giving it the illusion of age. It smelled of beeswax with a slight hint of coconut. And like all good Murder Mystery parties, Vivian had received a mysterious note directing her to the mansion and the game.

Dearest Vivian,

Tonight is our night of reckoning. Your past might be buried fifteen feet deep, and perhaps it will stay that way, but if you do not appear at Wolfsbane Hall at 7:00 p.m. on November 13, I will expose all your secrets to your family and the world at large.

See you then, liebste Schwester,

The Specter (or something like it)

The Phantom must have been a fan of Agatha Christie's recently released book, *And Then There Were None*, because the game's setup was nearly identical: threats to uncover secrets and being summoned to a mysterious, secluded mansion.

But the note also contained a clue.

Liebste Schwester

Celestine knew these words, but it had been far too long since she studied German. Her lessons ended after her family's horrific deaths and her being placed in foster care. Her foster parents only cared about the money they received from the government and did not continue Celestine's lessons.

"It's so macabre," Vivian said with an uninterested droll.

"*Liebste Schwester?* What does it mean?" Celestine asked, handing the note back.

"Dearest sister."

Celestine's heart pounded like a snare in her ears, and her

eyes flashed to James. *James*. Was her sweetheart the one torturing her—the Phantom?

Was there another option?

"They love calling me that or *wenig liebe*," Vivian said, her eyes tracking her brother and the twins.

"They?"

"All three of them."

"They all call you sister?"

Vivian sucked in an exhausted breath. "Of course. It's their favorite thing. Now, if you would excuse me, I have a bone to pick with my brother...and *cousins*." She added the last bit as an afterthought.

The fake blonde strolled off like a feline about to pounce on her prey, curls bouncing with each footfall. A part of Celestine felt sorry for the men, but the vengeful part of her thought they all deserved the storm coming their way.

Celestine rubbed her face, the ghost of a spider crawling up her skin. *James*. James? Truly, she didn't want him to be the Phantom. He was supposed to be her comfort, her escape, not her executioner. But then it could make sense. Celestine was nothing to James except a good fuck, and James was a bit of a psychopath. He didn't possess the ability to love.

A stinging sensation cued at the corners of Celestine's eyes, and she tried to suck in the emotions threatening to fall as she watched the men receiving their verbal whipping. The sound didn't travel far enough to reach Celestine's ears, but she still gathered that none of it was good.

Everett clenched his fists and turned the shade of a fresh apple, while James merely painted a stoic smirk on his sharp features and played with a metal contraption. Another one of his little inventions.

"Do you think I'm James?" the Phantom asked, a soft voice at the back of her neck, like a lover whispering into her ear. The sensation grated against her heart. All at once, wonderful and rotten.

"Were you listening to my conversation with Vivian?" Her voice came out breathy and far too intrigued. *No. Get it together, Celine.*

"I always listen to you, my sweet Celine."

"Don't call me that." She swatted at the disembodied voice behind her ear. It was no longer seductive. Now, it was infuriating. Celine was the Specter's name to call her, not this terrible beast.

"I like you in red."

"Well, red looks good on most blondes," she snapped back, and her eyes locked once again on James. Possibly the traitor speaking in her ear?

"Oh, this night is going to be a delight."

Celestine scoffed. "I am sure it will be for you, but mark my words: If you are one of my friends, and you've done this to me, I will never speak to you again."

The air around her sparked with heat, like a blanket coating her skin. The Phantom reacting, of sorts. But it was unclear what the warmth meant. It wasn't embarrassment, nor was it anger. "As you should."

"I hate you."

"And I enjoy you just a little too much." He chuckled, deep and husky, and the sound vibrated through her body, sparking a feeling she wished would vanish. Lust pooled in her core. One was not supposed to desire their torturer. "I always have and probably always will."

Celestine shuddered, and gooseflesh skated over her skin.

"Stop flirting with her." The painting of a grand duke awoke from its slumber, and it was not happy. At the sound of his voice, a star burst to life in Celestine's chest, filling her with its burning, energetic force. Her Specter was finally here.

And it mattered far too much that he decided to show up.

Darkness leaked out of the walls and curled around her legs. She physically felt them, like a sexual caress. Her breath hitched, and she clutched the wall to steady herself. She couldn't fall apart like this in public.

"She's mine," the shadows hissed at the other disembodied voice.

Mine.

"So she is." The Phantom chuckled. "To business, then?"

"Yes, after all this, sticking to business would be the best course of action." Celestine's shadow, lingering on the wall, spoke with the Specter's velvet voice.

A teardrop of sweat dripped down her back, and she swallowed. These enchanters were causing a storm within her body, and she needed to get control of herself.

Focus. Use them. Find answers.

Instinctively, Celestine squinted, searching the room to see what the men were doing. The light caught Dean's raven hair as he tried to calm down his cousin, Vivian. He had traveled to the commotion to rescue his brother. Despite nearly always having a scowl written on his perfect face, Dean had a far more stable energy than his twin.

None of them seemed remotely distracted; instead, they were all aligned in their resistance to Vivian. None of them felt like they were talking to Celestine, seducing her.

"It's past time to open your character card, Celestine." It was the Phantom's cold voice at the nape of her neck. "This show is rolling forward, whether you choose to accept it or not."

How did he know that was why she didn't open it?

"Your character will help you find the answer to your riddle."

Celestine crossed her arms. "I don't want your help, or

my character's." It wasn't true, but she felt like being obstinate. Something about him or this moment caused her to fight—if only a little. A change from her usual appeasement strategy.

"I need you to play." A shadow in the mirror beside her echoed with sound. It was another way to tell them apart. The Phantom didn't use multiple ways to speak. He was only a floating voice, and that was it. No flash or pageantry. "I need you, Cellie."

Celestine pinched her eyes shut and rested her head against the wall. These wicked spirits were breaking her. It might not have been their intention, but it was the result.

"Play the game, Celestia." Rocks crackled, the sound like stones shifting in a vase.

Celestine opened her eyes to see the Specter animating a statue. His narcissistic presence knew no bounds; he had to use various mediums to communicate. To titillate a crowd. But it wasn't a statue. It was the marble of the floor shifting. The Specter was in everything.

Comforting and terrifying all at once.

"I promise the game will lead you to the truth," the Phantom said.

Celestine gulped. "What are your promises worth?"

Neither of them answered. Instead, a guttural and empty silence writhed through the room—the silence of a casket inside a tomb. One that had been abandoned for thousands of years, the wood disintegrating and exposing the human remains to the harsh, unforgiving elements.

Celestine was all alone.

The last thing she wanted to do was trust the Phantom. But what other choice was there? So she gave in and opened the letter, letting the character flow into her skin, brain, and heart. Let it become a part of her for the night. But this time, the process was…different. Aggressive. It felt like being kicked in the gut. It felt like an assault.

Celestine flinched and hit the wall, knocking two paintings together. They swung back and forth as she steadied herself, catching her knees. The sound of the frames sliding against drywall slid through her ears.

Slide, scratch, slide.

Her heart hammered in her ears and at the base of her skull. Each beat sent a stroke of fear down her spine. Celestine tried to suck in a breath to regain her composure, but it was an impossible task. The magic was steeped in her skin and her head, and it burned like midnight rain during a firestorm.

But the weirdest part about all of it was that a character's history and script did not enter her mind. She didn't have any dialogue, no goals. There was no script.

Celestine's whole body shuddered.

Her red silk dress, which had been clinging to her curves, morphed, sizzling and transforming into a maid's outfit. It was a costume fitting the current period. Sometimes Wolfsbane's stories were set in the past, in the age of glorious crinoline skirts and over-the-top wigs. But not tonight. Instead, Celestine wore an A-Line cotton poplin dress with a scalloped white collar, cuffs, and a white cap.

Not alluring, glamorous, or tempting in any way.

Perhaps Babette would be happy…finally. Seeing Celestine's character brought so low.

Doubtful, though. Babette was never happy.

Celestine's hands squeezed her knees, and she slowly stood, rolling her spine one vertebra at a time, but she had to lean against the wall for balance.

"What in all the hell was that?" Celestine uttered, breathless.

Hello, Celestine. The French voice slid into her mind like spider veins growing up her legs. To say it was unsettling would be an understatement. It wasn't a script. It wasn't lines or cues. It was an actual voice—a presence.

"Who are you?" *What are you?*

There was no response. No ticking inside her brain. No words springing to mind. No job, no history, no personality. Nothing.

This wasn't a normal character card. Celestine was supposed to get information and instructions. But this was not that. This was an invasion. A physical force clutching at her mind like a parasite.

Was she being possessed? Was that a change with the Phantom's magic?

"Who are you?" Celestine asked again.

Wouldn't you like to know?

"Yes, I would, which is precisely why I asked."

You'll know what you need to know when I need you to know it.

What the fuck?

Irritation spiked in Celestine's blood, mingling with a shudder that ran through her full body. To say the words were sinister would be an understatement. This character—or ghost—was a villain. A *true* villain with nefarious intentions. Pulsations of anger ran through Celestine's body. The emotions felt foreign. Celestine's anger never tasted like this, like rotting cherry pie. Celestine's anger was a slightly sour candy. It was never big—never dramatic. But this anger was, and it was terrifying.

For now, simply do as you normally would.

Celestine swallowed.

I will let you know what to do when the time comes.

Wonderful, this character was as demanding as the Specter...and the Phantom. This was a night inspired by the Brothers Grimm fairy tales.

A loud commotion from the Entrance Hall pulled Celestine out of her worries. The red curtains lining the ballroom walls shook to the beat of the stomping footsteps. It sounded like a dragon arriving and pounding its claws against marble. Celestine couldn't see who it was—not yet. But she had a strong feeling...the only person with dragon-like qualities was Lorraine Ashbrook.

The twins' mother.

Celestine knew from reading about her in the papers and hearing about her from the men and Vivian. Lorraine was notorious.

Of course, Celestine was right. Lorraine strolled in, furs dangling from her body like diamonds. She looked as if she'd skinned a tiger and wore it as a prize. To the rich, the more furs one wore, the more prestige and money they possessed. And Lorraine only cared for prestige.

Her husband trailed behind her, carrying a bag, a traveling trunk, and a hatbox—enough clothing to last a month, not just hours. Archibald struggled with the bags, but he refused to put one down and carry them separately, as if he would get reprimanded if he did. Lorraine walked all over her husband, acting like a vicious, spoiled child smashing an ant beneath her boot. She said things like, "Oh darling, fetch me the caviar," with an exaggerated lilt, pulling out the words like they were strands of taffy. Everything about her was hyperbole. She couldn't just wear one pearl necklace; no, she looped eight around her neck, and they fit her like a straitjacket.

"Where is the doorman? I thought this place would be run better than this," Lorraine said, motioning to her servant—husband—to place her bags on the nearest table. Then she saw Celestine dressed as a servant and amended, "No, you do it instead. This is below you, Archibald."

Celestine raised her gaze to the ceiling, praying for patience and grace. "Yes, of course." She rushed over and picked up the hatbox.

Archibald flashed an apologetic grimace. "No, it's fine. You don't have to."

Celestine smiled in solidarity. "It's all right. I am a lady's maid tonight."

Lorraine ignored her servants, instead turning her attention to her sons. "What, no greeting for your poor, old, weary mother?" She had to be in her mid-fifties at most. Old would never be an apt description. Nor would the word poor ever describe her.

"Good to see you, Mother." Everett placed his feet on the table. It was a pure protest. "Don't boss Celestine around. She's not your servant."

"She's dressed as one."

"She does make rather a compelling point there, Ev," James said, glancing up from his hand of cards, unconcerned.

Dean leaned against the table, his arms crossed, looking like a statue of Hercules. "Mother, always wonderful to see you." He flashed his perfect porcelain teeth before walking over to his mother and wrapping her in an exaggerated hug, his hand lingering at his mother's neck for a moment, pretending as if he cared. It was merely lip service for the sake of the show.

It was clear neither twin appreciated their mother's presence.

Then why invite her?

Unless they hadn't. Another sign that none of her men was the Phantom. Could it be Archibald?

Celestine's eyes tracked toward him, and her brow furrowed. His shoulders were slumped, and an uncomfortable frown laced his face. It was like he tried to take up as little space as possible. It was a big task, considering the man had to be six feet four inches—at least. All the Ashbrooks were ungodly tall.

"See, that is the proper way to greet your mother." Lorraine shimmied her shoulders in a self-important way, highlighting her massive furs.

"Are you planning on moving in?" Dean asked.

"Can't a mother want to spend more time with her boys?" She ran a finger along her long strand of pearls. "We've been banned from these halls for so long. I simply want to stay as long as I can."

Banned?

Celestine didn't know this. Of course, she'd never seen the older Ashbrooks here before, but she'd assumed that was for entirely different reasons. Most of Celestine's sightings of the infamous family were in the gossip rags or from afar at prestigious events the men sometimes took her to as their arm candy for the night.

Everett scoffed. "Banned for a good reason."

"True," James said, laying his cards on the table and turning his gaze to Everett. "You lose."

Everett glared at the Royal Flush and said under his breath, "I always lose when my mother is around."

"Are you two still harping on about all of that? It's been ages." Lorraine plastered a candy-silk grin on her overly painted lips.

Everett crossed his arms like a scolded child. "I will never get over it."

"*We* will never get over it," Dean corrected with a whisper.

Celestine swallowed, watching the volley of comments back and forth and not understanding most of what was happening. It was a long-standing family drama.

"You are rotten little children. Terrible boys, how I ever loved you is beside me."

A large smile painted Everett's face. "What high praise."

"Oh, wonderful. At least this time, I wasn't included in that praise." Vivian wiggled her eyebrows and walked over to Celestine in a conspiratorial way. "Usually, I am the one she is constantly belittling. She has that in common with my mother."

"My poor nerves." Lorraine placed a hand on her chest. "I cannot stand your lack of forgiveness for a measly transgression from eons ago."

"Save us the dramatics, Mother." Everett's typically silly countenance was colder than Antarctica's tundra. It was the first time Celestine had seen him so serious, not his usual jovial self.

"Darling..."

She trailed off, because, at the same moment, the next guests entered the ballroom. The second branch of the Ashbrook family. Irene—James and Vivian's mother—walked in with her brother on one arm and her husband on the other. Her eyes were wide and full of excitement, tracking through all the magical elements of the room. "Oh, sweet, isn't this exciting? Ghost dancers!"

Walter grinned genuinely, as if he were proud of everything he saw. "Yes, dearest, it's wonderful."

"I can't wait until someone is murdered!" Irene said. "I've been waiting for this moment for what seems like forever. Finally invited to Wolfsbane Hall."

Her excitement radiated from her like an enchantment, reveling in the gruesome. Irene enjoyed watching things burn and often lamented that gladiator arenas were no longer in proper use. Her energy was like a current of unfiltered anxiety, like a small dog frightened of the wind.

Vivian groaned, leaned into Celestine, and, in a much too loud of a voice, said, "Don't let her airhead excitement fool you. She's a cunning, vindictive bitch." Her lips fell into a flat line. "My mother still hasn't forgiven me for her stretch marks or hair changing. Like I had any role in it."

"You've always been an ungrateful child." Irene took out her plum lipstick and reapplied it. "You both have been." She nodded at her son.

Celestine rubbed her temples, suddenly thankful for her family even though they were dead. Her mother had been great, and comparing the Ashbrooks to her was like comparing a dog and a wolf. Although similar, they were completely different species.

Gooseflesh rose on Celestine's arms as the jazz music cut out. A hollow hospital sound rang through the ballroom. The Phantom tore through it all. "Welcome, wretched family and the Specter's playthings, to our wondrous night at Wolfsbane Hall. I have invited you here for a multitude of purposes, but mostly to have fun. *My fun.* So revel in my revels." The Phantom's voice clawed into Celestine's skin. It was extra vicious and pointed. "You have all received your character cards and, surprise, every Ashbrook will be playing a variation of yourselves tonight. And because I am truly twisted, the remaining non-Ashbrook members of the cast play people from your pasts."

A sea of murmurs broke through the family, and Celestine's eyes rested on Frances, who had a similar expression branded on her face—an expression like crumbling poinsettias. A symbol of joy, rotting into ruin. The night was unfolding like an advanced strategic game, but unfortunately, it was unclear which game they were all playing—or even if they were playing the same one. Perhaps the Phantom was playing Chess while Celestine played Go and the Specter Backgammon.

The announcement continued. "I thought it might be a jolly good time for the Ashbrooks to live out their past sins and schemes through *my will.*" He laughed, the timbre deep and sinful. "And when you want to curse my name and unravel this game, remember, it was you who asked for it. It should go without saying: Be careful what you wish for."

His voice faded, replaced by music that sounded like nails on a chalkboard, filling the room with its sharp edges and delirious tones, enveloping the space. The sound waves were a physical thing breaking into Celestine's core like knives.

The marionette dolls from earlier fell from the ceiling, dripping like candle wax on a nearly dead candle.

The same singsong rhyme as earlier floated from their mouths.

Margret, Margret hanging down. It's cold this Winter's mourning. Too bad and oh so sad. You caused the Marquess's scorning.

The dolls repeated the song over and over again—a nursery rhyme from the eighteenth century.

"Stop!" Vivian called up to the ceiling. "You're truly not going to tell us which one of you pulls the strings in this place... still?" Her eyes moved first to her brother, then to her father and uncle, and finally rested on the twins, glaring with the force of a freight train.

"What does it matter which one runs it?" Irene asked. "The boys are thick as thieves. One running it is like all of them running it."

Celestine's brows arched downward, noting Irene only referencing the younger gentlemen in her statement.

"If it were only that easy." James tapped his cards against the table impatiently, as if all this was tedious.

"Could you, at the very least, stop the creepy dolls?" Vivian crossed her arms.

James shrugged. "They're not my dolls." A smile crept at the edges of his mouth. Unconvincing. But the dolls did stop their skin-crawling song, and lively party music descended as the ghostly illusions appeared again, dancing.

"I would suggest you begin your show. Ticktock, ticktock." The Phantom's voice cut in and swathed Celestine's skin like a cloak.

And as if on that cue, Everett sauntered over, his usual playboy demeanor kissing his features, but it looked slightly forced tonight. "My character wants to dance with you."

Did he have a regular character card tonight? Or did he, too, have a presence rattling inside his head?

His gaze ignited, stroking over every curve of Celestine's body. His stare was like a caress. And rosy blossoms spread across her cheeks, heating her chest, and she sucked in a breath. Everett had never used his seduction on her before, and a crumb of his attention could feed an army. Celestine suddenly understood why all the girls fell for this man—why they would all sell their souls for a night in his presence.

Dance with him. The character drummed in her mind, frustrated with the continuous distance between her and Everett. If Celestine was burning for Everett, the character was an inferno.

Oh, this character *wanted* Everett.

It was something to go off of.

Celestine gulped and tried to bring herself back to reality. "Since you are playing yourself tonight, what you really mean is *you* want to dance with me."

"Ah, yes, but I still have directives, like dancing with the pretty blonde maid, Margot."

Margot. A name.

Finally, it seemed the only way Celestine was going to unveil her character was through other people's reactions and words. And instinctively, she understood that figuring out her character might be the key to solving her other riddle. If the

Phantom was telling the truth, and the mystery game was wrapped inside the bigger mystery, was that the only way to unmask the Specter?

"So, what was in your character card?"

"It's filled with my history and mixed with false motives and directives for this show," Everett said. "Like dancing with you, but then that would make sense since you are playing *her*..."

He trailed off, lost in thought, and Celestine wanted to push him to divulge more, but her character, Margot, pinched her brain hard, causing pain to seep out of her temples.

Margot didn't like the prying.

"I think before the night's end, the Phantom will be torturing all of us with our deepest, darkest wounds." Everett's expression swirled with anguish. "That's why you're here," he said as if looking into Celestine's soul and seeing Margot instead.

Margot, responded, cupping Everett's cheek and forcing words to escape Celestine's lips. "I am here, my love."

Everett flinched.

One thing was clear: The Phantom was toying with him, and Margot was his punishment for the night—and maybe even his salvation.

"It's almost as if..." Everett blinked and then pulled Celestine into his arms, to a waltz position, as he inhaled the scent of her hair. "Margot," he breathed. "I have forever missed you."

12

Saturday, November 11, 1939
The Grand Ballroom

The piano sang a somber and hollow melody as Celestine's body slipped into the rhythm of the dance. It was a strange sensation, because while she enjoyed the movement and being close to Everett—he had always been her favorite Ashbrook—this wasn't a dance for her. It was Margot's.

It belonged to her character.

But the part of it that was so disconcerting was that Margot was completely in charge of the moment, and even more terrifyingly, she owned and used Celestine's entire body. It was like Celestine was trapped inside her mind; the character had cleaved all control, leaving her like a bird stuck in a cage, banging against the bars and getting her feathers caught on the rusted metal.

Celestine shivered.

She didn't know how to fight or take back control, but at the same time, Celestine didn't know if she should even try. Would it be better to let the scene play out and learn something?

Much like everything else tonight, this had never happened

before. Before, she'd always been the one steering the car. *Always*. But not now.

She was possessed by a spirit and stuck.

Her heart slammed in her ears, and her legs shook as they traveled through the three-four waltz steps.

Maybe Celestine should have fought harder for jurisdiction over her body and autonomy, but she didn't have the energy—mental or physical—after the Phantom and the fire. Perhaps her weakness was legitimate for once. At least now she knew she had been poisoned, so there was a reason for it.

Her feet followed the dance easily. Everett was a good leader. His frame was strong and confident as he glided her along the floor, but what was strange was the leaking of his emotions. Celestine could feel them like a tangible force. Everett churned with them, and so did her character. Connection, hope, and even love filtered through the connection between them.

For Everett, Margot was a memory bottled in a character card and unleashed on the party. Unleashed on him. Unleashed on Celestine. A boon and a curse. The Phantom's vengeance.

But why? What was the purpose?

As they danced, an illusion coated them, their surroundings changing. Now, instead of a ballroom, she was below twinkling lights, and the moon lit the sky. Celestine was barefoot, her feet sinking into grass that was painted gray by midnight. Willow trees swayed in a gentle breeze as Everett clutched her to his chest like she was a fleeting dream he wanted to hold on to forever.

"Margot?" Everett whispered, swinging her into a dip, his eyes liquid energy. A spark of passion ignited between them as he drew her up slowly by her nape. Their eyes met, lips hovering, nearly touching each other. "You even smell like her." The illusion settled over Celestine's skin. It was a shade darker than usual, like she lived on the edge of the Mediterranean Sea where the sun could kiss her cheekbones. Everett sucked in a breath, his fingers digging into the small of her back. "This is like the night I asked you to be my—"

"Take me somewhere private," Margot said, puppeting Celestine's lips.

He nodded and acted fast. The garden illusion broke as Everett tugged ~~Celestine~~—Margot out of the ballroom, down the hall, and into the privacy of a supply closet with barely enough room for either of them to stand without cramping each other.

Margot's back hit the wall, and Everett placed his palms on either side of her head, pinning her in. "Kiss me like you did that night," she breathed, her chest rising with her frantic heart.

Lightning struck inside Celestine's stomach. She bit her lip and stared at Everett. Could she just let this happen? Let the character lingering inside her brain use her body like this? But even if she wanted to fight it—to stop this—could she? Did she possess the power to overcome the parasite in her head? And worse, did she *want* this, too? She should have been horrified by kissing James's cousin. But she just couldn't manage to stir up any horror. Instead, only lust ate away at her core. Plus, a stolen kiss meant almost nothing at Wolfsbane Hall, because she'd kissed many men to further the shows. It was all an act, but the problem was that this didn't feel like an act, not for Margot.

And not for Everett.

So was it ethical? And did it matter what Celestine wanted, while Margot was holding tight to the control?

The tension between the two was a tightrope.

"You're not real," he whispered, his eyes swirling with pools of sadness. "You'll never be real again."

"I am tonight." Margot's hot breath caressed his cheek. "Please, I need you."

His attention focused on her lips, and he seemed to be deciding if he should give in to the demands of the character and his heart. It was a difficult decision to let go and accept this as true for this moment. Everett's lips moved nearer, hovering too close. Margot's breath hitched.

"Please," she begged.

Everett succumbed to the temptation, and his lips grazed hers, soft and gentle, light and tender, exploring her and the moment.

Celestine should've hated Margot for using her body for passion. It should've felt like a violation, but it didn't. She had once wanted to kiss Everett, but that was long before James came into her life and Everett had become her closest friend.

Would this be weird now?

Everett slid his hand up Celestine's thigh and stole her conscious thoughts. The sensation of Margot biting at her mind caused Celestine's loose grip to slide. Like in most things, Celestine chose not to fight it and let the other girl win, allowing her consciousness to recede to the back of her mind. Margot could have this moment.

Margot sucked in a breath and felt sensations for the first time in almost 300 years. Nothing save his skin against hers mattered anymore. A shiver ran through her whole body, igniting a fevered buzzing. Margot tracked her fingers along his chest, curling into his chiseled pectoral muscles as her tongue tangled with his. It was a kiss of remembrance. A promise and a resurrection. She would rewrite their story with their bodies, pressing together and forging anew.

Margot wrapped her legs around him, and he passionately

banged her into the wall, knocking over a broom and unknown chemicals to the floor.

"You're so perfect." He nipped at her neck as his hands slid under her dress, caressing her curves.

Fuck. Celestine's consciousness came back for a moment, realizing that she might be allowing a ghost to use her body to fuck her best friend. Once again, she should have been horrified, but she couldn't muster up that emotion. Because Celestine needed a release, too. She needed at least one more fuck before she died. And she was most definitely going to die tonight.

So, Celestine let go completely, allowing these two to do whatever they wanted with each other.

Margot whimpered. "I want more of you, Everett."

His lips glided along her jaw. "You can have all of me." His fingers played with the lace of her underwear as his lips slammed into hers again. He ripped off her underwear, wholly destroying them, and then his hands went to his belt. With a swift motion, he zipped down his pants and released his sizeable cock. Margot smiled. It had been so long since she had seen his cock, at least like this.

Spying as a far-too-horny ghost really shouldn't count.

"Yes, please," she whispered.

A loud crash cut through the tension, ripping them apart. It came from outside the door, rocks rattling against the floor, and it sounded like someone had knocked over a statue.

"Shit," Everett said. "We shouldn't have done that."

"No," Margot panted desperately, her chest rising frantically with every gasp. "We don't have to stop. I've waited to be with you again for nearly 300 years." She rested her forehead against his.

"Marguerite..." Everett pulled away and gripped her face

between both hands. Clearly, he didn't believe it until this moment. "Is it truly you?"

"Yes," she breathed, a tear tracking down her cheek.

Horror sparked in his eyes. "He really..." he trailed off, red climbing up his cheeks as he averted his gaze. "We can't, my love. This isn't your body." His head snapped back to her, and he placed a chaste kiss on her lips.

"We can."

"No." He shook his head. "As much as I want to, I can't. Not like this. Not with her. My brother is obsessed with her. I can't fuck his girl, as much as I hate him right now."

"Which brother?"

Everett cocked his head. "Touché."

Margot swallowed past the lump in her throat. "Fine," she whined. "But promise me, you will find a way for us to be together."

"I promise." He nodded. "Is Cece still in there?"

"Yes, but I pushed her far back into consciousness. I think she's sleeping." Another crash of rocks cut into their conversation. "It sounds like the show is progressing out there."

"Yeah," he groaned and helped plant her feet back on the ground before he tucked his cock back in his pants and zipped them up. "Sorry about your underwear."

Margot let out a small chuckle. "It's not new." She splayed her hands on the wall to keep herself from touching him again.

"Margot, love, please wake Celestine up. She needs to be conscious for this next bit."

"Fine," Margot said and imagined slapping the other girl awake. *Wake up, mortal girl. We have a scene to play out for you.*

Celestine's mind snapped back into place, but Margot still held the reins tightly. *What?*

Everett cleared his throat and stepped back, hitting the shelves on the opposite wall. "Right. Well, welcome back, Cece.

Time for past punishments, I presume." He nodded for Margot to start their play.

The air between them shifted, and Margot started their scene. "*We have to stop hiding this, Everett. I want to be out there with you.*"

"*I know, my love, and we will have our day in the light, but it cannot be today. My parents aren't ready...*" Everett trailed off as if in thought.

"*Ready to accept a French maid as your wife?*"

"*Wife.*" He smiled and ran his thumb along her jaw lovingly. "*I like the way that sounds. You're my wife.*" He gave her a gentle kiss on the forehead. "*I will tell them soon.*"

Heat spread through Margot, painting her chest crimson as she pulled her engagement ring from under her bodice. It was looped on a ribbon, because Margot was too poor to afford a gold necklace chain. "*We can't keep this secret much longer.*"

"*My love, I promise I will tell them soon. But I must go now; they're waiting for me.*" Everett quickly kissed her lips before rushing out of the broom closet.

The scene ended, and Margot released her hold, going dormant in the back reaches of their mind, letting Celestine glide back into control.

Celestine shivered everywhere, and the hairs at the nape of her neck rose. Covering her face with her hands, she sucked in a breath. What the fuck did she just let happen? A ghost possessed her body and nearly fucked one of her closest friends.

Celestine was too susceptible to temptations, too weak to wrench control from the spirit clawing at the back of her mind.

Shit. I almost fucked Everett, and I definitely saw his penis. What does that mean for our friendship? Dammit, Celine. Get yourself together.

All of this was rotten, and she didn't know how to handle

any of it. Or even what to expect. Nothing was familiar, and it felt like she had a thousand tiny cuts that would eventually bleed her dry.

At least one positive thing came of that interaction—besides finally seeing how good a kisser Everett was. She had also gained more insight into her character.

Margot was a French maid, engaged to Everett, and it was a *real memory*. It had to be, given Everett's response and the fact that the *thing* currently slumbering in the back of her mind was very much fucking real.

Something terrible had happened between Margot and Everett, and Celestine was certain it would play out through the show tonight. Her heart wanted to weep for Everett. One didn't feel that much love and connection just to squander it.

So what happened?

Rich men's promises were like fairy dust. Beautiful, but not real. Not tangible. Nothing to build a life or a future on. But Everett seemed like he would burn the world down for Margot. Except if that were true, why hadn't he told his mother about them?

Celestine bit her lip and smoothed down her hair, trying to compose herself and get her appearance back in order. She was quick about it, because she was quite accomplished at returning to parties after a secret rendezvous.

Her eyes caught on her shredded underwear, and Celestine rubbed her face. Fucking wonderful. She kicked them under the shelves. She would be called worse than whore if someone found those.

The door squeaked as it opened, and she crept into the hallway, slowly and quietly clicking the door shut again.

"I would never keep you a secret, Marguerite." Celestine reeled around to find Dean leaning against the wall, dark authority oozing from him. His arms were crossed, and he looked like an avenging god. "If I had you, I would let everyone know."

Celestine's insides tingled until she realized that this, too, was an act. He was speaking to Margot, not her.

The twins both loved the same girl. *Well fuck.* This was an interesting development. Was that what happened to Margot? The brothers fought over her?

Was that how it ended tragically?

"I wouldn't keep you a secret either, Celestine."

Her brows scrunched. Dean couldn't mean that. He was a creature of dark temptations and wicked games. There was no reason to be *into* Celestine for anything other than mental turmoil. Right?

Celestine didn't know how to make sense of this new world or what was even real. All of it? Everett's actions were based on her character, but would Dean's be too?

"We should get back to the party," Dean said when she still didn't come up with anything comprehensible to respond with. "We don't want to miss any of the excitement."

"Are all these scenes from your past?" The question fell from her lips.

It was coming together. If the murder mystery party would help solve the identity of the Specter, and tonight's play was all about revenge, then everything was about them and not Celestine. The play was a moment from the Ashbrooks' past. A moment centered around a French maid and forbidden love.

Was that how the Specter was formed?

Dean's response was simple. "Yes."

He pushed off the wall and turned his back to her.

Celestine nearly fell over herself to catch up with him. "And Margot...Marguerite, that's what you called her, right? She was real?" *And a possessive ghost inside my head.*

Yes. Margot answered the unsaid question.

Truly? Celestine asked.

Yes.

Not fucking terrifying at all.

"Yes, Marguerite was real." Dean tapped his fingers together, both distracted and dismissive at the same time.

"And you were both in love with her?"

"Yes."

Celestine swallowed. "I'm sorry."

"Why are you sorry?"

"It must have been horrible loving her and not being able to have her." Celestine wrung her hands. "My sister was ten years older than me when she died, but I can imagine if she were around and we loved the same man, it would feel dreadful."

Dean swallowed, his eyes swirling with azure fire, but he said nothing else, back to his usual ways.

Celestine fiddled awkwardly, wringing her hands again. She never knew what to do around him. "What happened to Margot?"

Dean let out a low growl. "I'm sure you'll find out tonight. I can't imagine the Phantom wouldn't make it a part of his sick play."

Dean walked with Celestine, a chasm of space between them. Lord forbid he touch her or guide her back to the ballroom on his arm—like a gentleman—as Everett or James would have done. Dean was just so frustratingly distant. But she longed for him to be the devil she saw beneath his eyes.

But he never would, or at least not with her.

What was wrong with her? She couldn't want three men. Three was too many. Right?

Clicking footsteps approached, mingling with the echoes of long-played, drawn-out arguments. Dean's eyes latched to hers, and quick like wildfire, he pulled her behind a red curtain just as the voices turned the corner. His hand covered Celestine's mouth, and his body pressed her into the wall.

"Will this ever cease?" Anger dripped from Lorraine's voice like water from a leaky faucet.

Irene snickered. "Probably not. If you wanted to live a certain way, you probably shouldn't have chosen this life."

The sound of the slap ricocheted against the marble floors. "You are worse than that whore we ki—"

"Ladies, ladies..." Firm footsteps rushed into the hall. "The arguing needs to stop." It had to be Archibald trying to break up the women.

His hand frozen against her lips, Dean looked heavenward, exasperation seeping onto his face. It was an expression that said, *For the love of God, again?* If it were a typical argument between his family, why did he need to hide Celestine's presence?

"Fine," Lorraine scoffed, and a dramatic huff accompanied the snapping of her heels, fading away.

"Now that she's gone, and no one seems to be around," Archibald said, and a crash sounded on the wall next to the curtain where Celestine and Dean were hiding.

"Oh, God no, not again." Dean's words were lower than a whisper and were covered up by the frantic passion erupting next to them. His father and aunt were kissing, and maybe more, in the middle of the hall. Oh, no, it was definitely more from the moans and flesh slapping together coming from next to them. A hallway quickie. Was everyone sex-addled in this house?

Celestine certainly was.

Dean shook his head and looked like he wanted to disappear into the wallpaper and never be seen again. Death might have been preferable to this. At every slight movement and moan, he flinched.

Celestine cupped her hands over his ears to relieve some of his pain. She couldn't imagine what it would be like hearing her mother rutting around with someone inches from her. Not pleasant. Dean's smokey eyes tilted down and captured Celestine's, and she had to suck in a deep breath, because she suddenly realized how close they were standing.

Far, far too close.

And his skin against hers was nearly unbearable. Both hot and cold, all at the same time. Like a metaphor for the two of them. He was always ice, and she was an eternal fire. Her heart beat into her throat as Dean's hand slid down to her neck, the movement a caress. All the while, he didn't take his eyes off hers. His irises were painted in either hidden seduction or ruthless hatred. It was hard to tell with him. A part of Celestine believed they might be one and the same. He hated her, but perhaps he wanted her at the same time?

Or she could be making it all up, because his hand dropped to his side a moment later, and his gaze slid away.

"Not in the hall," Irene said, panting and cutting through whatever Celestine felt toward Dean. *Thank God.* "One of our children could hear us."

Too late.

The pounding in Celestine's ears rattled her composure as Dean's aunt and father slipped away into another room to finish what they had started.

"Why do we need to hide from your parents?" Celestine asked.

"One should always hide from my parents." He looked like he was going to be sick.

Celestine laughed. "I understand why."

His parents are the worst monsters imaginable, Margot said.

Celestine chose to ignore the ghost. "But there was more to the hiding than that."

"There was." Dean skated out of her arms and held open the curtain for her to exit. His jaw was tight and his bones rigid, as if he were trying to rid himself of the feel of her. All the tension she felt building between them surely was only in her head.

He swallowed. "We should return. I assume someone will be getting murdered any moment now."

"Right." She gulped and gave a terse smile. "We mustn't miss the show."

As soon as they reached the ballroom, they were accosted by Lorraine, who rushed up to them in a tizzy. "Dean, dearest, have you seen your brother?"

"Which one?" Dean raised his eyebrows.

"How dare you?" Lorraine said with horror and let out what could have been described as a scoff. "The only one that matters."

"Oh." Dean slid his hands into his pockets. "I haven't seen Everett."

Lorraine ran a hand down the leopard fur on her coat. "If you see him, will you tell him we must talk?"

"I doubt he'll speak to you," Dean said. "He hasn't in years. Why do you think he'll start now?"

"He needs to get over it."

"He won't. Perhaps you should have considered the consequences of your actions before taking them."

Lorraine's face deepened into fury, and she looked like a Victorian painting that had red poured over the canvas. "Not you, too." Lorraine waved her hand dismissively. "Go fetch me a glass of wine. You know you're my favorite."

Dean released a low chuckle and shook his head. "Yes, Mother."

His eyes flashed to Celestine's momentarily, and they shared a grimace. If Dean hated Celestine, he hated his mother far more. He'd take any excuse to get away from her, and Celestine would have put money on him not returning if she were a betting gal.

"So, you're their new whore." Lorraine's lips pursed together as she examined her prey like a scientist about to dissect a strange animal. Glee lit up her every feature.

Celestine had been called a whore many, many times before. This didn't faze her. It was the nature of being a poor girl who ran with the rich and glamorous. A poor girl who openly flirted with and fucked said rich men. Everyone assumed she only hung around for the money and access to their abundant lives. It couldn't be that they needed her talent and skills to better their lives. No, she couldn't possibly be adding anything valuable.

"You're the girl my son is obsessed with," Lorraine continued, and Celestine laced a poisonous sugarplum smile on her lips. "Don't feel special. Occasionally, my sons latch on to a beautiful, poor ingénue to fight and obsess over. They promise her riches and a better life, but what does she actually get? Devastation."

All poor girls who chased after rich men received devastation. This wasn't news. It was one of the primary reasons the Ashbrooks were only for show, possibly a fun time, but nothing more. She knew it already. Celestine would never get to keep one for herself.

When Celestine said nothing, Lorraine added, "You're like all the rest. You'll be discarded sooner or later...or possibly even worse."

Definitely worse, Margot whispered at the edges of her mind.

Lorraine ran her fingers through her pearls as if drawing attention to her exorbitant wealth. "You'll never be good enough for him."

Celestine raised her eyebrows. "Which one?"

"Do not talk back to me. You are a maid unworthy of my presence or attention. You will answer when addressed. Do you understand me?"

Yes, Margot growled, and Celestine said aloud, "Yes."

Was Lorraine speaking to Margot then? Was this another scene playing out? Or was she talking to Celestine? Probably both.

"Nothing will affect our image, our reputation, or get in my sons' way. Do you hear me, girl?"

Yes. Perhaps this was for Margot's sake—for the show—because Margot rattled inside Celestine like a beehive, feeling attacked and furious. "Yes," Celestine repeated the character's line.

"You will not affect their future." Lorraine gripped Celestine's arms, her fingernails digging in. "You *are not* their future. Do you understand me?"

This felt like overkill. Lorraine liked to hear herself speak and couldn't be content with just one threat. She needed many.

"Yes." Celestine gritted her teeth.

"That includes Margot, your character for the night, and you, too, little *actress.*" She said the title as if it were a weed infecting her garden.

Ah, so she was speaking to both.

"Right," Celestine said disrespectfully.

"You are a pathetic actress in a tiny little town. You're beautiful, but that's the only thing you've got going for you." Lorraine truly enjoyed her insults, and she dispensed them as if they were candy. "You will never amount to anything." She clutched Celestine's chin. "Useful to use and play with, useful to fuck, but you'll never be worthy of one of them. Do you understand?"

Celestine didn't give her the respect of an answer. Lorraine might push her husband around, but perhaps, for once in her life, she would not give in. She wouldn't let this horrible woman affect her.

"Heed my warning, girl, or you'll end up just like her."

Her? Margot? Did Lorraine know what would happen to the ghost? Was she going to be the victim?

Fuck. Celestine hated playing the victim just as much as the villain. And she wouldn't put it past Lorraine to murder anyone.

She does like to murder. Margot scratched at the lobes of Celestine's brain.

A rotten feeling snaked over Celestine's skin.

Typically, the humans were Specter's little playthings. They came to get lost in their fantasies and an escapist story, to be in an Agatha Christie novel for one night of fun. But tonight, Celestine couldn't help but feel like *she* was the entertainment. The cast members were the puppets on strings. She felt like an object, a toy for these rich and powerful people.

But perhaps Celestine had always been a toy. Was she always the Specter's toy, and she just hadn't realized it?

"Ah, there's my little angel." James appeared behind them and wrapped his hands around Celestine, caressing the curve of her waist and pulling her into his solid body. "I've been looking all over for you." His lips grazed her ear, and he whispered, "You look like you need saving."

Celestine shuddered, and a shiver coursed down her spine.

Lorraine let out a disgusted scoff.

"Auntie, it looks like your target has finally decided to appear." James nodded his chin at a stumbling Everett, who had a half-empty bottle of bourbon in his hand.

He had left Margot and immediately sought out alcohol.

"Yes," Lorraine said, rolling her shoulders back. She sent a look of pure disgust at James before she prowled toward her son.

Celestine swallowed. She did not envy the Thrill-Seeking Casanova one bit. It was one of the murder mystery nicknames she gave him, because when he wasn't the detective, he was simply reckless.

But she didn't get a chance to ponder or witness his interaction with his mother, because James drew her into an alcove of the ballroom and pulled the scarlet curtains closed behind them seconds before his lips were on hers. Celestine's back hit the wall as James devoured her. He was a starving man, and she was his salvation. A feast he would savor all night if he could. His fingers cupped her ass as he pressed deeper.

Oh, he was... "James, we're in the middle of the show."

"And?" His lips left hers for only a moment before his tongue invaded her senses.

Shit. Celestine wanted this. She wanted his type of distraction. But they shouldn't. She'd almost just fucked his cousin in nearly the same way. And his mother and uncle had just done this.

"No." She pulled away, placing a hand on his chest. "This isn't appropriate."

"You need a distraction." He bit her lip. "You need this, Celestine. Don't lie to me and say you don't. I know your body is desperately in need of release after Dean just interrupted you and Everett."

"You're not mad about that?"

"No. Why would I be?" He sucked her lip into his mouth. "You're mine."

Fuck. His hands stroked up her legs, and he deepened their kiss, and Celestine couldn't lie to herself. She did need this. He was the best distraction from everything that occurred during the night. She didn't have to think about poison, mystery shows, or murder when she was with him.

It was just the two of them with an unstoppable passion.

Although the last time they did this during a show, she stabbed him seventeen times in the chest.

A moan escaped Celestine's lips as James trailed kisses down her neck.

"You are utter perfection," he said, nipping at her neck like a vampire.

"And you are a nice distraction."

"Is that all I am to you?"

"Do you want me to be more?"

"No, never." With one hand, he gave her ass a squeeze, and with the other, he stroked her thigh, fingers leaving indents. "You aren't for keeping. You are for fun."

Celestine inhaled sharply. That was never something a girl wanted to hear, even if she knew it to be true. She didn't get a chance to respond, because he sucked her lip into his mouth again and slid a hand between her legs. He chuckled when he found no underwear obscuring his way. He played with her curls for a moment before plunging two fingers into her core and stroking her walls. Deep circles. Deep, luxurious, forbidden circles.

Celestine let out a cry, and she came apart under his hand. She really must have been deprived to orgasm that quickly.

"You're such a good, wet girl." He silenced her, drowning out her cries of pleasure with his mouth as he continued stroking *that* spot. She ground into him, her hips bucking as his fingers fucked her so completely. "You're so ready for me, my love."

Celestine broke free. "I need all of you filling me."

James let out a low chuckle. "Of course, you do."

He pulled his slick fingers out and placed her on the ground before he unbuttoned his pants and unleashed his glorious cock. It was long, hard, and wonderful.

Celestine's chest rose with want. They'd done this hundreds of times, but it would never grow old because he was so talented with...everything.

James cupped her shoulders and drew the straps of her garments down until he released her breasts to the world. His tongue circled a nipple, and she gasped. Her heart beat in her ears. The anticipation of having his cock inside her was far too much. She needed him now, but he enjoyed torturing her. He got off on it. He loved to edge her. It was part of his sick games.

His hands caressed her inner thighs and, slowly, his tongue released her breast. He moved so sickly slow, his fingers hovering above her folds but refusing to give her what she wanted.

"Please," she begged. "I can't take much more."

James chuckled and stood back up to his full height. "My wicked little wanton." He nibbled her earlobe. "You will have all of me soon enough."

And as if in answer, his cock twitched against her upper thigh.

"Please." She reached a hand down to guide his length, but he caught her fingers in a firm grip and pinned them to the wall above her head.

"Bad little wanton," he growled. "I say when you have me. Isn't that right?"

"Yes," she breathed.

"Good girl."

He kissed her cheek and removed one hand from pinning her to line his cock up with her entrance then plunged in— plundering her wetness with his thick length. Her legs circled him as his cock filled her to the brim. She was so tight for him, and she would never get used to the sheer size of him.

He pounded his cock in, slamming her against the wall, fierce, taking no prisoners and allowing no surrender. He railed her with no restraint.

If the beginning of their lovemaking was slow, this was fast and unrelenting.

Celestine's arms fell as he released them, and she dug her nails into his shirt, her lips capturing his, biting him. They both could give a little pain with their pleasure.

"Naughty," he mouthed against her lips before he roared with his satisfaction. He came inside of her, heat filling her.

Celestine let out a moan as she came as well, trembling from her pleasure. Their frenzied sex came to a finish, sweat dripping down their backs, and their breaths were fast and exhausted. They panted into each other, trying to gain composure again.

James set her back on the floor and placed his hands on either side of her face. He rested his tired head on her breasts, and she stroked his sweat-slick hair with light fingers.

They stayed like that for a couple of minutes until James regained his energy.

"You're always such a good fuck," James said, patting her head and pulling away.

Celestine tensed, every muscle hardening with shame. She didn't know why those words affected her so deeply. She knew this was only for physical release. That was all.

James pulled up his pants and buttoned them, not even noticing the change. After all, he'd gotten what he wanted. "We should probably get back to the show."

"Right," Celestine said. She dragged up her dress and smoothed out her hair. "It would be foolish to miss the show."

"For you, it would be."

He placed a kiss on her forehead before walking through the curtains. She followed him to a table where Vivian played with a wine glass. A clink rang out as Vivian harshly set it down, already two to three drinks deep. This family might have a problem.

"You two have been gallivanting around, I see," Vivian said. "You smell like sex."

Celestine's cheeks heated.

"Don't be jealous," James said, sitting beside his sister, and Celestine glided beside him.

"I am only jealous your lover gets to be here. Mine weren't invited."

"Be glad of that."

"Oh, I am." Vivian examined her nails before pulling a long dagger from a sheath on her thigh. She began to play with the knife, tossing it back and forth between her hands. Something she did when bored sometimes. "Tonight is for torture." Then she turned her head to the ceiling and said, "I am hungry."

A booming chuckle filled the room. "If you must insist, sister dearest, let's have a feast. And possibly a murder." The Phantom's voice echoed off every surface.

Sister?

Celestine's eyes latched on to James, who shrugged. Was James the Phantom? Could that be true if he were being so calm about it? But then...did Dean imply earlier that he had multiple brothers? And Margot had as well...

Nothing made sense.

What was real? Was any of it?

Was sister just a title? Like a friend?

In a blink, the tables were filled with food—a feast for royalty. James's uncle Jon and his father Walter, who sat at a table away, smiled and immediately dug in. Everyone else seemed a little dazed.

A wave of dizziness overcame Celestine, and she had to grip her table for support. She sucked in a breath. The earlier exertion mixed with the poison was too much.

Her heart beat erratically—angrily.

Something hot dripped from her nose, and she used a napkin to clean it up.

Blood.

The damned poison was sinking deeper.

Sooner than expected.

The grandfather clock chimed. Eight o'clock. One hour down. One hour less to live.

A stroke of panic crawled up Celestine's throat. It was one thing to know death was imminent. It was an altogether different experience to be confronted with it. The jazz music and ghostly entertainment continued, clashing with the fermented atmosphere and Celestine's panic. The cast might be the only one's poisoned, but the family's issues were their own toxin.

Dean, Everett, and their mother were seated for dinner at one of the tables. Lorraine had ambushed Everett as he entered, and Dean had run interference. Everett sat with his arms crossed while Dean smirked and their mother lectured, unaware that neither man was genuinely listening. It was in the lines of their backs and the tension in their forms. Heated voices twisted through the empty space, slightly muffled by the entertainment, but they clung to the glass surfaces while the words themselves were muffled.

Curiosity was a beast in Celestine's chest. "Wolfsbane," she said, running a finger along her wine glass, "I would like to hear that conversation."

Celestine didn't often use the Specter's magic—or, in this case, the Phantom's—but sometimes it was necessary. Sometimes, asking Wolfsbane for help was the most prudent thing to do. Because with the chiming of the clock came a reminder that there were multiple games afoot, and Celestine needed to uncover the Specter's identity to live—and the Phantom's, to punch him in the face.

A mockingbird call whistled across the air, the house giving its answer. *Yes, Miss Sinclair.*

The house was the vessel through which the magic worked, and Celestine still didn't know how. She could ask the place to do something for her, and then it would decide if it wanted to listen. But she had no connection or ability to communicate with the house without the elixir. The elixir was like a telephone that connected them.

From the wine glass, like an echo, the voices played as if they were coming from a speaker. James lifted his eyebrows but said nothing, chewing on a new stick of spearmint gum.

"Must we truly go over all this again?" Lorraine growled at her son. "Get over it."

"It doesn't matter how many times you say that. It won't change anything." Everett took a large gulp from his bottle of bourbon. "I will never get over it."

Lorraine's head snapped to Dean. "And you're just fine with rehashing all this?"

Dean's smirk crawled further up his face like a spider. "Of course, I am. Why wouldn't I be?"

"Perhaps you should worry more about where your husband ran off to," Everett said with another large swig.

"I know exactly where he is." Lorraine's words came out in both a scream and a whisper. "Off making some more illegitimate children, I presume. You would think two bastards would be enough, but—"

"Do not speak of my siblings that way," Dean snapped back. "I put up with a lot of your bullshit, Mother, but I will not allow that."

Lorraine's lips fell into a hard line. "Of course not. He's probably your favorite brother."

James placed his hand over the glass and cut off the rest of the conversation.

"Oh, you didn't want to hear if you are Dean's favorite." Vivian slurred her words as a ghost waiter picked up another empty wine glass and replaced it with a new one. "This service is convenient."

"You're drunk." James leaned back in his chair. "And I already know I am Dean's favorite. He prefers less...emotionality, and Everett is an active volcano."

James wasn't wrong. Emotions poured from Everett like lava, continuously flowing. Although, Dean was emotional too —but the type of emotion that was hidden under a mountain of barriers.

Vivian clicked her tongue. "You're a blunt asshole."

"Ah, that I am." James confiscated Vivian's glass.

"And absolutely no fun." Vivian crossed her arms. "You're wrong about Dean. He doesn't mind emotion. You're the one who can't tolerate it."

Perhaps the truest statement Vivian had ever uttered.

A loud giggle sounded from the main hallway, and the jazz music cut out. The ghost dancers froze in their tracks, becoming statues. The ghosts, or whatever they were, always sent a shiver down Celestine's spine. She didn't know if they were real or just incredibly convincing puppets. Sometimes, when she conversed with them, they responded, but in other moments, they were like vacant old-time Gilded Age photos. Soulless and lacking any ability to understand. Celestine often wondered if the most realistic moments were actually the

Specter.

The laughter was absorbed into the room—sucked in, as if by magic—and it died out as Irene and Archibald entered, disheveled. A plum-colored stain grazed Archibald's collar. Everyone knew exactly what they had been up to. Celestine didn't judge. She'd just done the same thing with James, but she would never be the other woman. She couldn't betray anyone like that.

Celestine shook her head.

The Ashbrooks' relationships were as messed up as the Phantom's magic.

As if on cue, Lorraine howled her disapproval. She stormed up from her chair to confront her husband, pulling at his tie, probably hoping she could strangle him. "Is it not enough that you cheat on me? Must I endure it before our family and these vile plebeians?" Her eyes darted first to Celestine, and then Frances and then Babette, seated with the twins' uncles. "Have a little decency."

"Come on, it's not like we haven't known for eons," Walter said, sticking up for his brother.

Jon shook his head and sent pleading eyes to Walter, and under his breath, he said, "Let's focus on the food."

Walter patted Jon's leg but continued anyway. "I doubt there are any true secrets in this family."

The vein in Lorraine's forehead bulged, and she motioned at the cast members next to her brother-in-law. "These servant people didn't know."

"I mightily disagree, sister. All of Christendom knows."

Celestine's eyebrows scrunched together, and she tilted her head. "Besides, the Phantom isn't going to let us make it through the night without revealing our worst moments anyways." Walter picked up his fork and returned to his exceedingly expensive Wagyu beef and truffle fries. "Precisely why darling Celestine here is playing Marguerite, Frances is Angela, and Babette is Cauncy. All our dirty little secrets are on full display."

It was a striking statement, mostly because he bothered to learn the names of the cast. Almost no rich people did that. The three female cast members were merely the help, or objects for them to play with.

"Well, I, for one, am not playing this foolish game then—" As if in response to Lorraine's declaration, the lights went out, and darkness attacked the room.

A scream carved through the unease as suspenseful music —strings and harsh brass—crackled through the now frigid air. A reverberating drum pounded in Celestine's ears, her heart working too hard.

Another scream poured out.

"Oh, so delightful! This will be fun." Irene's voice came from Celestine's right.

Chaos lit the night with its sinister shadows, and Celestine felt something brush against her back. She shivered, her entire body going on edge, tight as a harp string. The squeaking of shoes, followed by the sound of a scuffle, came from her left, and indistinguishable male words mixed with gargling and another scream.

Then came a slap and a whooshing air hitting Celestine's face as if something had gone flying by. Her immediate reaction was to find cover. Rolling out of her seat, she ducked under her table. She really did not feel like becoming the murder victim tonight. Especially since, if she died in the show, she would be unable to name the Specter, and the poison would kill her.

Permanently.

Although, from the combination of events that had just transpired, it didn't seem like she was the target.

Sweat dripped down Celestine's temple, and she drew her knees into her chest. An eternity passed, or what felt like it, as she trembled beneath the table. One never got used to murder. They might be able to block it out and harden their hearts, but it wasn't an act a person could normalize—unless they were inhuman.

A popping sound cut through her thoughts, and Celestine clasped her hands over her ears.

Death lingered in the air, and she recognized the gurgling sounds of drowning in one's blood from a stab wound or a gunshot. Despite knowing the victim would most certainly resurrect, it was still terrible. However, this was the Phantom's show. Maybe nobody came back tonight.

The lights finally sparked back on, and the music died out. Everything returned to its previous state—everything except the dead body. Celestine poked her head out, the tablecloth resting over her head like a veil.

The smell of death clawed at the air—the scent of iron and unfulfilled dreams.

Lorraine's glassy, dead eyes stared up at the ceiling. Blood dripped from multiple wounds in her chest. An arrow protruded from her stomach, and a red tie dangled between her fingers.

"Let the investigations begin!" The Phantom's voice sauntered through the room as if he were present and enjoying his play unfolding.

A group of raven-haired heads—and Vivian's fake blonde —flashed toward Everett. He stood mere feet away from his mother's dead body. He stared down with a smile on his face.

Responding to the negative attention, he raised his hands in a gesture of surrender. "I didn't do it...this time."

15

his time.

What did it mean?

Oh, you're going to find out, Margot said inside her mind. Celestine shuddered. The sinister voice scratched at her corpus callosum like nails on a crooked chalkboard. This character's presence was radiating toxic energy, and it only seemed to be getting worse. She stared at the victim and smiled with sickening jubilation.

Celestine scratched her head.

There wasn't a world in which she was responsible for Lorraine's death, right?

Celestine remembered hiding underneath the table, cowering... Right? *Shit.* She didn't know. Not for sure. Her mind was barely her own. It was possible that she lost time and forgot things she'd done, like becoming the murderer. On a previous night, Celestine had been the murderer but not known it until the end of the show. Her character's delusions kept her from figuring it out until the very end. Those types of characters were never fun to play.

Usually, it was Wolfsbane that would erase her memory

after she had killed. It wasn't like this. She'd never been possessed before.

One thing was abundantly clear: Margot was a spirit of vengeance, and she wouldn't rest until she got what she wanted. Unfortunately, it was utterly unclear what she actually wanted.

Celestine raked her hands through her hair, massaging her scalp.

Swallowing, she crawled out from under the table, wiping off her knees as she stood. Stepping up next to Everett, she cocked her head, staring down at the murder scene.

It was time to investigate. One thing Celestine was an expert at.

Blood spread along the floor in a pool like lava slowly sliding down a mountain. It was everywhere: on the corpse, the floor, the ceiling, the tables, the walls, and even the people now lingering around the body. Crimson soaked into Lorraine's white furs, burrowing in between the hairs. Red and white. Celestine's favorite color combination.

It might have been an inappropriate thought, but there was no right way to act around so much death and stress. Celestine found that if she added levity or fascination to the gore, she was able to stomach it better.

She bit her lip. Lorraine's coat was ruined. It looked like a rabbit that had gotten caught in the jowls of a wolf. Destroyed, limp, yet still beautiful in its own way. Macabre really. This was probably another inappropriate thought. Celestine rubbed her head again, this time paying more attention to her temples. As she did it, her eyes tracked across the room, taking in the details.

No one was missing. The entire family and cast meandered across the room like figurines staged in a dollhouse. Walter and Jon were lounging at a dining table. Jon with a fork frozen halfway to his mouth while Walter, in the most ungentlemanly fashion, had his elbows on the table, his hands smashing against his face. Everett and Archibald hovered over the body. Babette clicked open her briefcase for the first time all night, her eyes sparking with covetous interest. Completely unconcerned, Frances and Vivian continued their poker game without even glancing up to see who was murdered. And, in pure Dean fashion, he was positioned against the wall, watching over everyone.

Either it was Celestine's brain-warping reality, or everyone else had barely moved. Truly posed like dolls. And like dolls, their expressions were waxen—almost indifferent, as if pleased by the turn of circumstances.

Celestine didn't blame them. Relief sank into her stomach, too. The only word to describe Lorraine being gone for the rest of the night was pleasant. She was a nasty piece of work.

Yes, she is, Margot said.

James strolled up behind Celestine and placed a hand on her back, a red stain lacing his shirt cuff. Blood. "Are you okay?"

"Yes," Celestine whispered back, her eyes finding Dean. Something was off about him...or maybe that was simply her excuse to look. But she noted everything from his pristine—bloodless—hunter-green suit to his recently polished shoes, to the expression spreading along his lips, the side of his mouth quirking up into a sinful smirk. The smirk that said, *Don't worry, darling. Devour me with your eyes until you're full.*

She swallowed, averting her gaze. She hated getting caught, especially by him.

Ghost violinists popped up on stage and played a somber, haunting song. Wolfsbane loved to underscore a dramatic moment like an epic movie in the theaters.

"Oh, it's wonderfully gruesome." Irene's voice cut through

the silence, and she clapped her hands. "An arrow and knives. I wonder if they felt different killing her."

Archibald walked over to his lover and placed a hand on her back. "Lorraine is going to hate this."

Irene's lips grew into an inappropriately wide smile. "Oh, yes, she is. Isn't it lovely?"

Archibald shook his head but said, "Yes."

"It's more than she deserved," Everett said, taking a large gulp of his bourbon.

No one seemed to disagree with the sentiment, giving everyone in the room motive, including Celestine. And it looked like multiple people may have killed her, or one person set it up to make it look like there were various killers. Knives and an arrow. Although...Celestine's eyes tracked to the balcony overlooking the ballroom, noting the glint of metal. Interesting indeed.

But how did Lorraine's death relate to the Specter's identity? If it was only one murderer, which Celestine was beginning to believe was the case, then was the killer the Specter?

The mysteries were linked, and Celestine began to realize she needed to focus on the fake game to find the answers to the real game. So Lorraine's murder now took precedence.

Celestine knelt, examining the corpse more closely, but she wasn't alone. Everett also knelt beside her.

"Since I am usually the detective, I shall grace us with my considerable abilities tonight," he slurred.

Celestine scoffed.

"But, brother, you don't have your ridiculous eyebrows or mustache tonight." Dean crossed his arms. "How will we be able to appreciate your skills?"

"It is truly devastating." Everett's tone carried through the hall like it was a chilly wind. "But alas, we must make do. I *can* still give you the accent."

"Please don't," Vivian said under her breath.

Everett wiggled his nose, ignoring his cousin's—half-sister's?—comment. He said in a thick Australian accent, "Blimey, what a mess. Everyone, stand aside." He stretched his arms out as if he were holding people off, but there was no one to hold off, because no one cared. "We must examine the body. To my side, Celestine...I mean, Margot. Please assist."

By assist, what he meant was to make him look good. Celestine had a feeling the Phantom didn't give him nearly enough direction or lines, because Everett's eyes were like a deer in headlights, and he bunched his hands into his pockets nervously.

It begged the question: Why even bother with this show today?

"I am already assisting." Celestine motioned to the fact that she was already hovering over the body. "You may continue."

"Right." He knelt beside Celestine. "Umm, what do we do now?" he whispered out of the corner of his mouth.

"Gloves," she whispered back.

"Righto." Everett held up his hands and motioned for Celestine to do the same. Magic swirled around them, sticking and forming rubber surgical gloves, and a tweezer-like tool appeared in Celestine's hand.

The visual examination came first. On the inner side of a wrist was a lipstick smudge. A different color from the color Lorraine was wearing on her lips.

Plum.

Like Irene's.

So only Everett could hear, Celestine whispered, "A projectile arrow to the left abdomen, most likely piercing the stomach."

Everett repeated her loudly and showily. The two of them

often did this during shows, so they were used to this dance. He was like Sherlock Holmes, and she was his Watson—if Watson was the one solving the crimes.

"One stab wound to the upper chest"—Celestine grasped the tweezers between her fingers, using them to displace Lorraine's clothing and examine the wound closer—"piercing the lung."

Everett repeated it.

"One stab wound to the middle chest." She rolled the body slightly over as Everett repeated the words. "And one final stab wound to the back left... Probably the fatal one, if it had pierced her abdominal aorta. But of course, we can't be certain of anything until the autopsy."

Everett chose not to repeat the last bit, because he wasn't overly fond of scientific accuracy like she was—or James was.

Celestine was about to stand, having gathered as much information as she could without a proper lab, but then something caught her attention. Red discoloration at the back of Lorraine's neck, under her ear. Celestine stroked it with her gloved finger. A tiny prick.

"No one move." Everett's voice boomed through the room. "We must uncover all the evidence."

Celestine stood and rolled her gloves off. She cocked her head, once again staring up at the balcony, measuring the angle of the arrow. She started to step in that direction, but Everett cut her off.

"I said no one move."

"The arrow."

"We can examine that later." He waved his arms dismissively. "Right now, we must start the interrogations. Everyone, grab a chair and sit in a row."

Celestine shook her head. Police didn't interview suspects together for a reason. But it was Everett's ineptitude that made his performance charming. It didn't matter how many times he played the role; he was always shit at it.

"I thought we weren't supposed to move," Dean said, raising one of his manicured eyebrows.

Everett rolled his eyes at his twin. "We must get to the facts." He motioned to Babette and Frances, because he knew they would appease him—especially Babette. They placed their chairs in a row, looking at the dead body and the detective.

"What is this? The new group therapy thing that is all the rage in sanatoriums?" James asked. "I don't particularly feel like being psychoanalyzed."

"There's not much to analyze in your head, brother. You're a psychopath. You have no feelings and like to cut things open," Vivian said, carrying a chair over to the row and sitting. "Perhaps we all *should* be placed in a sanatorium, seeing our minds are all so incredibly off-kilter."

"Sometimes, when dealing with our family, I feel like I already am." Dean shared a look with Vivian and placed his chair beside her.

Everett chuckled.

Frustration was painted across Frances's face. "Perhaps we should be serious, boys. Lives hang in the balance." It was a reminder to them that, while they might be behaving as if it were any other night, it was anything but.

James and Dean sat up straight at the words, their demeanors shifting. The men could often lack empathy and focus, but they still knew when to take things seriously.

Everett tried to smooth out his rumpled blue peacock suit, and Dean smoothed the lapel of his perfectly tailored prestige hunter-green suit. James fidgeted with the metal chain of his pocket watch, needing somewhere to put his hands. None of the men was particularly good at sitting still.

"Please, as you were," James said.

Everett nodded. "We must figure out the motive, means, and opportunity." But even Everett couldn't take himself seriously in this role anymore. He snorted and took a flask from his jacket pocket—a different bottle than he'd been nursing all night—and took a large swig. "Who am I kidding? Everyone has a motive to kill my mother. She is a vile creature."

Vivian tried to suppress her own laugh. "It is true, Aunt Lorraine is the biggest c—"

"Vivian, watch your mouth."

"Yes, mother."

"Not that it isn't true," Irene added. "We just don't say those types of words in polite company."

"Ah, so it's okay in private."

"Of course not."

Frances rocked in her seat. "So, if everyone has a motive, perhaps we could discuss that?"

As the detective, Everett took up his position once more and said, "Well, Vivian's motive is apparent."

"It is not." She stood so violently that her chair crashed to the ground.

Every Ashbrook possessed some sense of a hyperbolic nature, but Everett and Vivian usually took the cake with their over-the-top natures.

Everett simply raised an eyebrow. "Lorraine is single-handedly responsible for not letting you dance ballet. The only thing you love. And she orders animals killed for her custom furs."

"That doesn't rise to the level of murder. Besides, that's old news. She banned me from dancing years ago—and who in their right mind would kill over animal furs? I am devoted to my beliefs, but not that much."

"You'd be surprised what people would kill over."

"Your motive is much stronger than mine, and you know it." She crossed her arms in front of her chest like a toddler on a triad. "You hate your mother."

"Everyone hates her. That's her entire persona."

"But she killed your—"

"Do not finish that sentence," Everett growled.

"Motive is motive, brother."

Frances leaned in and sat up straighter. "Who did she kill?"

Wanting to hear the answer, Celestine leaned in slowly as to not draw attention to herself, hoping they would continue arguing with each other and giving away the answers.

"It doesn't matter," Everett mimicked Vivian, and drew his hands across his chest. "If that's my motive, then it's also Dean's."

All heads swung in Dean's direction. Normally, so silent and inviable. He wanted to remain so, but it was clear from the weight of the attention now on him that he couldn't

"I am not involved in this." Dean raised his hands. "Am I sad she's dead? No. But this time, I have absolutely no reason to do anything."

"But you have had reasons before." Everett wasn't letting his twin off the hook.

"You all have met our mother. Eventually, everyone finds a reason to want to kill her.

"Son, you might not have a motive now, but you'd do anything for any of your siblings." The twins' father, Archibald, moved for the first time since standing behind his lover and staring down at the body. He drew out a chair. "You are unquestioningly loyal to a fault—especially with Everett and James."

"Perhaps"—Dean slid his hands into his pockets— "but the question I would like to ask is, why is she holding your tie?"

"Everyone saw her accost me. She ripped my tie off during the blackout."

"While you were stabbing her?"

"And which brother are you covering for now, Dean?" Archibald met Dean's ire with some of his own. But it wasn't his frustration that caught Celestine's attention. It was the fact that Archibald was insinuating that Dean wasn't the murderer, but one of his brothers was, and that this had happened in the past. "Admit it, Dean. You'd bury the body for either of your brothers. You've done it before, and you'd do it again."

A dark smirk crept across Dean's face. "Of course, I would."

James cut in, trying to release the tension. "Well, at the very least, I don't have a motive. Dean wouldn't be helping me do anything."

Vivian scratched her chin and scoffed. "Of course, you do."

"And that is what?"

"Money. It's always money with you."

"I have more money than I could ever count."

"Maybe now," she said back. "But back when my character card took place, they removed your inheritance so that you wouldn't go into business. It stands to reason that all our cards are from—"

"Fine, you caught me. It is money," he said, with an even tone. It was nearly impossible to provoke a rise out of James— to provoke any emotion out of him.

Walter, who hadn't entered the conversation once, stood from the table where he had been picking at food and watching his family argue. "Alright. Could we take a little break from uselessly spouting out all our secrets and do something else?"

He walked over to the group slowly and calmly. His entire demeanor was vastly different from the rest of his family. He was even-tempered and solid, like a tree trunk with incredibly deep roots. But what was truly fascinating about his presence was that he actually did exude a calming influence over the rest of them. The Ashbrooks all sat back in their chairs, and almost as if they were a choir, they all breathed in unison and released heavy sighs.

But Babette wasn't here to be calmed down. She was dying, so in a thick French accent, she said, "And what about your motive, Walter?"

He shrugged. "I truly care nothing for Lorraine's state of living. Dead, alive, it matters not to me."

When no one counteracted him, Babette turned to Jon, the only other person in the room who hadn't spoken once. "And you, Jon, what is your motive?"

Jon flashed a dimple and tapped his fingers on the table where he was still eating. "Don't look at me. I'm only here for the food."

"Or," Vivian cut in, unwilling to let him get away with saying nothing, "maybe you didn't like her constant disapproval of your relationship with Walter."

"Except, I do not bother caring about the thoughts of an insignificant woman."

Ignoring the current conversation completely, Dean strolled over to Celestine's side—who, like a wallflower, was just wishing to stay invisible and watch the drama go down from the sidelines.

"It's all so terribly dull," he whispered to her.

Celestine shut her eyes and tried to take in a steadying breath, but it didn't work. Dean's words frustrated her to no end. He could be nonchalant and uncaring, because his life wasn't on the line. "I'm sorry you find my imminent death boring."

"I could never find you boring." He stepped in closer, and while he wasn't touching her, she could feel his presence as if he were. A shiver ran through her core, and she focused her eyes back on the scene before her.

"That leaves Irene and Archibald," Babette said, her intensity cutting daggers through them.

Vivian rolled her eyes once more. "Their motive is obvious."

Irene raised an eyebrow. "Oh?"

But it was Everett who cut in with the answer. "Adultery, obviously; everyone knows the worst kept secret among the nob—among San Francisco's social elite—is that you two"—he pointed to Irene and Archibald—"are fucking, and Vivian and James are his illegitimate children."

Celestine pinched her eyes closed at the final confirmation of what she already understood. They *were* all brothers. This meant that Celestine's earlier deduction was wrong. The Specter couldn't only be one of the pairs of twins. It also could be James.

Celestine felt it in her bones that the Specter was one of her men—not their father or uncles—but she wasn't entirely certain, so she kept all of them within her suspect pool.

"Well, *now* everyone knows," Irene spat out like a venomous lizard.

"Everyone already knew, Mother," Vivian sighed dramatically—like mother, like daughter. "Your lipstick is on his collar, and you're not even good at hiding it. I bet Celestine saw that as soon as he entered the room."

All eyes landed on Celestine, who gulped and nodded. "Yes, I noticed."

"He might pretend to be the genius detective"—she pointed at Everett—"but he's a fraud, and she's the real deal." Vivian turned and directed her following words only to Babette. "That's why the Specter truly adores her; her mind, not her...assets.

Babette scoffed.

Irene whirled on Celestine. "Maybe Celestine is the killer."

Celestine pinched her lips into a flat line and answered, "Me or my character?"

"You. I heard her threaten you and your relationship with her boys. Perhaps you killed her to remove the only obstacle between you and marriage to one of her sons."

"Only obstacle?" Celestine scoffed. "What about the fact that neither of them has even given me any indication they're interested?" After all, Dean hated her guts, and he'd never make such an offer. What was it with rich people thinking Celestine wanted them or their money? She just wanted to live in peace. "Besides, I'd be far closer to marrying your son—"

"Marriage, Cellie, I—"

Celestine ignored James altogether. "Firstly, I do not want to get married, and secondly, and not that it matters, James would never condescend to marry me. But if you want to accuse my character, Margot, of trying to marry an Ashbrook, then by all means. She does have a motive to get rid of Lorraine since she is engaged to Everett."

"Married," Dean amended.

Silence descended in the room, and it felt sticky, almost as if they had dipped their skin into hot tar.

Celestine's gaze landed on Everett, as did everyone else's. Would he finally admit it? He had a lot of explaining to do.

After enough pressure, Everett finally said, "So everyone has a motive. Now what?"

He still wouldn't admit out loud that he married Margot.

"Now, we investigate the murder." Celestine's gaze tracked once more to the balcony. The arrow had come from above. Celestine could tell by the angle of the wound. The murderer wouldn't have had much time to take the shot and get back down to the ballroom, so it was possible the weapon was still up there or stashed somewhere near it.

"That's what I was thinking, too." James walked over to Celestine, slid his hands in his pockets, and followed her eyes up to the metal glinting in the candlelight. "It's up there."

She nodded. One thing she appreciated about James above the others was his mind. He was a man of science. Physics. Rationality. And he understood her line of thinking. The arrow came from the balcony, so it was the logical location to search there first.

"Cellie and I are going to go search for the bow and arrow," James matter-of-factly told his family. "Try to be useful and look for the other murder weapon or the killer's change of clothing or anything."

"No, thank you." Vivian leaned back in her chair and

snapped at one of the ghost waiters to bring her more booze. "I'll stay right here. I have no interest in these silly games."

The character inside Celestine's mind flashed awake and barked out, "Of course, you wouldn't. You love to stand aside and do nothing when it matters."

Vivian's throat worked, but her eyes narrowed, and she examined Celestine like an impossibly complex math equation. "Hello, dearest Margot. I've missed you." She winked. "But you're correct. I have no interest in helping you. Not then, and not now."

Celestine's chest tightened, and fury burrowed into her stomach. A flash of murderous thoughts stroked through her mind as Margot's anger deepened. She wanted to skin Vivian alive, and strangely, Celestine wanted to let her. She didn't know why, but whatever had happened between the two girls was horrific. Celestine could feel it.

Margot retook control. "Do watch your back, Vivian." Margot's voice was dark venom. "James, let's go." She grasped his hand and pulled him out of the room.

Margot clawed at her mind, wanting to take over completely again, and Celestine decided not to fight it, slipping to the back of her mind, allowing the ghost to have the reins.

"Are you going to kill my sister, Margot?" he asked in his signature methodical tone.

"Yes, after I kill you." She stopped, turned, and slammed him into the wall. "And you know why."

James grinned. "Oh, I've missed you and your dramatic shows." His cold eyes devoured her face. "How are you going to do it? I like it when my Cellie kills me. It turns me on."

"You're sick." She shook her head, her hands still on his shoulders. "You've always been sick."

James lifted his chin. "Yes, I have."

I am going to kill you. Slowly, I am going to watch as you scream and beg for help, Margot thought. *Just like you did.*

But it wasn't time for that. Margot didn't want to help her weak, pathetic vessel, but this body was dying. If she were going to take it over and keep it forever, then she needed to solve the Phantom's riddle. Unfortunately, Margot also didn't know the answer. But the vessel was on to something. The answer to who killed Lorraine would most likely lead to the true identity of the Specter.

Keep it? Celestine screamed and pushed against her invisible cage. She would not let Margot have her body. But the ghost's control didn't budge. Margot's spirit was too strong. Ridiculously so. Celestine's arms grew heavy, and her veins throbbed as she felt herself being pushed further back into the recesses of her mind.

Margot removed her hands from James's shoulders and began walking again. "Keep up. We need to find the bow and figure out who killed your wretched aunt."

It didn't take them long to make it up the stairs and to the spot overlooking the dead body.

A crimson curtain was pulled to the side, and behind it rested a glimmering metal rig. A crossbow was screwed to the wall and held up with brackets. A fishing line was attached to a Rube Goldberg machine. When the marble reached the end of the machine, it would cause a chain reaction that would release the arrow from the crossbow.

Whoever set up the apparatus wasn't here when it went off. Had they even killed the proper target?

Margot would have known who was responsible for the machine without seeing the gum holding multiple parts of the apparatus together. But it was an undeniable clue. Celestine didn't miss it either.

"Ah, gum." Margot's lips slowly rose in a wicked grin. "So, you shot her with the arrow."

James raised an eyebrow. "And should I kill you for discovering it?" He pulled a revolver out of his pocket and pointed it at Margot's chest.

No, Celestine screeched in her cage, but of course, no one heard—except Margot, who didn't much care. If he killed Margot, Celestine would die. Forever. This couldn't happen.

No fear pulsed through Margot; rather, excitement churned in her blood. "Who do you think Wolfsbane likes more tonight?" Margot asked, her fingers reaching out and caressing the wall with her nails. "My love, do my bidding."

A loud sound snapped above Celestine's head, and she wanted to duck, but Margot didn't move. Instead, she looked on with joy. From the ceiling fell a wall of spikes, swinging down toward James. It sliced into his flesh, and impaled him to the wall. The gun slipped through his fingertips. Blood poured from the many holes now filling James's chest.

Celestine screamed in her mind. This was wretched. What if there were no resurrections? Would James stay dead forever? She clawed at her mind, trying to pull back control, but the vengeful spirit was too strong.

"Ah, it would seem she listens to me tonight." Margot referred to Wolfsbane. "I am sure you find this deeply pleasurable."

Blood dribbled from between James's lips, coating his teeth as he flashed a lopsided grin. "I assume this is for back then."

"Yes," Margot seethed. "This is for everything you did."

"And tell me," he wheezed, "what...what is it I...I've done?"

Anger overtook Margot, and she reached out and slapped him through the spiked cage. "I would have liked to do this much differently. If I had the time, I would torture you. Take you out to your railroad tracks and strap you down." She pulled out the words slowly, playing with them. "Then I would watch as the train tore down the tracks, barreling toward you. Do you think you'd feel fear?"

James flashed a dimple, causing more blood to leak from his face.

"Can you even feel fear?" she said, kicking a foot through the bars and pushing on his chest to move the spikes oh so slightly deeper into his body. "Doubtful."

"Perhaps"—he sucked in a pained breath—"you should tell me."

Margot scoffed. "Hilarious." She pushed his chest down again and watched his flesh move against the metal. "You told them, didn't you?"

An evil laugh gurgled through his lips. "Why, of course."

"Because all you have ever cared about is an interesting show."

"What else is there?"

Margot's nose flared. "Love, life, happiness. So many things, you fucking monster."

Margot didn't wait to watch the light leave James's eyes. She had thought she wanted to watch him suffer as life left his body, but she found his presence—even half dead, disgusting.

He'd die, and she'd go in search of her next victim.

Margot glared down at two more dead bodies, their blood painting a mural across the floor.

Beautiful.

Maybe James was right and she was also a psychopath like him. But she wasn't born one. She was made—made to crave the blood. Luckily, the self-righteous vessel was sleeping in her mind. She'd passed out when Margot killed again.

Dispatching the Ashbrook uncles took barely any effort at all. She simply ran into them in the hallway and used James's gun to put two bullets through their skulls. There was no need for a big show with Jon and Walter. They were useless when Margot was still alive, and now they were useless dead.

Ah, it was sweet how the lovers held hands as they died. Every Ashbrook had a secret, but their secret was wholesome. At another time, it wouldn't need to be a secret at all. Their sin? Loving the same sex when it was illegal.

To hide from the world, Walter married his lover's sister and moved them both into his house. Margot was pretty certain that marriage had never been consummated. Irene didn't mind the arrangement, because she'd been in love with

Archibald since she was a child, but he married another. It turned out he preferred his lover to his wife.

To be fair, anyone was better than Lorraine. A vampire, a beast, or even a gruesome reanimated corpse would have been better than Lorraine. So, while Walter and Irene never consummated their marriage, they still had heirs and children.

Margot shivered. What a disgusting thought. It was like imagining her own parents rutting in the sheets. Margot shook out her borrowed body but stumbled and had to steady herself against the wall. The vessel was sickly. It was something she'd fix once she had total control.

Her gaze latched once more on the dead bodies. The blood tracked toward her heels, the thick crimson crawling in a beautiful pattern—a Rorschach painting spidering out on the floor. It looked like a dove taking flight. She shuffled to the right so it wouldn't get on her shoes. They were horrific Mary Janes with scuff marks covering all sides. The Phantom had made her dress like a maid again.

Margot didn't know which one of the Ashbrook boys was the Phantom, but it certainly wasn't Everett. He'd never force her to wear something so heinous.

Turning her back on the dead bodies, Margot made her way further into the house. She had bigger targets now.

She'd killed Jon and Walter because they'd done nothing. They didn't watch with glee like James, but they didn't intervene either. A pattern with the Ashbrooks. A pattern she'd make them pay for.

Margot had two purposes in death: to find a way back to life and to get her revenge. And while it was almost a certainty that the Ashbrooks would come back to life—they were parasites like that—she'd still take the opportunity she was given. She would have her revenge. Perhaps it was foolish to murder the people who held the answers to the riddle she needed to solve to keep this body, but then Margot had always been a little too impulsive of a creature. Becoming...whatever she was, didn't change that fact. If anything, it intensified her darker, baser instincts.

She shrugged. She'd find a way to have both. Maybe she could torture the name of the Specter out of them before they died.

Warmth spread in Margot's chest as she scratched her head with the barrel of the gun she was still holding.

That was the answer.

Three murders down. Six to go. Perhaps five—she hadn't decided yet if she would also kill Everett. He'd deserve it, but then he was her one weakness. The one place where her revenge would falter.

Where to start?

Vivian maybe?

She'd be fun to cut open—perhaps pull out an eyeball or two—and Margot would force her to tell her everything she knew.

A twisted smile snaked across her lips. It didn't matter which Ashbrook Margot killed next. Any would do.

The vessel clawed against the edges of her mind, trying to stop Margot's tirade, but she didn't pay her any attention. *Ah, I see you're awake again. It doesn't matter.* The girl would never overpower her. Weak minds were easy targets, and this gorgeous, broken thing was one of the most pitiful she'd ever possessed. All the girl cared about was making the men in her life proud and being a good girl for her Specter. She pretended not to care what the Ashbrook men thought, but their approval was all she cared about. It was revolting.

Margot would never stoop so low.

A voice floated from inside the grand ballroom. "Well, this is too dreary, and I am bored. Who cares that we all have motives, means, and opportunity?" Irene said. "That's the point, isn't it? In most murder mysteries, everyone has a motive. That's why the Phantom chose Lorraine in the first place. I say we liven up this party."

Margot walked to the entrance so she could see the exchange.

"You could investigate the murder, then, instead of complaining about it in here," Everett said in an exasperated tone. "Or join me in drinking. I don't care."

Irene ignored her nephew and focused instead on the other twin. "Dearest Dean, play us a song on the piano."

"That feels incredibly inappropriate, Auntie." Dean sighed. "My mother is lying dead on the floor."

Irene's attention switched to Everett. "You're not as good at the piano, but would you deign to play?"

"No." Everett took a big swig of his whiskey.

Irene pouted like a child and placed her fingertips on the table. "House, please liven up the atmosphere."

To Margot's great surprise, the house listened. The house typically only responded to the cast. The guests in attendance didn't have elixir in their systems and, therefore, couldn't manipulate it. Yet the house did as she asked. The ghost musicians struck up a jaunty tune, and the ghost couples burst from the walls, dancing the jive.

Was the elixir even necessary, then? Was it all a lie? Margot wouldn't put it past any of the Ashbrook boys to design a house of enchantments that didn't even follow its own rules.

But it didn't matter. Margot had her mission—her rampage—and Vivian would be her next victim. But she wasn't in the ballroom, so her search needed to continue.

Yet as she lifted her foot to turn on her heel, her gaze touched Dean's, who was glaring...at her. The force of it felt strong enough to suck her soul out of the vessel. Margot shivered and kept moving. The last thing she needed was to catch that particular man's attention. At the end of the day, he was the most dangerous Ashbrook.

Unfortunately, he followed her out of the ballroom and into one of the narrow passageways that led to a staircase. So much for avoiding his notice.

Dean slammed her into the wall, his hand tightly around her throat. "Give her back to me."

"Oh." Margot cackled, her stomach tingling with amusement. "She's yours? Well, she's not home right now."

"Celine is not mine."

At the nickname, Celestine's consciousness snapped back into place, but she was still a prisoner in her mind.

"Sure thing." Margot stroked her hands like claws down his chest. "I am sure you wouldn't want her to touch you like this."

The muscle in his jaw tensed.

"Or maybe like this." Margot's finger curled under his belt.

No. Celestine wanted to scream, cry, or do something. The last thing she wanted was to be touching Dean like this without her consent and his. It was mortifying.

"Stop." Dean slammed Margot once more into the wall and tightened the grip on her throat.

Margot smiled, and her hands stilled, still on his belt. "I like it rough, but does she?"

I do. Celestine tensed. *Shit, what the fuck, Celestine? You absolutely are not going to cosign this.*

"Oh, she does." Margot laughed.

No, I don't. But, appallingly, she did. She liked the fact that Dean was touching her. Margot was right. She was a pathetic, desperate girl who desired men's attention.

Celestine wanted to pinch her eyes closed and die, but she couldn't because the demon was still in control of her body.

Dean's gaze raked over Margot. "If that's true, let her tell me that herself."

"As I told you before, she's asleep."

"No, she's not." Dean stroked his thumb along her jaw, and Celestine's cheeks heated. "I see her embarrassment on your cheeks."

"Maybe I am blushing because I want you."

Dean's lip twitched. "I have no doubt that you want me, Margot." Dean pulled her hands from his belt, and with a swift and authoritative movement, he pinned them above her head, pushing her deeper against the wall. Margot gasped, and her breath hitched. "You always wanted both of us." His breath kissed her ear, and she shivered. "You always loved playing with both of us, pitting us against one another."

Celestine's breasts rose with her quick breaths, and her core tensed, liking his taunts just a little too much. In this, Celestine and the demon in her mind were aligned.

"You like this?" He sucked her earlobe into his mouth.

"Yes," Margot whispered. "I have always wanted this."

Dean moved his lips to hover over hers. "I see death hasn't changed you." Suddenly, he stepped away. Margot's hands dropped to her sides, and her knees nearly buckled from the lack of pressure to keep them in place.

She let out a wanton whine.

"But I have changed," Dean said. "I am no longer a desperate boy. I am a man, and I won't play your foolish games anymore." Darkness overtook his features. "You will give us Celestine back by the night's end."

"Oh, will I?" Margot spat back.

"I will make sure of it." He took three heavy steps toward her again, and once more, he pushed her into the wall, circling her neck with his fingers, but this time, his touch was soft. His gaze caught hers. "I see you in there, Celestine. You might not believe it, but you are stronger than her. You can fight this and win." His thumb stroked her lip. "You just have to believe it."

Then he turned on his heel and disappeared down the hall.

Margot called after him. "You will fail."

"No, he won't." The dark, chocolate voice caused the hairs at the nape of her neck to rise. The Phantom. "You've been a bad girl, Margot."

She crossed her arms over her chest. "And?"

"You were not supposed to kill." His voice slithered behind her ear. "Should I assume you are actively trying to destroy my show?"

"I'm not actively doing anything." She pursed her lips in disapproval. "If you didn't want a character with their own thoughts and feelings, then maybe you shouldn't have summoned me."

"You are a piece on my chessboard, nothing else." The curtains shuddered, and the lights in the hallway dropped. "Nothing else."

Margot's eyes narrowed, and her arms gripped tighter around her chest. "I will be your reckoning, too."

A dark laugh encased her, the sound touching her every pore. "No, you won't," the Phantom growled. The hall's shadows curled around her limbs, caging—not allowing a single movement. "I own you."

"You don't," Margot said through her teeth, struggling against her binds. She winced in pain.

"You can try to ruin my game, but you won't be able to. For everything you do, I can undo." The lights in the hall flickered on, and there stood James in his striking dove-gray suit, very much alive.

"Hello, monster." James waved a finger at a time in a taunting fashion. "Miss me?"

Well, fuck.

"You will be a good girl and play *my* game." The Phantom's voice vibrated the glass of the hallway mirrors—nearly liquifying them. "If you don't, I will punish you."

"And how exactly will you punish me?"

"I will send you back to hell."

Margot swallowed, and her heart sped in her ears. That was the one thing he could do that would ruin all her plans. Margot needed time to fully possess the vessel. Excavating a soul was no easy process. It often took days, months, or even years to do it—though with one this weak, it would probably only be days. And once she did it, the Phantom couldn't threaten to return her anymore. He wouldn't have the power to do it then.

But he had the power now.

Margot sucked in a breath. "Fine. I will play your stupid games."

"Much appreciated. Now go with James to the ballroom. I'm about to make my next move." The Phantom's voice echoed in the hallway, and the lights returned.

"Well, we mustn't anger the Phantom further." James motioned behind him to the path that led back to the ballroom.

As James and Margot lowered themselves into chairs around a card table, lightning lit up the room and thunder shook the marble floors.

To Margot's utter dismay, the Phantom hadn't only resurrected James, he'd also brought back the uncles.

"Now that everyone has returned, let's truly get started," the Phantom said. "Welcome to our game within a game...

and possibly a game within a game within the game. Since you already know everyone has a motive, let's play a little game to get my clues...clues to all our various riddles tonight."

A small rectangular box appeared in front of everyone. It could fit in the palm of their hands.

"Open the box, and it will tell you the location of the first clue. Remember, tonight is about fun!"

Fun. Margot scoffed. Maybe *his* fun. But she knew tonight wasn't only for her revenge. It was a night filled with his. That's why he had pulled her spirit from the great beyond.

She bit her lower lip. An annoying habit the vessel had when in deep thought. Margot examined the box, as did everyone else. She had no idea what it was, but she was reasonably sure the vessel did. But she didn't want to give that soul any slack, and at the moment, she was forcing the girl deeper into the pits of her mind. Margot didn't believe Dean when he said the vessel was strong, but she wouldn't test it— just in case.

Instead, she would turn to one of the other two female cast members and see if they could solve the problem if they teamed up together.

Margot's eyes latched on to Babette, who was struggling with her puzzle alone. Perfect, they could team up. The pathetic soul would have also helped Babette.

Margot walked to the table by the other girl and leaned against it. "We could work this out together," she said, holding up her box for the other girl to see.

"Why would I do that?" Babette's eyebrows pinched together.

"Because discovering the true name of the Specter is nearly impossible."

"I'd rather see you die."

Margot cocked her head and smiled. "Ah, I see you hate my vessel, too."

"Vessel?" Babette raised a well-plucked eyebrow.

Margot sighed. It would take far too much energy to explain the situation to the brunette, and Margot didn't have the patience. "You don't want me dead."

"I do." Babette crossed her arms and quickly forgot her previous question. "You ruined everything. When you showed up, they stopped looking at me...stopped playing with me. You shine brighter than the sun and blind all who look upon you. They cannot see past you. It's not fair."

"That was a fun metaphor," Margot said mockingly. She hated desperate jealousy. It was pitiful and weak.

Babette ignored her. "You're a curse, and I wish you dead."

"Well, perhaps you will get your wish sooner than you may think."

Babette shook her head. "If you genuinely want to help me, tell me how to open the box and go away."

"I don't know how to open it." *And I don't think I would help you even if I did.* There was no use in helping someone who was so utterly combative. The vessel had put up with this girl for far too long, and Margot was over it.

The house shifted as Margot meandered through it, looking for Vivian. She was torn between solving the riddle box and hunting down the Ashbrooks. Yes, the Phantom would resurrect them after she murdered them, but she'd still get the satisfaction of the kill.

But the Phantom was one step ahead of her, and he was obstructing her path. Walls melted like candle wax and moved into each other, statues popped up along the hallways, their eyes following each of Margot's footfalls, and the ceiling swarmed with rotting fireflies.

"This isn't funny," Margot yelled up at the ceiling.

The ceiling let out a low chuckle.

"When I find out which one of you assholes is the Phantom, I will hunt you down and torture you for days."

But it seemed to be *her* torture that the Phantom was after right now. Because dragonflies and hummingbirds on strings dropped from the ceiling, some of them had their wings ripped off, and from their mouths played the cruel harmony from Margot's nightmares.

A nursery rhyme.

With a loud creak, the statues also opened their mouths

and began to sing in a sinister, off-key tone. *Margret, Margret hanging down. It's cold this Winter's mourning. Too bad and oh so sad. You caused the Marquess's scorning.*

The color drained from Margot's face, and guttural fear burned in her veins. Tears dripped from Margot's face as she fell to her knees and clasped her ears tightly, screaming. She couldn't hear this. Not this. Not again.

"Please." The word left her mouth as a hollow plea. "Please, stop."

"Open your box, and I will stop it," the Phantom's voice whispered right behind her ear. "Play my game, Margot."

"No." Her throat was raw. "No."

"For once in your miserable existence, just follow the rules," the Phantom said softly. While he was torturing her, he didn't seem to like it. He felt almost compassionate. "Please, Margot."

"Fine." Margot pinched her stinging eyes tight. "Fine."

She opened her eyes and drew the box into her hand. There was no way Margot would solve the puzzle. Though the last thing she wanted to do was admit that she was bad at something, it was undeniable. Margot wasn't brilliant. She wasn't stupid, either. She was merely average and, unfortunately, not the type of average who liked riddles.

The show wasn't made for Margot; it was made for Celestine. This meant she had to wake up the vessel.

Wake up. Please. I need you to tell me what this is.

The soul sparked to life and slammed so hard into Margot's consciousness that it was clear the girl was waiting to take her chance to come back into the spotlight.

Why would I help you?

Because if we don't solve the show, our body is going to die, and neither one of us wants that.

Margot sucked her bottom lip into her mouth. Celestine

was thinking hard about helping, and she said into their mind, *It's a stereogram.*

What the fuck is that?

It's a visual puzzle. If you look at it correctly, a two-dimensional image will become three-dimensional.

So, how do I look at it?

Hold your finger up in front of it and look at it through your finger.

But it wasn't Margot who did it. Celestine gritted her teeth and forced her consciousness to puppet her body, moving her finger in front of the box. A fairly easy puzzle, all things considered. Her vision shifted, and a mockingbird appeared at the center of the box.

She pushed it down, and voilà, it opened. As the box opened, the hallway cleared, and the song stopped.

Celestine inhaled sharply. She turned the small box over and poured a small slip of paper out. On it was a handwritten note.

I knew you would open it first, my brilliant Celine. The first clue to Lorraine's murder is stuffed inside the couch in the Pettitte Parlar —Your Phantam.

Parts of the note were misspelled. Celestine scratched her hand as Margot clawed at the sides of their brain. Celestine wasn't entirely in control, but she was fighting back. She might be a weak soul, or vessel, or whatever Margot called her, but even the weak could fight. Even an underdog could win.

So, while she had some ability to make choices, she got up and quickly made her way to the Petite Parlor. Stepping over to the couch, she lost her balance and was struck by a fit of dizziness. The palms of her hands barely caught her weight as she fell, and her knees knocked against the hardwood floor. At least she caught herself before striking her head on the coffee table.

Fuck.

Be careful, Margot yelled at the corners of her mind.

Because I want *to fall and hit my head.*

The poison was wreaking havoc on her fragile body.

On the bright side, now she was closer to the floor and in the perfect position to rifle through the couch. She plunged her fingers between the cushions, and they touched something sticky before they ran along a wet cotton men's dress shirt.

Celestine pulled it further out of the cushions. It was once a cobalt-blue Gossypium spun cotton shirt, but the blood coating it had made it nearly fully crimson.

One of the twins had changed their shirt. She knew it wasn't James, because Margot had just seen him in his dove-gray suit, and Celestine had fucked him in the same suit. So James didn't stab Lorraine.

So it was a twin.

The grandfather clock struck one. Two. Three. Four. Five. Six. Seven. Eight. Nine times, and dread pooled in Celestine's stomach.

This show was formed from decaying fairytales. It was beautiful and whimsical but altogether ghastly. And Celestine only had two hours left to live. To solve the murder and the riddle and get the antidote.

"Oh, that's rather gruesome," Vivian said in a singsong voice. She stepped into the room, followed closely by Babette, who had a devious smile on her face, almost as if the women had been working together.

At Vivian's entrance, the ghost inside Celestine sprang to life and fought for control. The battle was like a dance, with smooth lines, sharp turns, and cruel intentions. Celestine wanted agency of her life, while Margot wanted dominance and blood.

A burning sensation started at the back of Celestine's eyes, and her jaw locked from how hard she was clenching her teeth. The muscle in her forehead protruded as blood dripped from her nose, and she clutched the couch for support.

"Uh, Celestine, you don't look so hot." Vivian took a couple of hesitant steps forward.

"No—" Celestine tried to warn Vivian not to come any closer and to get out, but Margot zipped her lips closed.

Babette also moved further into the room, her smile slipping and concern etching her eyebrows. "Celeste, you're not —" She never finished the sentence.

Margot pinched and kicked and hit every inch of Celestine's insides. It felt like she was a frog being squeezed to death by an over-enthusiastic child.

She clutched her head and screamed, the pain becoming overwhelming. A soft hand gently touched her shoulder, but she couldn't see which girl was doing it. She highly doubted it was Babette, though.

"Breathe, Celeste." Babette's voice came from so near, almost as if she were beside her.

"You're going to be okay," Vivian said from Celestine's left. "You can fight this."

Did she know?

A hand rubbed a circle on Celestine's back, but it wasn't Vivian; she was standing two feet away, watching Celestine's meltdown.

Still far too close.

She wanted to yell at Vivian to leave—to get as far away from Celestine as possible. But the words never escaped her lips. Margot was too strong—too powerful—and she was winning this battle. Celestine was being pushed into her cage again, inch by inch, and Margot was closing the door. But she hadn't closed it yet.

Still, she had enough control to reach out, touch the floor, and say, "Wolfsbane, do my bidding."

Without seeing Margot's intentions, Celestine knew, and she threw all her energy at her prison door and tore it open.

She managed to get two words out of her mouth.

"Vivian, duck!"

Four arrows flew out of the eye sockets of the painting right as Celestine jumped up and tackled Vivian to the floor. "My character is trying to kill you."

Celestine landed on top of Vivian, straddling her chest.

"So it would seem," Vivian said. "Hello, Marguerite."

"Hello, Viv," Margot seethed. Celestine intentionally took a back seat in her mind—she wanted to see what the girls had to say to one another—yet her hands were still very much on the reins of control. If Margot tried to kill again, Celestine would step in—or at least, she would try. This was her body and mind; even a demon wouldn't change that.

Dean had said Celestine was stronger. She'd believe him.

"Don't call me that." Margot pushed down the other girl's shoulders. "It's Margot, and I am going to destroy you."

"Fine, Margot, but if you are going to *destroy* me"—she emphasized the word mockingly—"at least can you make it pleasurable. Like that one time at the lake."

Margot shivered and tightened her legs around Vivian's core. "I trusted you, and you betrayed me."

"Betrayed is such a big word."

"I helped you bury the body of the man you killed while fucking him—"

"*Accidentally* killed."

"I helped you hide your deepest, darkest secret, and you know how you repaid me?"

"With a kiss?"

"Shut up. Shut up." Margot grasped Vivian by the shoulders and slammed her to the ground. "You did nothing for me. Worse, you told your mother about me and Everett, and you found joy in my demise."

"I didn't mean to tell her." Vivian breathed heavily, her

tone dripping with clotted emotions. "I was so angry. I had just caught you kissing Everett and calling him husband after you told me you loved me and wanted to run off with me. I was so angry, I ran home in a tirade, yelling about it, and she overheard. I didn't realize what I had done until I stopped seeing red." Vivian gulped. "I never meant to hurt you."

"But you did."

"And you hurt me, too."

"At least you're not fucking dead."

"Aren't I?" Vivian said, looking around the room. "I feel like a walking, breathing corpse—and I may be. Who knows, really?" She shrugged.

"I'm going to kill you."

"Then do it." Vivian leaned up into the other girl. "Kill me or fuck me. I don't care which one you choose."

"I mean it, Viv."

"And I mean it, *Marguerite*."

They were lovers, too? Margot and Vivian? Margot and Everett? And Margot and Dean? Was James the only Ashbrook her age she hadn't pursued in some fashion?

She was just as much of a hussy as Celestine. It wasn't a bad thing; Celestine believed all people should live without shame and do what they wanted in love. However, it was astounding that the character shared so many similarities with her, despite the many stark differences.

Vivian reached a hand up and curled a blonde lock between her fingers. "He shouldn't have done this, not a real spir—" Her eyes narrowed further on the strand. "He knows better than this."

"I am sure he did it because my host has such a weak mind."

At the words, Celestine pinched the essence living inside

her brain with all her might—she was sick of being called weak.

Ouch. Stop that.

"Why would that be the reason?"

"Because as much as he protests, he wants me to stay," Margot said with a low, sultry voice. "In the vessel of his choosing."

"Doubtful."

Margot raised a brow.

"I know my brothers." Vivian's lips twitched. "The Phantom would never offer another soul this body. He's too obsessed with it and the girl inside, and that's not you."

"You were all once obsessed with me, too."

Vivian wiggled a bit underneath Margot's legs, seeing if she could break free. "Time changes many things."

"It hasn't changed you."

"Monsters never change."

INTERLUDE:

All that glitters was not gold—except when it actually was...

The Civic Auditorium was built for the World's Fair in 1915, and as such, the building was bedecked with finery. Gilded walls, rich velvet, and intricate murals. It was glamorous and powerful. Everything Celestine was not.

She gulped and pinched her eyes before walking onto the grand stage, with its lights glaring and the audience silhouetted. From what she could tell, there were three men in the audience. The Opera General Director and Opera Conductor were sitting relatively close to the stage, and one more man wearing a top hat was far at the back.

Celestine bit her lip and begged God—or whoever was up in the sky—to help her. Make it so she didn't stand out like a sore thumb.

Her shoes were covered with holes, and her dress had rips in the hem and bodice, which she had desperately tried to cover up with cleverly placed stitches, brooches, and lace formed from discarded plastic.

The Great Depression had not been kind to her, but this was the first step toward her future. She just needed to make it through these auditions.

Unfortunately, luck was never on her side, and neither were her nerves. Anxiety was a noose that strangled her vocal cords and wobbled her notes, and that could not happen during the biggest auditions of her life. But that was her luck. Celestine was an incredible singer, trained by her mother since the age of five. She had technique, tone, clarity, and near-perfect pitch except when she was nervous... Which, of course, always happened during auditions.

The song floated out of her like doves taking flight. Gentle, yet radiant. That was until one of the notes soured and curved sharply and then immediately flat as a counterbalance. After that initial struggle, all those notes faltered, and those birds flying gracefully in the sky turned to ash. And as she entered the B section of her Aria, she knew she'd messed up beyond repair.

There would be no respite from her suffering. There would be no hope. She'd either have to turn to prostitution to survive, or something far worse.

The director held up his hand, signaling her to stop. "That is enough. You can see yourself out."

Celestine bowed her head, tears forming at the edges of her eyes. She'd failed. Again.

Celestine would not murder another person. She was sick of blood pooling in her hands and ripping breaths from dying, frail bodies. She did not want to watch poison devour a body or clench her hands around a slender throat.

Never again. Nine years of death was enough.

Wolfsbane may bathe in blood, Margot might as well, but Celestine no longer would. She was done, and she was done with the parasite inside her brain taking command. No, it was her turn to take command of the ship and steer it in the right direction.

And Celestine had heard enough.

She climbed off Vivian and, without another comment, she slowly, silkily strode out of the room, walking by a wide-eyed Babette as she left. The brunette had watched the exchange with a mixture of bafflement and dismay.

Celestine moved purposefully through the house. She was beginning to understand the game. The Phantom had been moving his pieces on the board all night, placing pawns, setting traps, and dancing with his queen. Every person, every moment, every minuscule detail had a purpose.

Even Margot's rebellion.

He'd counted on it. He'd sculpted it. He needed it. Because he set up his dominos piece by piece, creating an intricate and impossible pattern before he pushed one down and watched the rest follow suit.

The Phantom wasn't just playing one game. He was playing many, all at once, and he was winning them all.

But what did he want?

It didn't matter. At the moment, only one thing mattered.

The name.

Vivian called Margot "Marguerite."

Marguerite.

So had Dean...and Celestine had seen that name earlier.

She creaked open the door to her bedroom, half expecting a trap, but she was only met with her slightly messy sanctuary. She was late to the show tonight, so while she hated messes, she hadn't had time to clean up. Books were strewn on every available surface. Sheets crumpled as if someone had just awakened from a nap, and soft candlelight illuminated the space, setting a slightly gothic atmosphere.

The news articles she'd rescued from the burning North Wing were on the nightstand—right where she had left them. But Celestine halted as she reached for them. Beside the stack was something entirely new. A music box. She shouldn't have paused, and she absolutely shouldn't have reached down and opened the box. Yet she did.

The haunting nursery rhyme wafted out. It was the same song that had been plaguing the night, but this time, it was a beautiful soprano melody, floaty and rich.

Margret, Margret hanging down. It's cold this Winter's mourning. Too bad and oh so sad. You caused the Marquess's scorning.

The sound crawled under Celestine's ribcage and nestled there like a caterpillar in its cocoon.

The hairs on the back of her neck rose, and she sensed *his* presence in the room. Either the Phantom or Specter. But she said nothing, not letting them know she'd felt them there.

They could wait.

The nursery rhyme bent with the presence of the ghost. The words faded away, and only a soft lullaby remained, a mixture of piano and violin notes that felt more like a bubble bath than a haunted nightmare. Although it would always be a mix of the two in Wolfsbane Hall.

Celestine ran a finger along the burned edges of her articles before reading the top one once more.

The article was dated December 26, 1760, and the headline read: *Suicide or Another One of the Marquess of Winterly's Misfortunes?*

The main article gave more details, but was still full of judgment and conjecture.

Duke Breython's maid was found dead on Christmas Eve, an apparent suicide. The Marquess and his brother are heartbroken by Miss Marguerite's death. The girl was said to be rather close to the Marquess and his twin. So close, that some sources say the brothers shared her as their mistress. Twins are supposed to be close, but not that close. Others say Marguerite was their mother's lady's maid and nothing else. Either way, her body was found hanging in the west tower at Breython's great house. It is believed to be an apparent suicide, but this writer is unconvinced. As we know, the duke's eldest son, the Marquess of Winterly, is no stranger to heartbreak and death. His first fiancée was found drowned in the lake at her house, his second ran off with the stable boy and eloped in Scotland, and his third was found trampled to death by her horse. Is the Marquess simply the unluckiest young man in Britain, or is there something far more sinister happening in the north count—

The rest of the article was far too burned to finish, but Celestine had read everything she needed. Margot, the demon, the ghost in her head, had been killed. There was no way she killed herself, not when she loved Everett—and playing with Vivian and Dean. Of course, Celestine had guessed much, and Margot had said as much. But there was something so disturbing about confirming the fact. It made it all the more real and reaffirmed that there was nothing ordinary about the night's show at Wolfsbane Hall.

The song, the newspapers, and Celestine's character all pointed back to 1760 and the suicide. But it wasn't a suicide. It was murder.

Yes, it was, Margot said in their head.

A murder in 1760. Shit. Were the Ashbrooks immortal?

Something like that.

Something like immortal? What did that even mean? But more importantly, Margot's death was vitally important to the show tonight. Perhaps some of the answers Celestine needed were in the past, and who would know the past better than the one who lived it?

"Who killed you, Margot?" Celestine asked aloud, but it wasn't the ghost inside her who responded. It was *him*.

"So you've figured it out?" the deep whiskey voice whispered from behind her ear, and his breath stroked her neck.

She whirled around, trying to catch him, but her hands fell as if through smoke.

Never physical.

She knew this, yet she still tried.

"Which one are you?" she asked, her pulse thrumming in her neck.

The air around her warmed and moved as if a presence were there. "Can you guess?"

She didn't have to guess. This was a show, and it was a floating voice that was far less flashy than the Specter. "Hello, Phantom."

"Very good." An invisible hand reached out and brushed her bicep. A full-body shudder coursed through her. Just another reason it wasn't her Specter. He never touched his toys.

Her heart hitched, and her hand fell to her bed for support. Her broken, fragile heart couldn't take much more of this.

"Who are you torturing, Phantom?" she breathed. "Me or your family...or both?"

"I would never torture you." His hand traveled up her arm, the force of his touch hard enough to leave indents but not hard enough to bruise. The shadow stood behind her in as physical a form as she'd ever seen it take, and he was touching her—actually touching her, as if he were genuinely present.

She gulped, unsure of what to do.

"You poisoned me." She leaned back into his touch and was met with a physical, albeit invisible, chest. She closed her eyes and soaked into the feeling.

He rested his chin on her head. "Only a little."

She curled her arms into her chest and pinched her eyes tighter, trying to keep her tears from falling as fury churned in her stomach. It felt like melting porcelain dolls and disintegrating phoenixes—like destroying beautiful things. A metaphor for the Ashbrooks. Men who destroyed beautiful girls.

Celestine slammed the music box lid and stepped out of the hollow man's embrace. Nothing good would come from taking any comfort from the Phantom.

"Go away." She twirled around and tried to look as menacing as possible, which was much like dressing a puppy up like a vampire. It was still a puppy.

A shimmer of light reflected around his tall body, and he stepped toward her, saying nothing.

Celestine's nose flared, and her eyes stung, still holding

back her tears. She was so sick of giving rich, dangerous men her tears. "I hate you."

"I know." His presence rattled, retreating from the room, leaving a desolate echo in its place.

Celestine crumpled onto her bed and pulled her knees into her chest.

A glittering image hovered above her as if the Phantom had returned, but the presence felt different.

"Specter?" But even as the name left her crimson lips, Celestine knew it was wrong. This was not her Specter. It was something so much worse.

The ground shook like an earthquake. Celestine clutched her bed frame for support, and the shaking increased. Was it another big one, like the 1905 earthquake that took half of the city to the ground? For a moment, Celestine believed it, but then she remembered this was Wolfsbane Hall.

As if on cue, a sickeningly white light, like at the hospital, licked through the room, and all the air burrowed into the walls like creatures trying to flee a predator.

Celestine's feet scraped against the hardwood floor; she needed to escape and get out as fast as possible, because whatever force was in front of her was malicious. It was like Death coming to collect his soul.

Get out, Celestine! Margot screamed. *Get out. She's coming for us. Again.*

21

It was too late. There was no way Celestine's feeble body could outrun anyone.

The force in front of Celestine solidified, forming into the one person she never imagined it could be. Shock nestled into her bones, because once someone was murdered in the show, they never came back to life until the mystery was solved.

Murder victims never resurrected early.

And yes, the Phantom had resurrected James and the uncles, but that was because they weren't supposed to die. That was because Margot had ruined the show.

But this?

Lorraine's translucent ghost body hovered over her. That was not possible.

But...

Lorraine wasn't back. Was she? Just another of Phantom's tricks?

"Phantom?" Celestine croaked, her throat too dry from the lack of air in the room. "Help."

A vicious smile crossed Lorraine's pale, sharp cheekbones. She looked like a sculpture of Hera coming to kill one of Zeus's poor, unwilling lovers.

"He can't help you now, girl." Her voice was a weapon. A scythe.

Lorraine rushed forward, and Celestine tried to dodge and scurry past her would-be murderer. But Lorraine was both too fast and too magical. Celestine's sanctuary rotted into a nightmare. Her sheets became manacles holding her down, her floor became a black pit, and her perfect books became a cage she couldn't escape.

Celestine was fucked.

She was a young woman in a serial killer's lair. It was like glaring at Death, except Lorraine was far worse than Death. She was the Devil, or something close.

"No," Celestine and Margot screamed in unison as Lorraine's sticklike, witchlike hand circled her throat.

She lifted her like she weighed nothing and slammed her onto the bed, causing Celestine's remaining books to fall into the black pit.

Lorraine tightened her fingers. "You will not ruin my boys."

The air squeezed from Celestine's lungs as she reached behind her head; she tried to grab a pillow, book, or anything she could use to hit Lorraine over the head. But there was nothing to hold on to. The wicked woman had made sure of it.

"They are mine and only mine, forever."

What an overbearing, fucked-up mother. Men were supposed to cleave from their mothers at some point. It was a natural part of life. That was probably not the most appropriate time to have such thoughts, but Celestine had never died knowing it would stick before.

As darkness consumed her, she wished she had kissed Dean just once.

An utterly useless thought.

Death's claws raked down her spine, and her head lolled to the side, her limbs growing limp.

She was dying, and it wasn't even because of her feeble heart. Or maybe that was precisely the reason—she was being murdered because of a man. Men.

How awful.

Blackness was a snake coiling around her neck, a straitjacket locking her down forever in a trap of her own making. She should have listened to Dean last week, run away and left San Francisco and Wolfsbane forever.

She didn't want to die like this.

Dying was inevitable, but maybe she could have lasted a couple more years and become a world-famous actress that all the women would admire and all the men would want to fuck.

It wasn't until the light left her that Celestine realized she hadn't been weaponless. She could have asked the house for help. She, too, had elixir in her veins. She could have used the Phantom's magic.

Then fight, Celestine. Fight.

But wasn't it too late?

It's never too late. This time, it wasn't Margot inside her head—she'd been strangely dim since the attack. It was Dean, or at least an echo of what Dean would have said. And channeling the man of her nightmares—or dreams—she kneed Lorraine in the breasts.

The force was hard enough to knock the older woman away momentarily.

"You're dead," Celestine wheezed, coughing, her mouth, throat, and lungs burning. "The dead don't—" *Come back alive during the show. Only after.* She finished the sentence in her head, because all the air was ripped once more from her lungs.

"The dead can't die twice, girl," Lorraine hissed.

It didn't make sense. Celestine must have been hallucinating, being sucked so far into unconsciousness that words were distorting themselves. It made no sense, but then delirium had its claws in her brain, sinking in and pulling all rational thoughts from her mind. It was possible she'd said something entirely different altogether.

Lorraine placed both of her knees on Celestine's chest, preventing her struggle.

"This won't be the first time I save one of my sons from an unworthy match, and it probably won't be the last."

Celestine's eyes fluttered shut, and she was hit with an eerie vision.

Lorraine pressed the full weight of her body down on Margot as Irene slipped a noose around her neck. The rope was looped over a metal bar at the top of a tower in a Victorian castle. Margot tried to kick and claw, but her pannier skirts were far too bulky and cumbersome to get any traction, and she was no match for the two women. Worse, she'd been drugged. Her limbs were growing dim and drunken.

Irene tightened the noose, and Margot's fingers curled into the fringing edges of the coarse rope. Then Irene grasped the other end of the rope and pulled.

"No," Margot tried to scream, but it came out more like a gargle. "I love them."

"You cannot possibly love both of them," Irene spat, placing all her weight on the rope, levering it until Margot's feet scraped against the floor. "You broke my daughter by marrying her wretched son."

"Everett isn't wretched," Lorraine said.

"But you admit Dean is, then?"

"Of the two of them?" Lorraine questioned. "Yes, Dean is far more wicked. Everett is mostly the harmless one." Lorraine pulled again on the rope, and Margot's feet left the floor. Dangling. Dying.

No, *please, I am not ready to die. I am not prepared.*

Margot bucked, kicking her legs out like she was in a swimming pool, but the action only pulled the rope deeper into her skin. After a minute, her eyes rolled back into her head and her limbs fell limp.

As Margot died for a second time, in the vision, she was expelled from Celestine's mind. Dead once more.

"The difference this time, Mother, is that I will not allow it," Dean said, towering over his mother with a wine bottle in hand. "I am not Everett. I am the Beast of Winter, and I do not stand by and do nothing when something I care about is in danger. This you should know by now."

He brought the bottle down on his mother's head hard enough to kill her...again. The woman slumped on top of Celestine's limp body as her eyelids drifted shut once more, consciousness a faraway aspiration, much like her dreams of Hollywood.

Her hand fell limp at her side as Dean cradled her into his chest and walked her to his private study. Consciousness was a tango. Quick turns, sharp edges, and a sensual seduction.

No, that wasn't right.

Perhaps the smell of rosewood, musk, and oranges wafting into her nostrils was confusing her, because Dean's scent was pure debauchery.

Decorative wallpaper, golden wall sconces, and a smattering of ancient mirrors, paintings, and sculptures blurred together as a kaleidoscope of color. Pain swarmed all over her body. She'd thought that if she'd only been choked, only her neck and upper body would hurt.

Nope.

Everything. Her muscles, her bones, even her sinews. Everything.

Celestine's heart banged hard in her chest, overworking. *Boom. Boom. Boom.* It was both fast and lethargic at the same time.

"Do you only touch me when I'm passed out?" Her head

drooped against his chest, and she tried to hold it up. "That's very inappropriate, you know?"

"Yes."

A fog of sleep rolled over her mind, and she yawned. "Disappointing."

"Do you want me to touch you other times?" His voice was a low rumble.

I want you to touch me all the time, Celestine thought, or at least she hoped it was a thought. Begged it to be only a thought.

"You're hurt and not thinking clearly." It was more of a grunt than words.

If only I didn't think it all the time. Sleep's talons sank into her skull, and she completely passed out.

Celestine clutched her throat as she jerked awake, rising up on an obscenely comfortable couch. A piano played the song "Poor Wandering One" from the operetta *Pirates of Penzance*.

Dean's strong fingers moved over the keys with beautiful efficiency, hitting every note like he was worshiping them. Celestine wanted those fingers to worship her, too. And that would not do.

"You don't have to just watch. You could sing along. After all, you are an angel of music."

She could. She was a soprano and often sang in the Specter's shows. But Celestine didn't want to. Not to mention, her throat was formed from hot coals.

"And are you my Phantom?" she croaked.

A grin crawled up his face. "Maybe don't try to sing right now."

"Why are you playing the piano?"

Dean didn't even falter as he spoke. Every note was perfect. "Don't you love the piano, or is the Specter a liar?"

"He told you." It was more of a painful breath than words.

"Yes."

As always, Dean was frustratingly vague. One-word answers were starting to drive her crazy.

"Right, and why the song?" she asked.

Dean shrugged. "It felt fitting."

The movement of his shrug didn't hurt his playing; his fingers were still perfectly stroking the keys. Her core pulsed. *For the love of God, Celine, stop using the word "stroking" to describe it.*

Celestine gulped and tried to distract herself and her body by continuing the conversation. "Am I the poor Wandering One, or are you?"

Dean flashed a dimple. "It is a good question." He paused his words as he played the last notes. "I think it may be both of us. I am cursed to wander the world forever, never getting what I want, and you wander these halls with no true goals, following the mad whims of a ghost."

Anger twisted inside her, but the problem was that Dean wasn't wrong. At one time, Celestine would have done anything for the Specter. That's what the female members of the cast did. That's why they were given a spot at Wolfsbane. The Specter wanted loyalty above all else, and Celestine was forged from one thing: loyalty. Always trying to prove her love, doing anything to feel worthy.

Everything Dean said was correct. But she hated it.

"And what is it that you want?" Her lips fell into a hard line, and she curled her fingers into the leather of his couch.

Dean closed the piano's lid and walked over to the couch.

"How are you? Not just your neck, but *you?*" He slid in next to her.

Celestine's brow furrowed; she was caught off guard by the question. "You're the only person to ask me that. Ever." Besides Frances. But Frances mothered everyone. That was her thing. That was why the Specter wanted her.

"Well, my brothers are. . ." Dean ran a hand through his raven locks. "Sometimes single-minded."

"What are you?"

He raised a well-manicured eyebrow, a gesture that said, *Oh, wouldn't you want to know, little bird?*

Celestine rubbed her face. "I don't know you at all. Tonight is the first time you've tolerated being in a room with me, the first night you've truly spoken to me."

"Ah..." His eyes went icy, although there was always a little ice in them. "I can also be single-minded. Avoiding you could be considered evidence of that."

"Why do you hate me?" Celestine's breath caught in her throat, and she wrung her hands, hating that she cared about the answer.

"I very much don't hate you." His words were charged, dark.

Celestine bit her lower lip. "I don't understand."

"You need to stay away from me, Celestine. Everyone around me dies." He glanced at the bruises forming on her neck and the charred marks still on the bottoms of her shoes. The gaze made it clear that he didn't have high hopes for her living. "You should get as far away from this place and us as possible. Everyone in my family is a villain. Especially the Specter. When this is all over, you should pack your things and leave."

Celestine's brows flicked together. "It's always the same

thing with you. You're always trying to get rid of me." Except even as she said it, she didn't truly believe it this time.

"You saw what my mother did." His voice was a velvet snare. "You felt what she did to you. She'll never stop. And I'll never be free of her. It's our curse for what we did."

"We?"

"Play the game. I am sure you'll find out. You've already uncovered many of our secrets," he said. "The Phantom isn't letting anyone get away with their secrets tonight."

Acid crawled up her already raw throat. "Or you could simply answer my questions."

"Now, where is the fun in that?" he asked, but he clearly didn't mean it. Dean was the only Ashbrook who didn't enjoy the show.

"You could help me."

Dean shrugged.

"What the hell is your mother? That wasn't human. What are the Specter and the Phantom? Are you all that way? Are you immortal?" Celestine rushed the questions out, as if saying them quicker might mean he'd answer one of them.

"I can't tell you precisely what we are, but I assume the game will provide the answers," Dean said. "And yes, *we*. Every member of my family is a powerful immortal capable of using magic similar to that of the Specter and Phantom."

He demonstrated this by causing trees to sprout out of the wooden floor. Orange trees.

Blood rushed into her ears. "Are you the Specter?"

"You know I cannot tell you that."

"Why?"

"Because the magic binds us."

An anchor dropped into Celestine's stomach. She would never get a straight answer out of him if he were the Specter. But perhaps she could figure it out through different questions. He played the piano and had played one of her favorite Gilbert and Sullivan shows. He demonstrated an intimate knowledge of her.

"What's your favorite book, Dean?"

His head cocked at the abrupt change in subject. "I don't read much."

"Why?"

Silence cascaded through the room. Dean's gaze fused to hers, and inside the depths of his eyes were swirling emotions —indecipherable ones. "The truth?"

"Yes."

His Adam's apple bobbed. "Because reading makes me feel stupid. It's challenging and draining."

Celestine bit the inside of her cheek and waited for him to continue. In her experience, if one person stayed silent, the other would usually fill the silence. It was a dangerous game to play with Dean, because he could stay quiet for days.

"I don't speak much in general, because I am not good with words," he said. "I am not eloquent, and I often mix things up. It's hard to be the one brother who is such a major disappointment to my family. Everett is everything that I am not. He's smooth, brilliant, and academic; James is the engineer. He builds things, tests them, and understands how people and things work. I am just...me. Quiet, dangerous, and—"

"Mysterious?" Celestine couldn't help herself; she cut in, and her gaze caught on his hunter-green suit jacket.

"Yes, I guess that." He ran another hand through his hair. "I am the protector. The fixer. I step in when my brothers get in trouble, which they inevitably do." He paused for a long moment in thought, but Celestine was exceedingly patient. He had to be the Specter. "But you never answered my question. How are you feeling?"

Her cheeks tingled and pinched. It was like he cared,

refusing to let the question drop. The problem was that Celestine didn't know the answer, not really. No one ever cared about her or her emotions, so she had learned to suppress them deep down into the abyss of her chest. But she thought on it for a moment and slowly said, pulling the words out like taffy, "I'm...so angry. All my life, I have been abandoned, first by my father walking out on us when I was five and then by the brutal murders of my mother and older sister." She didn't know why she was sharing all this with him. "No one stays. No one fights for me. I am just an object to be used. And I don't want that anymore."

24

Saturday, November 11, 1939
Dean's Private Study

Dean said nothing. *Nothing.* Once again. He was calamity-made flesh, and the tension in the room was suffocating her worse than Lorraine's hands had. And she didn't know why having him say something—having him affirm her—meant so much, but it did, and he wasn't giving anything.

Of course, he wasn't. He hated her. A tear leaked from her face, followed by another, until a cascade of them fell. Her tongue grew heavy, and she refused to say another word.

He could have her tears, but she'd give him no more secrets —not that her secrets were worth anything to begin with. She was foolish to think someone would actually want them or even cherish them.

Dean cleared his throat, reached out, and wiped a tear, then another, and another away. In the process, his legs slid in next to hers, kissing them.

"I am not good with words or comfort," he said in a low baritone. "And I can't promise not to leave you, since I stand by my earlier statement that you should get as far away from here as possible, as far away from my family, and especially me, while you can." He paused and scooped up another tear with his thumb. "I know you deserve someone to choose you."

Celestine lifted her head, and her gaze locked on his. "Dean." It was only a breath.

Her heart thrummed in her chest as he leaned in and pressed his forehead to hers. "We are only devastated by you." Then he kissed her forehead and leaned back, giving them space once more.

"Holy hell." Everett's energetic voice was followed closely by James's deeply methodical tones. "I wondered when you'd finally give in."

Dean cleared his throat and caught his brothers' gazes, one after the other. "I was merely comforting her."

"Sure," Everett said disbelievingly.

The side of James's mouth quirked upward. "Well, perhaps it is my turn to comfort her, then." He strode over to her, his hands in his pockets, and he looked like midnight sins coming to roost.

Dean nodded. "As you should." He stood, and without another word, he disappeared from the room.

He literally disappeared into thin air.

"Ah, we're no longer pretending we can't do that," Everett said with a jungle-cat grin.

"There's no use when she knows we're not normal," James said. "You can thank your mother for that."

"What are you?" Celestine's voice was still so pained and raw. It felt horrible to talk, and whispering hurt more.

"We can't tell you that yet, my love." James sat next to her and pulled her into his lap. His fingers examined the bruises forming all over her body. "I am going to kill her...again. But this time, I get the knife."

"Only problem is she won't stay dead." Everett loosed an

exasperated sigh. "Trust us, if we had figured out how to keep her dead, we would have done it long ago."

"Everett." James glared at his brother, the look so dark, it made Celestine shiver.

"Ah, yes," he cleared his throat. "Well, I see that you are okay, my sweet Cece, so I am going to go...examine my cuff-links. It's a very important job, that."

"Vital," James agreed, and turned the force of his attention back to Celestine. A seething anger like she'd never seen before painted his face. "No one hurts what is mine."

"Am I yours?"

"Always."

It wasn't love. It was possession—obsession, and she didn't know how to feel about it. But she didn't mind.

"I'm sorry I let Margot kill you earlier." Her nails bit her palms.

"Oh, my sweet Cellie. I know that wasn't you." He ran a finger lightly over her wrecked neck. It was sweet. James was only ever soft with her. No one else. And when he cast the weight of his attention on her, there was no one else in the world. No one could hurt her or cause her pain. He was her protector.

"I'm okay, James."

"No, you're not." His voice was silky like butterfly wings. "And I hate that I wasn't there to protect you." He kissed her cheek.

"You can't always be there." Celestine swallowed, and pain spiked through her throat. She winced.

His gaze darkened. "I am going to tie her up and torture her over and over and over. Maybe I can't kill her, but I hurt her. I can make her pay for this."

"I don't want you to make her pay." It was a lie. A big part of her very much did want him to make Lorraine pay, but

Celestine was over the violence. She was over the games. "Just help me take my mind off it."

Heat sparked in his gaze. "I would like to fuck you on my eldest brother's prized couch, but you're far too broken for that—and he'd probably torment me for days for it." He stood with her still on his lap, scooping her up in his arms like she was weightless. He always acted like a Hollywood movie hero. "But perhaps I can try to kiss some of these wounds better."

"James, I can walk." She shook her head, but she enjoyed it when he got like this. She loved both his domineering and softer sides. That was what was fun about him. He could be both.

"I know, but why should you?"

He carried her to the billiard room, still cradling her. He kicked open the door with one leg, walked her over, and placed her down on the billiard table, his legs straddling hers.

James shrugged off his jacket. "I haven't gotten to see you all night." He cupped her face far more gently than normal.

"I did kill you." She laughed. "That was technically seeing me." *And we fucked in a corner...*

"Oh, shut your trap, my love." He ran his thumb over her mouth. "Actually, on second thought, open it for me." He tipped her chin back and gently touched his lips to hers. "I am sorry about tonight," he said against her lips. "About the Phantom, the Specter, all of it.

He made it sound like he was responsible for part, if not all, of it...although that wasn't possible. The Specter and the Phantom were definitely different people. But she couldn't think long about that, because he pulled her deeper into a kiss without letting her respond. James comforted with his body, with passion. Never words. He didn't like long stories or feelings And sometimes, all Celestine needed was the physical. She needed to forget about her troubles, forget about the Specter and the Phantom.

"Let me know if it's too much," he breathed into her. "Let me know if you need a break, because I don't want to hurt you."

She nodded and moaned into his mouth. Her throat was on fire, but maybe, just maybe, he could distract her from it.

He smiled into her lips and used his tongue like he was apologizing for something. Wetness gathered between her legs, and Celestine whimpered as James knotted his fingers into her hair. All she wanted was him. He invaded all her senses.

His fingers stroked over her neck, moving the sleeves of her dress down. But when they caught on her shoulders, he ripped the dress off completely. He growled when he was still met with her bra, so he tore that off, too, and her breasts bounced free.

Taking her breasts into his hands, he deepened the kiss. She gasped into his mouth when he flicked her nipple and circled it with his thumb.

"Oh, God, yes," she moaned. "I want more."

James tasted of champagne and unfiltered lust, and he smelled like a mix of dry cedar, black tea, and comfort.

Celestine's body trembled, and she tried to pull him closer, take him deeper, but she tilted her neck just slightly and caused pain to spike through her entire body. She flinched, and James immediately removed his lips from hers.

He shook his head. "You're too hurt for this."

"No," she pleaded, but it came out far more like a croak.

"Cellie, it's in your voice." He leaned his forehead on her head and let out a low growl. "We can't do this."

"Please, I need this distraction, *your* distraction." Her center was pulsing, needy, and it must be fed, but it wouldn't if

James thought she was fragile, breakable. "I need you in me, not coddling me."

His expression was mangled.

"Please," she said again, begging.

He gave her a chilling side-eye. "I won't damage you any further, Celestine. You almost died."

"I didn't."

"And you're a wanton little liar." He smirked.

"James, I will always be breakable. It's a part of who I am."

"I know," he growled again. Crimson desire spiked in his eyes. "Trust me, all I want to do is fuck you. But I don't break my experiments when they're teetering on the edge, and I won't break you."

"Then don't fuck me." A seductive expression climbed her lips. "Be creative." She spread her legs wide, exposing her naked folds.

"God, you will be the death of me." But his smile widened, his hands dug into her thighs, and he began to kneel.

One of his hands slid up her stomach, and he pushed her down so that her back would rest on the table. Billiard balls rolled across the table with sharp clinking sounds as they hit one another. James lifted her legs over his shoulders.

"You're so wet for me." He glided his fingers through her slickness and thrust one inside, and she nearly came from that mere touch.

"More," she whimpered.

He obliged and thrust a second finger into her then leaned in and circled her clitoris with a talented, smooth stroke.

"Oh, fuck." She bit her bottom lip and rolled her head back, accidentally hitting another billiard ball.

Fire erupted everywhere his tongue touched her. Celestine's hand reached out and stretched through his silky hair.

"I think you're enjoying these ministrations."

Celestine whined at the absence of his tongue, and he chuckled as she pushed his head back down. The sensations he coaxed and the way his hands and tongue moved were like magic.

"I-I am... Oh my God." Her eyes rolled backward, and his fingers curled into that magic spot, and she came apart completely, screaming at the wallpapered ceiling.

James didn't stop his fingers or his tongue until she stopped trembling, and once he did, he stood back up and caught her mouth with his. Celestine tasted herself on him, and pure fire consumed her as he placed two fingers back into her core.

"Thank you," she whispered into his mouth. As she curled her fingers into his hair, something horrible happened. Liquid began to drop from her nose.

Celestine's nose was bleeding. She pulled away, but not quickly enough; blood got all over James's lips and tongue.

"I'm sorry." A sense of terror gripped her stomach, and she clutched her nose, but she didn't have anything to stop the bleeding. James handed her his pocket square, and instead of cleaning off himself, he licked up the blood with a smile.

Horror struck through her.

"Don't look so disturbed, sweet Cellie," he said. "You drink blood every night."

Her eyebrows knit together. "What? I do not."

"What do you think is in the elixir?" he asked.

Celestine bit her lip, and confusion slithered up her arms like snakes. "It doesn't taste like blood. It usually tastes like cherry wine and chocolate." A confused expression carved itself into her face.

"Does all blood taste like metal?"

"Human blood, yes."

"Ah, and therein lies your answer."

Celestine gasped, and her scalp tightened. Everything tightened. "The Specter, and you? You're really not human?"

James shrugged, but eventually said, "What did you think the Specter was?"

"A magician, or magic itself..." she trailed off, unsure what to say.

"Not immortal?"

Shock had stolen her speech, even after everything she had witnessed that night. This was too much.

"Yes." He cupped her head. "We're immortal. But you already knew that."

"How did you become immortal? What even are you?"

"Ah, now, those are the right questions."

He grinned and stepped away from her, turning on his heel. "You'll probably want to ask the house for another dress." Over his shoulder, he said, "You need to get back to the game, because it looks like the poison is digging its claws in deeper."

Then James stepped out of the room as if all of this—the kiss, the orgasms, everything—was just one of his experiments. Like he was the Specter, and tonight was his show. Or he was the Phantom. But most of all, she was hurt because it was incredibly insensitive.

He was so confusing. He could be warm, possessive, and her rock, and then a moment later, he turned into a glacier—so cold she couldn't ever build a home on it.

After Celestine asked the house for a new dress—this time with undergarments—she made her way back to the Grand Ballroom. She needed to find Frances and Babette and share information. They were in this together, and they would find the solution together—even if Babette didn't want to.

Unfortunately, Babette was nowhere to be found, but luckily, Frances had found Celestine as soon as she'd entered the room.

Enchantment was on full display in the ballroom again. A nightingale's song drifted through the room, and starlight filled the space with a warm glow, creating an illusion of the night sky playing out on the ceiling. Ghostly dancers swayed to a country dance, and fake translucent patrons gambled all over, mainly at Irene's behest.

Everett was drunkenly "playing" the piano, hitting the wrong notes every so often, but Celestine narrowed her eyes, wondering if he was doing it on purpose. He was probably forced to play by his overbearing aunt.

On her way to the room, Celestine had grabbed a pen and paper to write down all the clues and everything she had learned from the night. She sat at a table on the edge of the room and began to write, Frances sitting next to her silently, allowing Celestine to do her investigative thing.

Lorraine was holding Archibald's tie. Gum was on the crossbow. The Ashbrook twins and James had access to the crossbow before the murder...

But so could have anyone, because Celestine had left the ballroom to kiss Everett in the closet.

The twins changed their shirts, and Dean's was covered in blood. Everyone had motives. They were all Archibald's children. The Ashbrooks are immortal. Lorraine and Irene killed Margot. Everett married her. Vivian loved her. But what about Dean?

Celestine never really knew anything about Dean. Except...

Dean was the Marquess of Winterly, and all his fiancées either died or ran away.

But what did any of this have to do with tonight's show?

Was Margot the motive? But for which man? Or was it like *Murder on the Orient Express*, and there were multiple murderers? But most importantly, how did it all lead to the Specter? Because the show was supposed to reveal his identity. So, was the night's murderer also the Specter?

Celestine sighed.

Her eyes locked on Vivian, who was sitting at the bar drinking a martini. When Vivian noticed her stare, she raised her martini, a wicked smile on her face.

"You have your calculating face on." Frances finally spoke.

Celestine's attention shifted back to Mother Hen. "Yes."

"Eat." Frances placed a grilled cheese sandwich in front of Celestine. "I know you, girl. You haven't eaten a thing all night."

Celestine tapped her fingers on the plate in a frustrated fashion, but she secretly appreciated Frances's mothering.

"I know you're not okay, my Celeste."

Blood jammed in Celestine's veins. "No, I'm not."

Frances snatched at her fingers. "Your hands are tinted blue. The poison is affecting you worse than the rest of us."

She hadn't noticed that symptom yet, and she fought the urge to pull her hands away and hide them. Celestine never wanted anyone to see her sickness. But she wasn't surprised at all that she was more susceptible.

"Well..." Celestine sighed. "I was just strangled."

Frances gasped. "What? Tell me everything."

So Celestine did. She told her everything from the game and her information on the Ashbrooks to her suspicions about Dean. She had once imagined that Dean could never be the Specter. But now she wasn't so confident. All the clues pointed far more strongly to him being the main murderer in Lorraine's game, and then there were the clues that led her to believe he was the Specter.

His piano playing, muddled words, and distance from Celestine made him seem to know her intimately despite never speaking to her. Sure, that could have been because his brothers told him, but she was far more convinced it was because he was the Specter.

The clues could lead to James and Everett, too, but there was something about Dean that felt right. But she didn't even want to think about the implications of that.

It all meant Celestine was fucked. Because she loved the Specter, and she wanted to kiss Dean more than anything. But he would never want her back. He was her impossible feat— her Mount Everest. A mountain that no one in the world could possibly summit.

At the end of Celestine's story and suspicions, Frances hugged her, comforting her. Frances shared all the information she had gathered during the night. The only new information was that she'd seen James walking up to the Balcony, where they'd found the crossbow minutes before Lorraine's murder.

Frances was also convinced the Specter was Dean.

When they had finished in hushed whispers, Jon, James, Walter, and Vivian walked up to the table.

"How's the game going for you? Any answers yet?" Vivian asked, sliding into the chair next to Celestine.

"No," Celestine lied.

"Well, are you at least enjoying yourself tonight?"

"I hope you're kidding," Celestine said, glaring at a drunken Everett banging on the piano like it was the drums. He was far more out of it than usual. "I am enjoying myself as much as he is." She motioned to the man with a nod of her chin.

Everett always played with vices like they were dares. He drank too much, played with too many girls, and lived life as if every moment should be consumed by risks, but he seemed extra intoxicated tonight. Usually, he had a sense of decency to his vices...not tonight. However, Celestine couldn't blame him. The Phantom had resurrected his dead wife's spirit and stuffed her into Celestine's head.

She shivered at the thought. She still wasn't over it. She hadn't much time to think about Margot, the way she had tried to take over her and expel her from her body and then was brutally killed and forced out of Celestine once more.

"Ah, yes," Vivian agreed. "Everett is more miserable than usual tonight. He can't even pretend to be jubilant and have a good time. He doesn't like reliving the worst moments of his life—who would?" She shrugged. "And he blames himself for Marguerite's death."

Dean appeared next to his blitzed brother. He placed a hand on his shoulder and whispered something into his ear. At the words, Everett stopped smashing the keys and glowered at his older brother. Celestine imagined Dean had threatened him to stop hurting his piano. It was a baby grand.

"Dean also blames Everett," Vivian added, her eyes also on the twins. "They may look identical, but those boys have very different views on responsibility."

"Dean is the heir," Walter—their biological uncle—said. "Heirs are raised with an incredible sense of duty hanging over their heads. Everett was always the spare, and therefore way more reckless."

"Reckless in love," Jon agreed.

Walter shared a knowing look with his lover. "Yes, but I can understand."

Vivian ignored her uncles, who were nearly jumping each other's bones in front of her. "I am surprised it's taken this long for them to tear each other apart."

Celestine's head whirled to Vivian. "What do you mean by that?"

"One of them is certainly responsible for tonight." She glowered at them and downed her wine like it was a shot. "And he is forcing all of us to confront our gravest mistakes. The Phantom is playing ten games all at once. Torturing all of us with the worst moments of our lives."

"What was your moment?" Frances asked.

Vivian sucked in a long breath. "My character card was all about my ex-lover, who died in my bed. It was all very scandalous back in the day."

"In fairness, it would still be a big scandal today," Jon said with a large grin.

Vivian rubbed her face. "And, of course, all the drama with Marguerite."

"Did you kill your lover all those years ago?" Walter stroked his chin, watching her.

"Would it matter?" she snapped. "If I did, it's not like I'd be the only murderer in this family."

"A confession now wouldn't matter, considering it happened 127 years ago." Walters's voice turned soft. "And no matter what, I will always be your dad, and I will always go to battle for you."

Vivian's eyes widened, and she pinched her lips, holding back a well of emotion spreading in her chest. She had one great parent. It was clear from the way Walter—and Jon—looked at her.

They casually spoke about being immortal in a deeply unsettling way, almost as if they had forgotten Celestine was sitting there.

"Speaking of our tortures," James finally spoke, trying to distract the group from the heavy emotions spiking between his sister and his father. "My character card was all about the train accident of 1893 that killed forty-seven people, and many thought I should be hanged for it. All the good that would do."

Jon chuckled. "It would be hard to kill a dead man."

"Besides, it's not like I was the only one responsible. Dean is the silent partner and mastermind behind most of our endeavors." James steepled his fingers underneath his chin. "I build things, Everett seduces things, and Dean plans things. He's the brain that keeps things going. I've never seen anyone beat him at chess, unless he wanted them to win."

Celestine froze. Chess, piano, and a dislike of reading. The mastermind.

Dean *was* the Specter.

She knew it in her core. He was the one who spent every night with her as she fell asleep. It *had* to be Dean.

Celestine's revelation was cut off by Irene and Lorraine entering the ballroom and speaking loudly.

"Lorraine and Dean ruined the game." Irene's seething was followed by a long, dramatic pause. "She was supposed to die"—she pointed at Celestine—"but I was supposed to do it."

James interrupted. "Neither of you were supposed to kill—"

"And Lorraine, you gave it away that we can come back from the dead," Irene screamed, her arms flying hyperbolically around like she was a conductor of an orchestra. "You let her discover that we are not humans."

"Mother, I am fairly certain you're the one who just announced that to the entire room," Vivian said, shaking her head, her cheeks tinged with amusement.

Ignoring her daughter, Irene continued her tirade. "Dean, do you have anything to say for yourself? You saved the girl."

"And killed me again," Lorraine said through gritted teeth, her hands on her hips.

"Killing Celestine is terrible form," he drawled. "You deserved to get killed again for it."

"Yes." Vivian took a big sip of liquor. "How could she possibly guess the Specter's true identity if she were dead?"

Everett pounded on the piano once again with a fearsome velocity. "Mother, you must pay for your sins. Just like everyone else here." He drunkenly slurred. "I will make sure of it."

Then he slid sideways off the piano bench and crumpled to the floor. But he didn't stop speaking. "You tried to kill Celestine, because you didn't want her to take one of your boys, just like Margaret. You've killed all of Dean's fiancées until he started scaring them off so you couldn't. You're genuinely terrible, and I will make you pay for it. You deserve to get murdered seven times over. I wish you could stay dead."

Lorraine gasped. "You don't mean it."

"Oh, I do." Everett's eyes dropped closed.

"Everett, you're soused." Dean shifted him with his dress shoe.

James tilted his head like a snake examining its prey. "He's not just soused. He's also high. How much smack did you take, Ev?"

"It was laudanum, and it was loads," he slurred with his cheek against the marble floor.

"I'll take care of him." Dean pushed him once more with his shoe. "Sober him up, if you will."

"I'll never be heartless like you, Dean." Everett yawned then passed out.

"Well, that display was lovely, but can we get back to the point?" Irene crossed her arms like a child and pouted. "Dean ruined my fun. I wanted to kill the girl."

Vivian slammed her hand on the table and stood violently. "You can't kill Celestine; if she is dead, you will ruin our actual game. Mother, don't you want to see the real show?" Vivian let out a dramatic sigh, mocking her mother. "We didn't come here for the Murder Mystery Party. We came for the Thriller. We came to watch the cast struggle and die from poison, not your strangling fascination."

Anger whirled in Celestine's stomach at the word. *Fuck all of them. They were all in on it the whole time.*

Celestine's insides felt like quicksand. Cracks formed in her heart like fault lines spidering out. "You're all in on this?" Her eyes grazed over all of them and landed on Vivian. "Even you?"

Vivian averted her eyes and pretended to pluck lint off her dress, and an anchor dropped in Celestine's heart. How could she have believed that at least one of the Ashbrooks was on her side? She should have known.

She was so foolish.

They were all villains—all monsters. But Vivian's betrayal somehow felt so much sharper than the men's. With the Phantom's presence, Celestine knew one of the twins or James had betrayed her. She'd somehow gotten used to that fact, but she never imagined Vivian would be in on it. And not only that, but she was enjoying it. She said the family came to watch the cast desperately try to discover the Specter's identity but fail.

They came to watch them die like animals in a cage.

They came to bathe in her blood.

Yes, all Wolfsbane Hall patrons came for a horror show—that was the point. But never had they come to watch the cast be tortured. They came to watch their friends, family, or lovers in horrible situations, but there had always been resurrections —an out.

There was always hope.

Not anymore.

But worst of all, the men, including Vivian, knew it was a hopeless night, and they came anyway—for entertainment.

They were gladiators in ancient Rome.

Celestine fell back in her chair and rubbed her temples. If they were betting on the cast's deaths, did that mean the riddle was even more impossible than Celestine first imagined? Did the riddle even have a correct answer?

Celestine played with a sequin on her dress. After James had destroyed her earlier outfit, she'd asked Wolfsbane to provide her with another. It had, except what it chose was forged from passion. It clung to her curves and fell down her waist like liquid silver, dripping like mercury from a broken thermometer. The waist was gathered into a tightly knitted corset that split at the middle, showcasing her considerable assets.

Bile rose in her tight throat, and she turned to Vivian. "Have you placed bets, too?"

Irene clapped her hands. "Oh, yes, it's been immensely fun. I have you dying next. I also have you being the first one to guess the Specter's name wrong."

Dean, under his breath, said, "And you *will* be wrong."

"Probably why you wanted to kill her, Mother." James's voice was pure wildfire, ripping through a forest and coming for rich houses.

"It doesn't count if you kill her." Jon pulled a notepad out of his suit jacket pocket. "She has to guess the Specter's name wrong."

"But if she dies, then she won't be able to guess, and I will win anyway," Irene said, petting one of her over-the-top furs. "I only bet she would die first."

"Well, you are going to lose, Mother." Vivian tapped her fingers on the table nonchalantly. "Celestine will win this absurd game."

"True," Everett said, leaning against the piano and still very drunk.

The sentiment didn't make her feel any better. They set her up and watched her like a little pathetic mouse in a maze. They were all sick. Who cared if they thought she'd win it?

The only people she could trust in this house were Frances and Babette. *Fucking Babette.* What had the world come to? Everything was so fucking rotten.

The valves in Celestine's heart clenched.

"Was Lorraine's death just a charade?" Celestine swallowed, the burning sensation her only comfort. It fucking hurt, but at least it meant she was alive. "And all your secrets being exposed... Has it all been fake?"

A soft wind skated through the room, and her voice carried on it like a haunted requiem. Her song was met with the thrumming dark harmony of the Phantoms as he said, "Oh, no, Sweet Celine, they're playing a game as well. They just always enjoy the suffering of others, but trust me, lovely, their deepest, darkest secrets have been plaguing them all night long. Everyone is playing a slightly different game tonight."

"Which has been quite horrific," Irene called at the ceiling. "We would all appreciate it if you would stop it."

A rotten laugh coated the room. "You all wanted to come here and play a game." Lightning struck, followed by thunder that shook the ground. The candlewax sconces all swayed at once and then burned brighter. "This is the one we all deserve."

Celestine's skin prickled. A cascade of things hit her at

once, but the strongest thought—the one that raged inside her like a tidal wave ripping apart everything it touched—was that she'd truly had enough. It was all too much, and there was only so far a person could be pushed until they pushed back. Celestine had spent her whole life being the good girl, being kind, fitting in, not rocking the boat, and caring for the needs of others.

Her whole life, obeying others,

But what about her needs? What about her life?

"I think…" Her chin quivered, but she rolled her shoulders back. "I'm done."

Celestine didn't want to hear their response. She didn't care anymore. So she turned on her now sparkling heels and walked out of the room with purpose. Clicks measured her footfalls as she left. *Click, clack, click, clack,* just like her heart.

Celestine was done being the Specter's little pet. She was over being his marionette doll. Celestine never did anything for herself in her life, and if she was dying, now might be the best time to start living only for herself. Unfortunately, she didn't have much time to live, a reminder that became abundantly clear when crimson began to streak down her face.

Not again.

She grasped the closest material to her to stop her nosebleed. It happened to be a rich, velvet curtain that was used more for decoration than for its practical utility. Celestine cursed.

Fuck. My body is fucking falling apart.

Babette and Frances were not suffering nosebleeds. She'd asked earlier, and they had looked at her with wide, confused eyes. So it was only her. Figures.

Everything affected her far deeper than others. It was her curse.

When her nose stopped bleeding, she tried to move again

but was hit with a strong wave of lightheadedness. Blood loss, weak limbs, and poison eating away at her were not a great combination for her dizzy spells, which started occurring at a concerning frequency three weeks ago.

Celestine pulled on the now blood-soaked curtain for support and leaned her head against the wall, begging for support from God or angels or whatever being was up there watching. If devils existed—and were sitting in the other room —then angels could exist, too. Celestine wasn't particularly religious, but the closer she got to her inevitable demise, the more she wondered what would be next.

Heat grew beneath her fingertips, the curtains growing hot but not uncomfortable. It was more like a warm hug. She narrowed her eyes and stared at them. The house was morphing again, but Celestine didn't know why. The walls turned her favorite color—dark red, closer to maroon than orange.

Wolfsbane was apologizing—or something like it.

Or maybe it was the Phantom, because moments later, he spoke, a booming voice that could be heard all over the mansion. "Alright, my lovelies, it's time for a game. Everyone has gotten far too comfortable, and we cannot have that." His voice shifted like a snake coiling. "Tonight is about secrets and lies and guttural betrayals, and what kind of host would I be if I didn't follow through on that promise? So welcome to my House of Horrors."

Everything froze for a moment, a picture in time—the time before horrors—because as soon as time slipped back, every-thing shifted. The house started to decay and seethe like an evil creature. The walls dripped black tar, the floor churned, and moss grew over it, but it was dry and empty of life, so much so that if she moved her feet, all she heard was a crunch.

"The house will stop its torture when someone finds the

missing murder weapon—the knife," the Phantom continued. "Here is your only clue: It lies beneath the silvered tree."

If it were possible, the house would have descended further into chaos. Blood dripped from the ceiling, a drop landing on Celestine's palm. At first, she thought it was her nose bleeding again, but when the rain began to fall, covering every inch of her body and dress, she understood.

Blood dripped down her eyelashes and covered her nostrils, and she felt as if she were drowning. But the worst part of it was the metallic scent, which was so strong it gave her a headache.

But the chaos didn't stop there.

Window shutters smacked against the outside structure as if a tornado were pulling them out. The sound was an eerie pounding, and to that melody came screaming. Monsters popped out of paintings and chased down the ghosts, filling the air with tormented screams. Off-key violin strings underscored the broken song.

The Phantom was even torturing the ghosts.

The walls creaked and buckled, glass spewing onto the surface. But it wasn't just any glass; it was enchanted silver shards—torture mirrors. From time to time, the house would bring them out and torment anyone who walked by them, playing either their worst fears or the memories someone tried to forget.

The secrets people needed to hide.

Things like hit and runs, affairs, real-life murders, or dark family secrets that needed to stay in the dark. The house pulled everything from someone like taffy, and like taffy, it was sticky and hard to remove once it was fashioned onto it.

Celestine hated every single time the mirrors awoke.

Because they sank deep into her, playing with the confines of her reality.

Tonight was no different.

Celestine's greatest shame played on the shards like a silent picture show. To her left played the moment when her father walked out their door for the last time. Child Celestine never cried during this memory, because she didn't know it would be important. She didn't know he'd never come back. She didn't know she'd never see his face again—a fact that would scar her forever because, over time, her memory of it faded.

She couldn't even say now what color hair he had. Was it blonde like hers, red like her sister's, or brown like her mother's? Celestine didn't know.

He was just a shape, a tall man-shaped hole in her life.

On the right mirror, the shard played the worst moment of her life. A couple of years after her father's disappearance, Celestine woke up from her Sunday mid-afternoon nap—after Sunday mass, Celestine always wanted a nap—and she discovered her mother's ravaged body. It appeared to have been torn apart by a beast. But it wasn't just her mother who was dead. A chunk of her sister's red hair sat in the middle of the floor, and her blood painted the room like modern art splatter-paintings.

But no matter where she looked, Celestine couldn't find her sister's body. Whatever monster—and it was a monster—who'd attacked them ran off with the nineteen-year-old's body. Celestine was nine years younger, and her sister was like a second mother to her.

For Celestine, this time it was her greatest fear playing down the hall: Dean leaving her. Everett telling her she was worthless and James never speaking to her again—never fucking her again, kissing and flirting with other girls in front of her.

Treating her like the trash one took out and abandoned on the curb.

Her greatest fear was being alone. Alone because everyone had left her—because that's what people always did.

The one mocking her now was a moving picture of her dying, over and over again, with no one there and no one to care or grieve her death.

Celestine's vision tunneled in on it, and her heart hitched—which was ironic, because in the vision, Celestine held her chest, her heart failing, and her face turning blue. But no one was there to compress it, to try to get it moving again, to try to restart its rhythm.

Always her fucking heart.

Celestine swallowed and blinked then turned and walked out of the hallway of horrors.

The problem with trying to torture a dying woman was that there came a time when she no longer felt anything, when apathy clung to her skin and refused to let the fear in, because there came a moment when acceptance overcame all darkness and peace won out.

Peace was far stronger than fear.

Celestine replayed the clue in her head. *Here is your only clue: It lies beneath the silvered tree.*

There was only one silvered tree in the house. It wasn't even hard to solve—the Library. A large, framed painting of a silver tree was at the center, surrounded by a cove of books.

She shook her head. Far too easy. However, given the obstacles—the horror house—she understood why it was easy. It was so easy, in fact, that she wasn't the first one to solve it. The Ashbrook twins were already there, deep in argument.

"Why did you have to do this?" Everett snapped in a low, hushed voice. "You're not as perfect as you would assume."

"I know I'm not," Dean responded with a cool, measured tone.

Everett crossed his arms, no sign of his previous intoxication. "No, you're a hypocritical prick. Manipulative and awful."

"Oh, that's brilliant coming from you, seeing as you love your puppets so damn much."

"At least I don't torture the ones I love—the love of my life."

"No, you're right." Dean laughed, thick and crooked. "You did absolutely nothing."

"Why don't you take the plank out of your eye, brother, before you point out the speck in mine?" Everett quoted the Bible, which was strange, because Celestine didn't think of him as that devoted. "What you're doing is far worse."

"At least she's alive..."

A long, tense pause rattled between the twins. They both looked like ancient statues. One, Apollo, emanating a sickly light, and the other, Hades, cloaked in shadows. "Perhaps you should find the knife now, Ev?"

"As you wish, my lord," Everett mocked. He walked over to the painting and easily pulled the knife out from underneath it. As soon as the knife handle hit his flesh, the house morphed back into its normal state. "I've found it. I found it." He held up the knife and turned on his falsely cheerful mask and voice.

James, Vivian, and Jon burst into the room, pretending to play the game with vigor. When James reached his brother, he grabbed the knife out of his hand and reprimanded him. "You got your fingerprints all over it. Idiot."

A bright, fake smile danced on Everett's face. "I'm not good at silly games."

Neither of the brothers was that reckless, and both had touched the knife. They weren't helping the investigation. They were obscuring it. Why? To what end?

"You're so book smart, but oh-so stupid." James rolled his eyes.

Dean cleared his throat. "I don't mean to be *that guy*, but you also just touched the knife."

James's eyebrows dropped. "Well, fuck."

Celestine clenched her fists, her nails biting her palms. She was so fucking over this. James was not that stupid. He knew exactly what he was doing. She was done with manipulation and done with the Ashbrooks. She would go to her room, pack her bags, answer the riddle, and leave.

And if she got it wrong, so fucking be it.

"Oh, child, you look like hell." Frances stepped into Celestine's path as she exited the Library. Using the hem of her skirt, Frances wiped off some of the blood still lingering on Celestine's face. "Did you take a bath in blood?"

"I might as well have," Celestine said, pursing her lips. "How has your investigation been going?"

Celestine probably should have been working with Frances and Babette more during the show, but she had become so wrapped up in her character and all her many issues and vendettas. Now, though, they needed to work together.

"It's been going better than I expected." She scratched her head, and with her other hand, she pulled a piece of paper out of her pocket. "I know you said you think the Specter is Dean, but I am beginning to believe it's James."

Celestine narrowed her eyes in question.

"I was racking my mind, and Dean doesn't fit. The Specter is flashy, methodical, and twisted." Frances held out a piece of paper, and all her notes were written on it. "Dean isn't flashy. He doesn't like it when you are the murderer, and he would never force you to do it. It's not in his character."

"It could be," Celestine said. "What do we even know of Dean? He never speaks."

"Just because he doesn't speak doesn't mean we know nothing about him. We can gather far more from someone's actions. See, look at this." Frances pointed to the paper. "His actions don't match the Specter, but James's do."

Celestine hesitantly took the paper from Frances. She wasn't convinced. Dean was still the far more logical answer. He played piano, mixed up words, and knew far too many intimate things about Celestine. Only the Specter would have had that knowledge. Not to mention, he was the one who called her Celine. But Celestine took the paper anyway.

Tiny script was scribbled all over the paper, but the biggest handwriting said *gum, crossbow, wanting to be murdered, deeply methodical, sick enough to design the games.*

Celestine bit the inside of her cheek and returned the paper to Frances.

"If tonight's mystery is also supposed to lead us to the name of the Specter, then it would have to be James, too." Frances tucked the paper back into her apron. "The gum on the crossbow is a clue to James. It has to be him."

Celestine shook her head, unconvinced. There was an equal amount of evidence, if not more, leading to Dean.

"I feel it in my bones, Celeste. James is the Specter."

26

Saturday, November 11, 1939
Celestine's Bedroom

After taking a much-needed bath, Celestine rested her wet locks on her pillow and placed her hand against the wall, like she used to do when she fell asleep listening to the Specter playing the piano. It was a goodbye.

Despite everything, she would miss him.

Love was such a fickle and terrible thing.

Tears gathered like beads on her eyelashes.

Celestine sucked her lower lip into her mouth and let out a long breath. The Specter was here. She knew it. If she had one magical power, it would be that she could always sense his presence. He was here, like he always was at the end of the night. The version of him she got in secret.

Her Specter.

"Celine…" Her name played like music on his tongue, like a symphony of sorrow and longing. It floated like the Phantom's, but unlike the Phantom, it felt like he was coming from the other side of the wall, as if he were standing there. Waiting and listening for her.

And fuck, she missed him. *This* him.

Emotions trilled in her stomach, like the music of his voice. Too many to count or name. Everything she'd ever felt for him colored the inside of her body. Bloodred like fiery passion, dust-gray like heartbreak, honeyed-yellow like comfort, vomit-green like revulsion, and on and on it went—the colors of her soul.

She touched the wall and pinched her eyes shut, her nostrils flaring and her cheeks stinging from the weight of her heartbreak.

"Who are you, Specter?"

She didn't bother with pleasantries, because she already knew the answer. She knew he was Dean; she knew it in her bones. Everett and James didn't have the capacity to be everything that the Specter was. Everett wasn't serious enough, and James was too blunt, too cold. And Dean was a dark mystery, like her Specter.

Every bit of her knew it to be true. There was no other answer. But she wanted Dean to do the right thing. Drop all the games and just be honest with her—be with her—one last time.

When he didn't respond, she asked again, "Who are you, Specter?"

"Don't call—" it was all breath.

"Who are you, Winter?" she asked, but she knew the answer. It was in the riddles, in all the games from the night. The Marquess of Winterly, the eldest son of the Duke of Breython. He had been telling her all along.

"I can't tell you that," Dean said as the Specter on the other side of the wall.

She stroked the wall with her fingertips before laying her hand flat on it. She imagined him doing the same thing on the other side. "Why?" A tear dripped down her face. "Why?" Another tear dropped. "Why?" She sucked in a shaking breath. "Why?" Her eyes stung as tears littered down her cheeks. "*Why?*"

He sucked in an audible breath. "Because I am terrible. I am your villain."

"Yes, you are."

A long silence licked the room, and Celestine curled her knees into her chest, feeling the fine cotton against her legs.

"Celine…" He said her name like a prayer.

"I hate you."

"I know."

"And I don't…" Her voice caught. "Specter, I ha—"

"Don't call me Specter," he said gently once more. "Just not tonight. Tonight, all I want to be is yours. Only yours." He stopped, as if in thought, and she waited for him to continue. "Every night, I spin fictions, I tell you tales, and you read me mysteries, but for one moment, on one night, all I want is to be real with you."

Her heart doubled in her chest, and a spike of pain shot through her left arm. She clutched the heel of her palm to her chest and tried to massage the pain away. Both physically and emotionally

"Why? Why me?"

"Because you are my match and my conscience."

Celestine stared at the canopy of her bed, taking in the details of her carved rosewood. She wanted so much for what he said to be true. But words from pretty gentlemen were hollow things. They were as fleeting as time.

"Dean…" she said, breathless.

"Yes?" But it wasn't the Specter who answered; it was a voice from the doorway—a shadow of a tall, dark, and wicked man. The villain of storybooks.

Celestine sucked and inhaled sharply. How long had he been standing there? Watching?

She must have asked the question out loud, because he

responded, "Only a moment. You stormed out, and I was worried..."

Confusion raked through her. Dean didn't look like he'd just been speaking with her on the other side of the doorway. He looked like a dark, brooding, and avenging prince.

"You didn't have to come," she said, because she didn't know what else to say. What was there to say other than, "You are the Specter!"

It was an accusation.

"You know I cannot confirm that." He tilted his head and examined her. His gaze landed on her every bruise, her swollen limbs, and her loose silk gown that barely left anything to the imagination.

A muscle in his jaw ticked, but he didn't look away. Rather, he took three large strides into the room and hovered above her like the Angel of Death coming to consume his next victim.

Heat and desperation pooled between her legs, and she longed to reach her hand down and relieve the ache, but she absolutely could not do that while he was watching her.

Tension painted the space between them. It surged and sucked all other energy out of the room except the unbearable need tingling in her core. Celestine licked her lips and tossed her legs over the side of her bed, sitting up, bringing them even closer together.

If he was the Specter, was this the actual moment he wanted? To talk to her as Dean, in private, unmasked but also masked...somewhere in between because they both knew the truth now?

She gulped but lifted her chin to catch his gaze in hers. Refusing to look away. "What is my favorite color, Dean?"

"Bloodred, like the color you stain your lips every night." His hand hovered near her chin as if he wanted to caress her, but maddeningly, he still wouldn't erase the space between them and touch her.

Truth burned in her blood. It was him—her Specter. James and Everett didn't know her favorite color; she'd never once told them, and they never once cared enough to ask.

But Celestine was no fool; she would test her theory and prove it right. Just because she could.

Her eyes fell on her chessboard. It was her move. "Pawn to H5." She tilted her chin back up to him in a challenge.

His gaze glanced down at the board, and thoughts poured across his face like ink in water. He was deciding if he'd take her bait.

"Queen to G6." He took her pawn, but he was out of moves, and the pinching at the corner of his lips showed that he knew it, too. He was going to lose the game.

"Queen to G6." Neither of them physically moved the pieces. They didn't have to. The board was memorized in their heads. Instead, they kept their gazes locked on one another, having a conversation without needing to say the words.

"Bishop G1." Blackness cloaked the edges of his eyes, but it was not dangerous or dark; it was just him.

"Queen G1."

A smirk lifted on Dean's face. "A sacrificial queen."

She cocked her head like a hawk. "Isn't that what I am to you?"

"Never." He stepped closer and finally—*finally*—touched her, his hand cupping her face. "Never."

"It's your move." Celestine's words came out as a sensual plea.

He leaned down, his lips hovering over hers. "Bishop to G1."

"You are trapped," she breathed.

"Yes." His thumb caressed her lips.

Her chest rose with frantic desire, her breasts rising with it. "You've lost. Concede."

"I concede it all to you and hold nothing back." With that, his lips crashed down on hers.

For a beat, she stiffened from the shock, frozen like a lake in the dead of winter. Dean Ashbrook was touching her—not only touching her, he was kissing her. And damn, she wasn't going to waste this moment. So when her brain caught up, she swung her legs under her so that she could kneel on her bed and get closer to him.

Her fingers curled around his suit jacket, and she whimpered from not being able to be closer to him. If she were going to have this moment, she wanted all of it. She wanted to claw at the rough flesh of his back. She wanted to climb him like she would a mountain.

Because he had always been her Everest.

Running her tongue along his lower lip, she forced him to open further to her, and he was happy to oblige. More than happy, because he cupped her ass and pulled her closer to him, the motion allowing her legs to wrap around him.

Kissing him was like both waging a war and suing for peace. It was all tongues, teeth, and hands roaming all over each other's bodies, but it was also gentleness and reverence.

And it was also confusion.

She had spent nine years wanting to taste him because, if she were being honest, from the moment she first saw him scowl at her, she was hit hard with longing. She spent nine years trying to convince herself that she hated him and wanted nothing to do with him. She spent nine years pretending he didn't matter, pretending she didn't notice his presence every time he entered a room, pretending he wasn't gravity drawing her in.

Nine years convincing herself she would never be worthy of a man like him, convincing herself to love anyone but him.

But Dean was her unquenched desire, a sea of broken promises and dark phoenix fire. Kissing him was like both the sickness and the cure.

Their foreheads met, and Dean said, "Tell me a secret, Celine. Something so real that no one else knows."

"And what if the Specter already knows all my secrets?" Her voice trembled, thick with her want. "What would I tell you then?"

He nibbled at her lip playfully. "I know you have at least one secret. It's a massive one. I can sense it."

She did, but she didn't want to tell anyone. Just because she finally knew who he was and was finally able to touch her Specter, it didn't mean she should give away the one final thing, which was *hers*. "I do, but why would you deserve it?"

"I wouldn't."

"Tonight is about unveiling your secrets, not mine."

"True." He wrapped one of her blonde curls around his finger. "Then tell me this. If you could have a future with one of us, would you?"

Yes. Of course, I would choose you. But she didn't allow herself to say it out loud. "It's not a question worth pondering, because it can't happen."

"I know." The confirmation was a blow. But he still had his hands all over her, and his eyes drooped with passion. He wanted to kiss her again. "If I could freeze time in a moment, it would be this one."

Dean let out a low groan and lowered her to the ground as if he had just realized that he still had her strapped around him. Her feet were jelly on the floor, and he steadied her with a chuckle.

Once she'd gotten her shaky legs under control, she stared

at him and said, "I would choose you." She gulped. "But what if I told you my big secret is that I have no future?"

His large, veiny hands squeezed her shoulders. "Of course, you do. You'll get far away from my family and become a movie star."

No, I won't. Not in this lifetime. "Not if I die from the poison." Dean flinched.

"But if I am destined to die tonight, then I think I would like to kiss you again...kiss you like I have no future." She curled her fingers around his tie and pulled him to her once more, and she kissed him like it was the last thing she would do—because it probably was.

Her heartbeat danced with his, and she pulled him into her so much deeper, asking him never to let her go.

"Let's make this moment last forever," she moaned, desperately wanting it to be true.

Celestine crashed her mouth into his with a frantic frenzy of passion. She was going to put everything into this kiss. Everything. She was leaving nothing on the table, because she was on Death's checklist.

The pure passion and hunger of the kiss caused her knees to weaken, and instead of steadying her, Dean scooped her up into his arms and laid her down gently on the bed, because she was poisoned and fragile. She allowed it, but she didn't want to be so weak that she couldn't even hold herself up for a kiss.

She was too damn fragile.

His lips never left her during the whole motion, so he ended up on her bed, hovering above her as they deepened their passion even further.

Dean's eyes locked on hers as he stroked his fingers through her hair, sending shivers down her spine, her body hypersensitive to him. Celestine bit the inside of her cheek and breathed deeply through her nose, not wanting him to see how his touch rattled every piece of her. She needed a mask of her own, because they couldn't keep this moment forever. It would end, and when it did, she wouldn't be able to keep him.

But, oh, how she wanted to keep him.

Celestine had kissed countless men. She seduced patrons, fucked some of them, and played with the fires of passion every week. Heck, even tonight, she'd kissed Everett, kissed and fucked James. But nothing—and she meant nothing—compared to this. Every kiss before this moment was child's play, simple practice. But this one? This one was bottled wild-fire and the well of unending life.

It was every promise and every dream she ever had all wrapped into one.

It was home. Because *he* was home. The Specter was her home and always had been.

Celestine growled. Too many layers of clothes separated them, and she hated it.

Everything heightened between them. Every vessel in her body was hot and needy. Celestine had to touch him. Him, not his clothing.

"You're wearing far too much clothing." Her hands clawed up his chest and under his jacket, forcing it off his shoulders. Then she twirled her fingers into his hunter-green shirt and ripped open the buttons. If all the men she'd fucked could destroy her clothing, she could ruin some of theirs from time to time, too.

He chuckled, a hand sliding up her leg and underneath her silk dress. "You're a naughty girl."

"Yes, I am." She sucked her lip into her mouth. "Now, be a naughty boy."

He hummed into her mouth and clutched her by the throat, all dominance and masculine energy. Everything about him was swimming with control and command. Her dark prince. And she was his equal.

With each new caress, her body grew tighter and tighter with need. She was a bowstring, taut and ready for release.

But she really shouldn't fuck him. It was too dangerous for her heart.

Her teeth nibbled at his tongue for a moment until she bit down hard. They were war and peace; right now, she was choosing a little bit of war because she wanted to test something. The elixir was formed from their blood, and it tasted like them. So she bit down again, causing his blood to gush into her mouth.

There was a hint of metal with orange liquor and coconut.

Celestine stiffened and jolted back, horrified, pushing him off her.

No. It was so wrong. Gooseflesh rose on her arms, and her heart skittered. No. No. No. No. It couldn't be.

Dean wasn't the Specter at all. He was far, far worse.

27

Saturday, November 11, 1939
Celestine's Bedroom

She stepped back, her leg knocking into the wooden bedpost, horror lacing her bones. He took a step toward her, confused, and she held out a hand to stop him from moving any closer.

"No." Her voice came out as liquid flames.

"Celine..." His brows knit together. "What's wrong?"

Thick emotion laced her tongue. "How could you?"

Wetness gathered at the back of her eyes, but she wouldn't release any more tears for him. But they gathered like raindrops on her lashes. Dammit, why the fuck did she have to cry so much. It felt like it was all she'd done lately.

She was so dumb. So fucking stupid. She should have figured it out much sooner. The game Specter was so different from the one she loved. Game Specter was flashy and impatient, caring nothing for feelings or the impact of his actions.

But the ~~Specter~~ Phantom in her rooms, he was patient, with a dash of dominance and warmth. He was home. It was so different, but she had thought it was because he didn't like anything getting in the way of his genius. The truth was unfathomable. There were always two of them.

Always a Specter and a Phantom.

Fuck. Fuck. Fuck. It hurt so much.

Always two.

It was why he never wanted to be called the Specter. Why he went by Winter, it all made horrible sense. He never wanted to be called the Specter in her rooms, because he wasn't the Specter.

He never had been.

He was the Phantom.

Bile rose in her throat, and her broken heart murmured. Angry and sad all at once. She closed her eyes and hit herself in the head. How could she fall for it?

Dean took a step toward her. She didn't see it but felt it, heard it in the intake of his breath.

Dammit. The Specter—no, the Phantom—had been her sanctuary, but now he was her prison—her tormentor. He'd tricked her, poisoned her, and played with her like a marionette doll with all its strings cut off.

She hit herself again. She was so fucking stupid. "You're the Phantom." She opened her eyes to see the betrayal. He was a man formed by decaying trust and broken hearts; he was her devastation.

His expression was one of surprise, but he quickly locked it up and slid a hard mask over his features. In his blue eyes, she saw the recognition—the truth.

She didn't give him a chance to speak. She couldn't hear one more lie out of his mouth, but honestly, she didn't want to hear the truth either. Not right now. She'd get it from the true Specter.

"Don't follow me." She held her arm straight out, blocking him.

Fury coiled in her stomach like a king cobra, and she no longer had any tears left. Her eyes had dried up, and they would never water for him again. Apathy was her new friend.

Celestine ran and ran and ran down twisting halls and up the grand stairs, heading back to the Library, where the largest mirror in the house rested.

It was a mess as she walked into the room, possibly from the earlier search during the Phantom's game. But books had been thrown open on coffee tables and the floor. Some had cracked spines, and others had their pages bent, scattered across the marble floor or on intricate throw carpets, their paper mangled. It was horrible, but she couldn't focus on it.

Celestine could always count on the Specter to appear in a mirror. He loved using mirrors to toy with people, appearing in them, haunting them, and morphing them into something far more tantalizing.

Mirrors were one of his *things*.

Celestine steeled her spine and glowered up at the silver glass. "Specter."

It only took a moment for him to appear to her, almost like he was waiting for her to call out to him.

A blue, glittering silhouette appeared in the mirror, its surface rippling like the water of a lily pond. "Yes, my sweet Celestia?" His voice was too bright, like the sound of a hospital hallway. The tone was white—sterile—not warm or charming in any way.

Celestine shivered and didn't say anything. She had no idea what to say or how to start. He must have realized the staggering nature of her discomfort, because smoke poured out of the edges of the bookshelves and through the cracks in the wall, forming a solid figure. A man. The smoke stepped behind her and wrapped his hands around her, cradling her into his chest. She felt his presence all at once, crooked and toxic, yet warm and lifegiving.

She didn't want to get comfort from it, but she couldn't help it.

The Specter could be awful, but then there were moments like these when he was so loving and tender, making her the center of his world. It made every pore in her body light up, and it made her feel like she could forgive anything—and she had.

Whenever he hurt her, he'd always do this, always pull her back in, apologizing and loving her like no one had before, and she would always forgive him.

Every time.

This time, the smoke felt like being wrapped up in James's arms, and she leaned her head into its chest, taking a big breath of him. He smelled like he had just eaten a handful of raspberries and drank a whiskey. And maybe she was manifesting what she wanted, but James usually smelled of ash and raspberries.

And foolishly, she leaned into him, accepting the comfort even though she knew he'd betrayed her too.

"What is it?" the smoke whispered into her hair.

She snuggled into him, seeking his comfort for her following words. "Do you talk to me in my bedroom after the games?"

"No..." His voice was anguished. "My magic is blocked from there."

"By whom?" Celestine's voice cracked, but she didn't need him to tell her the answer. She already knew. She'd confirmed as much with Dean, but she still had to hear it out loud to make it feel real.

The smoke twisted around her, snaking up her legs as if trying to touch her everywhere, yet he still said nothing. Time stilled, and the moment dragged on like molasses dripping from a jar. He knew the answer but was measuring how to say it.

The silhouette in the mirror shifted uncomfortably. And

the busts on the bookshelves came to life, all their eyes staring at her as if trying to look into her soul and see what would happen if they told her the truth.

The pages in the books surrounding her flew open, turning on their own accord, yet in a rhythm. It was musical, all the movements taken together.

All the statues, the mirror, and the smoke spoke as one, like a thousand voices. "The Phantom."

Her heart stumbled, and the snake in her stomach coiled in on itself as if seeking shelter from a storm.

Dean was the Phantom, but he was also the person who played chess with her and spoke to her about everything as she drifted off to sleep.

How could he be both her comfort and her pain all at once? It wasn't fair. It was torment.

He was her betrayer. Her Judas, her Brutus. He'd been her best friend, her rock, her firm foundation. He was the one who truly knew her. The one who talked to her every night before bed like a lover...like a true partner.

And he had destroyed it all.

He had destroyed *her*.

It hurt so fucking much, but she didn't even get a moment to grieve or process the pain and what it all meant, because a sharp scream pierced through her devastation.

A scream that traveled up from below.

Something dreadful had happened downstairs.

28

Saturday, November 11, 1939
The Green Room

Celestine's worst nightmare was laid out before her. Frances's lifeless eyes stared at the ceiling of the Green Room, Babette cradling her body and howling. "No, no, no, not you. Not you." The scream was raw, guttural, and hysterical.

The brunette rocked back and forth, back and forth, her eyes glazed over and hollow and her hair falling messily over her shoulders, all the while never stopping her haunting whispers of, "No."

As she watched the scene unfold, the heartbreak tore through Celestine's chest, too, but she had no tears left, and the fact that she couldn't get herself to loose even a single drop for the woman who had been her mother figure for nine years broke her even more.

Who couldn't shed tears for the ones they loved?

Celestine's nostrils flared, and her jaw grew tight and tender.

Even Babette could manage it, and she wasn't nearly as close with Frances. In fact, it was news that the brunette even cared this much for the older woman. Celestine honestly didn't know Babette could care about anyone.

Had Celestine missed it? Had she been too focused on herself and the Specter to see the other girl?

Babette wouldn't want anyone to see her acting this way. The girl was formed of dissociation and distance, not wanting to get close to anyone. And she certainly wouldn't want anyone to witness this level of pain.

Celestine walked to the door, shut it quietly, and then returned to Babette, kneeling beside her. She stretched out her hands to the floor and spoke with Wolfbane inside her head, asking the house to bar anyone else from entering the room and hearing Babette's anguish.

"Not you." Babette's eyes twitched to Celestine's and flared. "Of course, it couldn't have been you instead. You should have died first."

Celestine smiled sadly. "I know. I always thought I would be the first to die among us, too."

Babette scoffed and gently tucked Frances's hair behind her ears. "You're like a cockroach. Impossible to kill."

"I guess I could be a cockroach. I can scurry very quickly, and I do have an oval face, but I don't really have the hair for it. I am not a redhead. Although I don't know if you could call their shells hair, ya know?"

Babette tried to suppress an amused laugh. She hated that she found anything Celestine said amusing.

"Is there anything I can do?" Celestine asked.

"Why are you always so nice to me?" Babette visibly swallowed. "It's so irritating. Always so good, so perfect. Never anything out of place. It's obnoxious."

Celestine sucked her lower lip into her mouth, chewing on it as she thought. "It's because I pick people who will never love me back... It's a character flaw. I guess I am just used to being treated poorly."

"Me, too. I pick terribly." Babette's eyes locked with Celestine's, and there was a heavy weight in them. The weight of all the stars in the universe. The weight of the universe.

A shattered silence descended in the space between them. The air was cold and thick. Confusion licked at Celestine's core. She'd never had a positive moment with Babette, never able to find common ground or respect between them before, but it felt like there was a shift in the air—like they might be able to change their future. Possibly even be friends or, at the very least, friendly.

"So, she guessed who the Specter was and got it wrong?" Celestine asked, her eyes falling back to the cold, broken, lifeless body of her friend.

"Yes." Babette's voice was hollow.

"Why did she guess?"

"Because there were only forty minutes left to guess, and she was convinced." Babette wrung her hands. "She didn't think there was any possibility that she was wrong."

"Who did she guess?" Celestine asked, but she was fairly certain she already knew the answer.

"James."

Celestine nodded, her heart leaping into her throat. "So the Specter is officially not James or Dean."

"Officially?" Babette raised a dark brow.

"Dean is the Phantom."

Which meant that the Specter had to be Everett? There was nearly no chance that the uncles or Archibald were the Specter. They weren't around the mansion enough, not to mention the younger Ashbrooks all but confirmed one of them was the Specter.

So it was Everett.

As if summoned by her thoughts, Everett appeared out of thin air in front of them, causing Celestine to jolt and clutch her heart, it surging far too fast.

"Come on, dolls. You're gonna miss the climax," Everett said with great jubilation. "And trust me, you don't want to miss this part."

"Fuck," Babette uttered softly. "You shouldn't do that. It's jarring."

He flashed a dimple and traced her with his gaze. "Is it?"

"Of course, it is," she bit out. "But of course, you wouldn't care about that because you don't care about anyone. But by all means, show us to your next show of horrors. We've been having so much fun already tonight. Why not a little more?"

Celestine's eyebrows crinkled. Babette had never talked back to him before. Perhaps she was done with the men and Wolfsbane Hall's games, too.

A sickeningly sweet smile blanketed Everett's cheeks. "Then follow me."

They did. Both girls were wary and walking as if on eggshells. Nothing about the night was expected, but more so than that, everything about the night was tainted. So much had ruptured that they would never think about it or their jobs the same.

Everett led them back to the showroom—the Ballroom. Once again, the ghosts were dancing and putting on an illusion, a show, a dance of secrets and lies. But there was something different about this show. It was putrid, like maggots and worms crawling out of a corpse. Celestine shuddered. Whatever was about to happen wasn't going to be good.

Everett went over to his brothers, who were standing in front of a table of champagne glasses, discussing something in hushed voices.

Babette and Celestine shared a look of camaraderie, both of them fully understanding that they were done. Something had shifted between them forever. It was small, but it was something.

"Oh no," Babette whispered under her breath as Lorraine and Irene walked up to them. The last thing either girl wanted was to talk to the monstrous matriarchs of the family.

"The final two," Lorraine said with a twisted smile.

Babette rolled her eyes. "Was that supposed to be hard? There were only ever three of us." Venom dripped from her ruby lips, and she reached out and slapped Lorraine across the face. "Fuck you and your fucked-up family. Frances was the best of us."

Lorraine lunged at Babette, but Celestine stepped between them.

"I won't hesitate to hit you, too, girl," Lorraine said, balling her fist and moving it toward Celestine's face.

She shut her eyes tight, bracing for the pain and force of the punch, but nothing happened, and Celestine peeled an eye open, confusion littering her expression.

"Touch her, and I will lock you in a cage for five hundred years," Dean said, holding his mother's fist. "And I will let Everett...and James torture you."

Lorraine's face turned a shade of deep crimson, but she said nothing else, lowering her hand.

A silence soaked the space between them like the ocean waters in the north. Frozen and deadly.

But Irene cut through it and said to Celestine, "How are you still alive?

Lorraine crossed her arms. "Because she's our sons' little whore, and they will do anything to keep her alive in this game."

"Even I think that's too much," Babette said beneath her breath.

Dean seethed, his anger taking on a physical presence, causing the floor to shake between their feet, but he wasn't the only one angry. Fury also broiled in Celestine's blood.

Her jaw tight and hands curled, Celestine said, "I'm alive, because I am clever and not foolish enough to guess the riddle before I am beyond certain."

"And how is that going for you, girl?" Lorraine asked, a sickening amusement dancing on her face. "It doesn't even matter what I do. You'll die soon."

She was more right than she even knew, but Celestine rolled her shoulders back and refused to let this ancient and horrible woman intimidate her.

"Perhaps I will."

"Oh, this is so fun," Irene clapped and said in a high-pitched voice that sounded like a fork dragged across a plate. "It's been fun watching the others struggle, but I don't think you've struggled enough, little blondie."

"Yes, have you even been trying to solve your games?" Lorraine asked in a mocking voice. "It seems like you are merely a lazy, lowly whore who has no thoughts in her tiny little brain. You deserve to die."

Whore again? At the very least, be a bit more creative...

"That's en—" Celestine started, but Dean cut in, "Mother, you will—"

"No, you won't." Celestine stepped in front of Dean and pushed him out of her way. This was her fight, and Celestine would no longer cower. "I don't need you to rescue me, Phantom. I can do it on my own."

She faced Lorraine, her voice a noose preparing to strangle the other woman. "How dare you judge me. How dare you call me despicable things, and why? Because I am a penniless orphan? Because I wasn't born with money and power? It's not the seventeenth century anymore. Old money is waning and becoming irrelevant. Soon you will be just as powerless as me." Celestine shook her head. "And as for *your boys*, I flirt with them, and yes, I fuck them, because I can. It is my job to be a flirt...and they enjoy it. I am paid to be the pretty, desirable ingénue that women want to be and men want to fuck. It's all an act, and while I do have genuine feelings for your sons, and before tonight, I would have considered them friends, but after all this is over, I don't think I'll have even an ounce of feeling left for them. So don't worry, Lorraine, you will get everything you wanted, and this time, you didn't even have to kill anyone."

Celestine finished her speech with conviction, but her feet wobbled. The energy used had far overworked her. She took two wobbly steps and hit the table hard, using it to steady herself. Dean reached a hand out to steady her, but she shook him off.

"Get away from me." Her voice was raw. "I never want to see you again."

"Celine..."

Rage clawed at her back. "No, Dean," she said in a low, dark whisper. "Never call me that again. I hate you."

Her stomach twisted into knots, and she didn't know how to unravel them. It was all far too much. Anyone would have cracked under the pressure.

Irene clapped slowly and sarcastically, a taunting note in her voice. "Oh, the show is getting so delightful. Star-crossed lovers, a brutal breakup, and a betrayal."

Vivian stepped in front of her mother and glowered. "For once, Mother, can you just stay out of it?"

"But this is why we came!"

James interrupted the display by clicking a knife against his wine glass. "As is our family tradition, shall we make a toast to our good fortune and wondrous show, which is about to meet its climax?"

Wine flutes filled with champagne appeared in every person's hand. Everett made his way to Babette's and Celestine's sides, but Celestine was still breathing too hard, her heart storming in her ears and her vision blurring in and out. She'd had too much excitement for a lifetime.

"Celeste, you need to sit," Everett said, forcing her into a chair. When he had her entirely sitting, his twin raised his wine flute into the air.

"To secrets," Dean said with a wicked smirk.

Everett nodded and raised his glass. "And lies." He tipped his glass into his mouth and downed the drink in one gulp before the toast was even over.

"And grand manipulations," James added.

Vivian raised her glass. "And this hell of a night being over."

Then every Ashbrook raised their glasses and clinked them together. Babette and Celestine shared a look of concern but raised their glasses to match the family. But before Celestine and Babette could drink, Everett stole the wine flutes from their fingertips and downed them both in quick succession.

When they stared at him with wide eyes, he merely shrugged and said, "What? I was thirsty." He winked.

Within a second of taking his third drink, Everett crumpled into a heap and was clumsily caught by Babette. "Fuck, you're heavy."

But he wasn't the only one who fell. All around them, every Ashbrook fell to the floor.

"Not again," Walter whined as his knees buckled and he fell to the floor.

Dean was the only Ashbrook left standing, because he hadn't sipped his drink yet. But his gaze tracked between them, and a sinister smile crept onto his face. "To Death." He held up his glass and gulped it down, his eyes locked on Celestine's. "Solve the riddle, dearest Celine."

And he, too, collapsed to the ground.

Babette lowered Everett to the floor and felt for his pulse. When she couldn't find it, she grew frantic and tried to listen for his breath. But nothing.

"He's dead. They're all dead."

The night was formed from chaos. Had the three Ashbrook brothers just poisoned their entire family? All three of them? Or just Dean? And why drink it himself?

Celestine sucked in a sharp breath and lifted herself weakly to stand vigil over them, but her legs were still jelly. Babette had Everett's head resting in her lap, and she was whispering a sweet lullaby, but it was unclear if she was whispering it to him or to help keep herself calm.

"Should we assume they are going to stay dead until we solve the show?" Babette asked, stroking Everett's dead hair.

"I have no idea." Celestine's gaze traveled over all of them. Bodies were strewn all throughout the Grand Ballroom, like a child's discarded toys. "Most of them have already died tonight and come back from the dead."

"Right." Babette let out a long-suffering sigh. "So, any ideas?"

"I say we just leave them."

Babette snorted. "They would deserve it."

"Yes." Celestine took three slow steps, but when she

couldn't make it any further, she sat in the middle of the room and crossed her legs. "I hate them."

"Sometimes I do, too."

Celestine was done, both physically and mentally. Her body could barely move anymore, so she stretched out, lay down, and stared at the ornate ceiling. A mural of a lion fighting a wolf was painted in heavy detail. It was unclear which of the two beasts was winning, and it wasn't just a battle of strength. It was also a battle of wits.

Celestine rubbed her temples. With being so close to the end, the poison was wreaking havoc in her body, and her heart was beating arrhythmically. She placed a hand on her chest, felt it, and counted the beats.

Beat.

Beat.

Beat.

But they were too far apart. Her heart was slowing.

Beat.

She was dying.

"So you're in love with Everett?" Celestine asked, her eyes staring at the sharp canines of the wolf.

"Yes," Babette said softly. "This kind of feels like the closest I've ever been to him." She combed his hair back lovingly. "But, unlike you, he'll only ever see me as a friend."

Celestine slid her fingers along the marble. "I don't think he likes me like that, nor do I like him that way. I don't think he allows himself to love anyone after Marguerite."

"Instead, he drowns himself in pleasures like drugs, boundless girls, and you..." The implication was that Celestine was fucking him. But she never had.

"Tonight is the first time I have ever even kissed Everett, and that is only because I was playing his long-lost murdered love."

Babette scoffed. "But you throw yourself all over him." Ah, and this was the actual reason why Babette hated her. "You're saying you've never fucked him?"

It was an offensive way of asking, but Celestine chose to ignore the insult. "It's my job to be desirable, and the only Ashbrook I've fucked is James."

"They're not all for your job," Babette said, "James is your lover—"

Celestine sat up to look at the other woman. "James and I have fun together. We both make good distractions. It's not any more than that."

"And Dean?"

God, Celestine didn't even know what Dean was to her. The love of her life? The end of it? He was the one she wanted with every ounce of her being, and the one she also wanted to murder with her own hands. If she were to strangle someone in real life, it would be him, but she'd never be successful. He was a wall of muscle. It would be like a mouse trying to crush a cat.

Dean Ashbrook was too much to put into words.

"He's…" she started, but nothing else came out. "He's my ruination."

Babette laughed. The sound was meek but filled with thick understanding. "That makes sense." She let out a huff. "You know, I always wished to be you."

"And I always wished we could be friends. You seemed so beautiful and fun. It was my deepest desire for a long time. And then…"

"And then?"

Celestine snorted. "You were wretched."

"I was." Her brown eyes were nearly black in the flickering of candlelight.

Celestine swallowed past the lump in her throat. "Then I stopped wanting to be your friend."

Babette placed Everett's head softly on the floor then shifted to sit up straighter, her eyes flicking to Celestine. "Do you still want to be my friend?"

Celestine traced the marble pattern with a finger. "Sadly, yes. I want impossible relationships."

"Then maybe we should try." Babette's voice was quiet and tentative.

"Truly?"

"Yes."

A piece inside Celestine's heart clicked into place. "Alright. We can try while I am still around." She rubbed her chest again, another shot of pain rushing through her system. "But I don't think I'll be here very long."

"You're leaving?" Babette's chestnut locks bounced as she cocked her head and examined the other woman.

"I can't stay here much longer."

Celestine felt as though she was swathed in sorrow, every regret she had ever had playing in her mind. Her eyes focused on the gilded pillars holding up the elaborate ballroom. Everything about the house was stunning and foul, and butterflies of grief stormed through her veins. Leaving was never easy. Change was a cage. Humans often disliked change because they valued stability and safety.

Change never felt that safe, at least not at first.

"We could start by solving this show," Celestine said.

Babette nodded. "Let's find the Specter."

"So, what do you have?"

"The evidence points to four and a half suspects for the show, but I know they all didn't do it." Babette's eyes landed once more on Everett.

"The boys, Irene, and Archibald," Celestine said as a confirmation.

Babette played with the lace of her skirt. "Earlier, I dusted the knife, shirts, and crossbow for prints, and it pulled all three of the Ashbrook brothers' prints...which isn't surprising, since Vivian was playing with the knife at the beginning of the show, and James and Everett touched it after." Babette paused, thoughts flowing through her brown irises. "So the real question is: Are we dealing with one murderer or multiple?"

Celestine curled her lower lip into her mouth. "Do you have the evidence?" Celestine hadn't kept it. She'd tracked it in her head but hadn't gathered it and stored it to look at it again.

"Yes."

"Then let's go over it again."

Babette jumped up to get the evidence. Celestine tried to follow, but as she tried to stand, she still felt impossibly weak, so with a frustrated huff, she remained seated. She needed to save her energy, because she knew that, at some point, she would need to use all that she had left to run.

Babette motioned for her to sit and wait. Then she ran through different parts of the house and brought everything back, placing it in front of Celestine so she could see it all.

When she was finished, she had gathered the knife, two bloody shirts, one in green and one in blue—apparently, Babette had found the second bloody shirt earlier in the night —Archibald's tie, James's gun, and the crossbow.

"Should we dust for prints again?"

Celestine shook her head. "No, I trust your work. You are good at your job."

Babette's face lit up, but she tried to shake off her reaction, not wanting Celestine to see how much her words meant.

"But..." A thought sparked inside of Celestine.

At the beginning of the night, Everett had said, *"It wasn't me this time."* And Walter had said, *"Not again,"* when he died. And the entire night was about the Ashbrooks' secrets: secret murders, money problems, fraud, and corporate accidents.

All pieces of evidence pointed to a different family member.

The tie: Archibald

The knife: Vivian, Everett, and James

The shirt: Dean

The gum: James

The lipstick: Irene

The only people who didn't have evidence pointing toward them were the cast, Jon, and Walter.

Perhaps Jon was only truly here for the food. Celestine laughed. Of course, he would be. Jon and Walter seemed to be the only members of the family who cared about the others. And Celestine didn't believe they had anything to do with the murder. But everyone else?

Did they all do it, like *Murder on the Orient Express*? After all, that was Dean's favorite Agatha Christie book.

But it didn't make sense.

She was missing something.

Celestine's brow furrowed as she remembered Babette's briefcase. The girl had been hiding it all night. "Babette, what was in your briefcase?"

"A lot of things. Love letters between your character and Everett. Proof that James was responsible for a train accident, information about the deaths of all of Dean's former fiancées. It was full of blackmail. My character was blackmailing the entire family."

Celestine rubbed her temples and thought.

Did the answer lie in their secrets? Why had both Babette's and Celestine's characters been so central to the secrets? It wasn't just to punish the Ashbrooks. Dean was more clever than that. His every action always had multiple purposes.

So, why all the secrets? Celestine went through them all again, and she landed once again on Marguerite. The entire night revolved around her and the murders of every Ashbrook bride.

For the first time in the whole night, Celestine wished Margot hadn't been exorcised from her brain.

The girl had all the answers.

The secrets lay with Marguerite.

But then Celestine suddenly remembered that she might already have the answers she needed: the fire, the letters—everything was connected, including her venture to Specter's rooms. Plus, Babette's blackmail would help create a full picture, too.

She needed to get the newspapers and letters. They had the answers from hundreds of years ago. But she still didn't have the energy to move. "Babette, can you do something for me?"

"Yes."

Celestine instructed Babette to go to her room to find the newspaper articles and also bring back her briefcase. Yes, Lorraine had ruined Celestine's room earlier, but after the attack, everything had returned mostly to normal, including all the books and papers strewn throughout the room. So, within minutes, Babette was back with all the newspapers and gossip sheets. They were all about the Ashbrooks' history. Babette's letters matched almost perfectly what Celestine had discovered in the North Wing.

Celestine's hands traced the letters and turned through them as she read aloud.

"Article 1: 1760 Duke of Breython maid found dead on Christmas Eve of an apparent suicide.

"Article 2: 1760 Marquess and twin heartbroken by Miss Margaret's death.

"Article 3: 1893 Business tycoon embroiled in scandal at the railroads. Should he be charged with murder for the train crash?

"Article 4: 1758 The Beast of Winter, Marquess Winterly, has another fiancée mysteriously disappear.

"Article 5: 1776 The Beast of Winter Sullies Lady.

"Article 7: 1810 Young Lady Breython is caught with a dead man in her bed, and a scandal ensues.

"Article 6: 1761 The Duke of Breython and his family were mysteriously poisoned on Christmas Eve during the annual house party. Thought to be dead, the family made a miraculous recovery and is all in good health and good spirits. It is still unclear who might be responsible for the poisonings, but some believe it is the vengeful spirit of Marguerite that comes back to haunt the family, as it is precisely one year since her demise."

All the articles related to one of the Ashbrooks' secrets that had played out over the night, even the last one. The family was poisoned.

As if summoned by her thought, the same old nursery rhyme began to play again. The marionette dolls were once more coming to life to sing the song.

Margret, Margret hanging down. It's cold this Winter's mourning. Too bad and oh so sad. You caused the Marquess's scorning.

Wait, the song was about death, but the rhyme got it wrong. The rhyme assumed that Dean was the one in love with Margot, but what if it were Everett.

Winter and Marquess referred to Dean, and all the articles about the Beast of Winter referred to his dead lovers. But what if it was never Dean? What if everything was Everett all along...

What if all the girls who were murdered or died were also really tied to Everett and not Dean? They were twins...

What if everything was always Everett? Including Wolfsbane Hall.

Celestine tore through the love letters to better understand them. What if Everett was the true murderer tonight and his brothers had helped cover it up like they always had?

If the answer to the murder led to the Specter, then it had to be Everett, because they knew James wasn't the Specter. After all, Frances had died, and Dean was the Phantom...

So, the Specter was Everett, and perhaps the letters from Babette's briefcase contained the truth.

She flipped through them quickly again, skimming and finding pertinent information.

Letter 1 was useless.

My Dearest M, it feels like ages since we've been together. My heart aches without your touch and your sweet smile...

She skimmed the rest, but there was nothing of great note. Celestine flipped to the following letter.

My Dearest E, I cannot bear this separation...

Celestine flipped the page again and again until she stopped on:

My Dearest M, I found the apothecary you suggested. It was filled with all manner of mystical objects. You may be right about the existence of the supernatural. I will write back when I have more information.

But he never wrote back. Because the date on the letter was three days before her death. The following letter was written to his mother.

Dear Mother, I will treat you in the same manner as you treated Marguerite. —Everett

Next letter:

Dear Mother, I have successfully turned your prized son and heir against you. —Everett.

Next letter:

Dearest Family, it ends tonight. I will have my vengeance. —Everett.

So Everett was the murderer.

Babette took the letters from her hands. Reading them, too. "It's Everett," she breathed. "It's always been Everett."

"Yes, but..." But it still didn't quite fit. Because too much happened for him to have managed it alone. Why use the arrow and the knife if it was just one killer?

Why was Dean covered in blood?

What was it that Archibald said earlier? *Dean was loyal to his brothers and would do anything for them. They were thick as thieves...*

So, did James and Dean help murder Lorraine, too? Are they Everett's accomplices?

Had they always been? Not just in covering up the deaths, but causing them, too? The bloody shirts, the crossbow, the knife, and the small, needle-sized prick at her neck. Three weapons. Three men being framed? It was damning evidence.

But the most obvious answer was usually the correct one.

They weren't all being framed. They were all the killers. Celestine closed her eyes and reimagined the murder.

The lights went out, Lorraine got into a confrontation with Archibald, and Irene came to his defense, at which point Lorraine slapped Irene and tore off Archibald's tie.

Then the men acted. Everett had stolen Vivian's knife during the scuffle, and James shot the crossbow. The twins either took turns with the knife, or maybe only Everett used it, and Dean stood by as a sentry.

But it wasn't only the knife. The prick on Lorraine's neck. She'd been drugged, too. He was slowing her down during the fight. Then it slipped into place. When Dean had hugged his mother when she arrived, he lingered and slid his hand across her neck. He'd drugged her and stabbed her.

The noises, the evidence, everything made sense with that sequence of events.

"No," Celestine said slowly. "It was all three of them."

As each word left her mouth, the click of a gear turned. Magic filled the room—an enchantment laced into the walls, the floor, and even into Celestine's very cells.

A full-body shiver stole over her body, and memories soaked into the room, playing out like a silent picture show. It was a ghostly image playing as if on a projector, like the new movie in theaters, *The Wizard of Oz*. Just like that movie, this one had color and sound.

It was a dark and stormy London night in 1761. The three Ashbrook brothers were walking down a street in Covent Garden.

Dean faced his brothers. "Are you two sure we want to do this?"

James shrugged, his typical nonchalance twirling on his face. "They killed Marguerite. They deserve our vengeance."

"Right," Dean scoffed. "And this idea of yours has nothing to do with the fact that they are withholding your inheritance because you want to invest in that mechanical thing."

"It's called a steam engine, and it is the way of the future." James checked his pocket watch. Clicking it open and closed a couple of times in a perfect rhythm.

"The future, Dean. How can you argue with that?" Everett flashed his signature honey-sweet smile, just as false then as it was now.

"Are you sure this woman is not a witch?" Dean asked. "Witches are dangerous; we know that. We don't want a repeat of what happened with Great-Grandmother." Young Dean was brighter and had more energy. He wasn't the broken, dark, brooding man he had become, but he was still the exceedingly responsible one.

"Perhaps a witch is exactly what we need," Everett said. "We should curse our mother. Curse them all."

"Witches don't exist." James shook his head.

"You and I both know they do." Everett glared at his brother. "Great-Grandmother—"

"Was a fraud. Science exists." His voice was solid stone, stubborn and unbudging. This woman is just going to give us a concoction that will teach our parents a lesson."

As Dean opened the door, a bell shook above their heads, and they walked into an apothecary. Ivy laced the ceiling, and there were shelves and shelves of corked bottles. Weeds, herbs, and pastes lingered inside them. Books and gadgets rested on the shelves between bottles, from clocks ticking backward to butterflies trapped in jars and an actual barn owl staring at them, watching their every move.

On one shelf, a bottle glowed with red light. Dean shuddered and said under his breath, "Are you sure she isn't a witch?"

"Ah, the lordlings." The Herbalist smiled with a thick knowing, her eyes cutting through all of them. The stare was so jarring that all three men shifted on their feet uncomfortably as they flicked their eyes to each other for support.

"She is expecting us?" Everett mouthed to Dean.

The Herbalist shimmied her shoulders. "Of course I am, Lord Breython. Your brother told me you wanted to kill your parents for murdering your wife."

Everett's head snapped to James. "You told her that?"

"Not at first." He held out his arms as in surrender. "That came up after many, many conversations...don't worry, I trust her."

The Herbalist shifted a couple of bottles behind her desk before she walked out and met the men in the middle of the room. "We have a better plan for your parents. They can be more useful alive, especially with where your bloodline stems from." She said the last bit under her breath, and a snake of anxiety climbed the rungs of Dean's ribcage. "Besides, they deserve torment for what they did. Death is too easy."

Everett raised a wary eyebrow. "What will we do instead?"

"You're going to poison them with this." She turned on her heel

and walked to the corner, where she lifted a large red jar filled with liquid. Then she walked and placed it on the counter.

A shiver ran through Dean. He knew that jar was not in any way good.

The Herbalist—or witch—confirmed his suspicions when she said, "It will cause them to go into a coma, in which they will experience your torment. But you must ensure you also take the elixir, or it won't work."

Dean did not like any of it. The woman was dangerous. She was not their salvation or their solution. She was darkness. He could sense it clinging to her skin and caking her pores.

"Why?" he asked, crossing his arms.

The witch met his defiance with strength, staring him directly in the eye. "Because the magic requires an anchor—and puppet master, which you three will act as."

"Magic?" Dean turned to his brother. "James, I think she is a witch."

Everett nodded. "She's definitely a witch."

"I am beginning to believe it as well," James said, examining the jar, but he didn't seem horrified like Dean. No, he was intrigued. There was something deeply wrong with him.

The witch cackled and smiled as if this was the most obvious thing in the world. "Make sure you all get a large portion of the potion. It won't work in small doses. I wish it did."

The vision shifted, and the men were at a ball with their family. Skirts twirled through the room in a choreographed waltz. The rich elite laughed and danced, soaking up the atmosphere. Wallflowers stood at the side of the room, their eyes tracking eligible gentlemen as they hoped they might walk up to them and ask for a spot on their dance card.

The horror that happened next played out much like the one had in the present day. There was a toast, and the family collapsed.

The scene shifted, and they were all in a hospital. The men were *the first to wake, and their nurse was the Herbalist from the apothecary.*

"Good morning, little lordlings."

"What did you do to us?" James asked, his voice scratchy. His hands traced over his body, patting his arms, chest, and legs, making sure they were solid, because something felt utterly off—wrong. It was as if he were both solid and translucent at the same time.

He wasn't corporeal anymore. Not really. It was something in between life and death. But he also wasn't a ghost.

He was alive but also dead.

Dean rubbed his hands over his face, and in the process, he blinked out of existence, his body turning spectral.

"What the fuck?" Everett whispered. "What are you?"

"A witch." The Herbalist's face stretched into a crooked and rotting smile. "And not all at the same time."

Dean reappeared and leaned over to James, muttering, "I think witches do exist, James," continuing their conversation from before they entered the apothecary.

James nodded his response. "I think it's a strong possibility, yes."

"What have you done to us?" Dean glowered at the witch, his expression murderous.

She shrugged in a self-satisfied manner. "I've made you into immortal creatures known as Specters. Part human, part witch, part ghost. Both alive and dead, with some useful magic And since your ancestors were once witches, you will be the most powerful Specters in existence."

"We're what?" Everett gulped. "What powers?"

Her nose wrinkled. "You'll find out." She cracked her neck. "Just be happy we didn't make you into vampires. Vile creatures, those."

"Vampires?" Everett asked, fear coating his voice.

Dean balled his hands into fists. "Why do it?"

She laughed, a deep and sinister sound, her eyes turning black. "Because rich lordlings will be useful to us." Amusement lit up her face. "Your magic feeds off manipulation, which shouldn't be hard for young lordlings like yourself. But be wary, because if you go without manipulating someone for too long, you will cease to exist and die."

James cocked his head, fairly certain the witch was lying about something, but he didn't know what it was.

# 30

The vision cleared, and intense pain shot up Celestine's jaw and radiated out through her arm. She clutched her chest, knowing the pain was coming from her heart. *Her time was up*.

But she needed to fight through the pain and the weakness. She had one last riddle to solve, and now she understood it all. She knew the answer but wanted to see their faces as she solved it and left them.

Groggily, the family started to wake, their movements stiff and slow. Death still clung to their bones.

The Murder Mystery Game was officially solved, but it was not over. Everett, James, and Dean had murdered their mother together, almost as if they were one person. Although they weren't, they were still three cruel men with their dramas and schemes.

The game tonight was like multiple Agatha Christie novels, both *Murder on the Orient Express* and *And Then There Were None*.

But the show wasn't over. There was still the dénouement.

Still, eleven minutes left of the show and to give the final answer. Babette and Celestine had to unmask the Specter. Eleven minutes left to live and solve the final riddle.

That didn't seem as easy as it appeared. She thought the answer to the Murder Show would be the same as the identity of the Specter. But Celestine thought there was only one Specter. So, was she wrong? All three brothers worked together to murder Lorraine, but Dean was the Phantom, and James wasn't the correct answer. Right?

Celestine thought that was right, but then everything in the show was so fucked up and cursed that she didn't even know what was real anymore. She'd thought she'd had the answer many times before, but then she'd been wrong. There was a reason no one had unmasked the Specter before.

One Specter.

One name.

One answer.

Right?

It seemed so obvious. Dean and James had helped Everett with his revenge in the past. They had helped him murder his family and make them pay. They had always been his accomplices. They were now, too, but Everett was the Specter.

It was the only thing that made sense.

There had always been a Phantom and a Specter during the whole time that Celestine lived in Wolfsbane Hall. All the inconsistencies between them made sense. The game Specter and post-game versions were vastly different creatures because they were. The version of the Specter after the show was calm, caring, and stable. Because he wasn't the Specter at all, he was the Phantom.

So the Specter was Everett, but there was only one way to know for sure.

Shakily, Celestine placed her palms on the floor and tried

to lift herself up. She managed to do it slowly and with a lot of effort, but she needed to do this.

Celestine leaned down and grabbed the knife from the evidence pile, and with unsteady steps, she walked over Everett, painful step by painful step, each footfall sending a jolt of pain through her body.

Once she finally made it there, she reached out and pricked his arm with the knife and dipped her finger into his blood, placing it on her tongue.

"Ouch, why the hostility, doll?" Everett flashed her a withering glare.

Celestine stepped back as if slapped. His blood tasted like cherry wine and chocolate, the main taste of the Specter's elixir, especially on the nights when the shows were the flashiest.

The Specter's elixir.

Everett was the Specter.

Babette must also have reached a conclusion, because she whispered, with alarm lacing her soft alto voice, "It's you."

A tear ran down her face, and she wiped it away quickly with the back of her hand. Apparently, she didn't love the fact that she was in love with the Specter. But she was in love with the Specter, and Celestine was in love with the Phantom...

They really had chosen the wrong men.

And, of course, it had to be twins.

So stereotypical.

Babette glowered at Everett, a kaleidoscope of emotions playing across her face. She worked her hands in the skirts of her dress as she just stared at him. "How could it be you?" But she hesitated for a moment before saying it out loud and finishing the game.

Celestine let the other woman have this moment, because she hadn't needed to be the winner. She didn't care about being the one to solve the puzzles. She never had; she just happened to be the cast member who solved most of the Specter mysteries during her tenure.

As Babette opened her mouth, Celestine clutched her chest once more, and she realized something was terribly off—a dark feeling churned in her stomach.

"Wait," Celestine started, "Don't say—"

But she was too late because, to the entire room, Babette announced with extreme confidence, "Mr. Phantom, my answer to your riddle is: *The Specter is Everett.*"

Pain gnawed at Celestine's bones, and the answer to why something felt wrong hit her.

It was the elixir.

When Celestine murdered James, the elixir tasted of champagne and raspberries. Not cherry wine. Every time James was the murder victim, the elixir tasted of champagne.

Babette was wrong.

Celestine gasped.

Shit. Shit. Shit.

Babette clutched her head and let out a guttural scream. Blood dripped from her mouth, eyes, and ears. She stared at Everett, her eyes wide and glazed with confusion.

"No," Everett said in a low baritone, and he stepped forward, catching her falling body, cradling her in his arms. He fell to his knees and held her, stroking her hair as she choked on her blood. "Shhh, you're going to be okay. It's going to be okay." He pulled her body into his chest, and tears cut down his face.

Celestine watched on in shock, the large grandfather clock ticking the time away, haunting her with the last minutes of her life.

There were only seven minutes left.

But Celestine didn't even care about that, because the

scene was horrific. There was no right answer as to who the Specter was. It had been a trick question the entire time.

There was never one answer.

There were *three*.

Three fucking Specters. But Celestine wanted to confirm it before she said it out loud. Pivoting around, Celestine sucked in a breath and called upon all her remaining energy. She picked up James's gun off the floor and slowly trudged to her room.

The pain of each step caused pained tears to skate down her face. In the corner of her room was her nightstand, which held her stockpile of elixirs. She swung open the glass cabinet and sifted through the elixirs. She brought several up to her lips.

Her body gave out, and she fell to her knees, her broken heart pounding monstrously in her ears. Her fingers shook as she grasped the vial from November fifth and took a sip.

Champagne and raspberries.

Fuck.

That was one.

She turned to September seventeenth. It had been a special show that was more subdued and mental, more like a chess game than all the pomp and circumstance of the usual shows. She took a swig.

Orange liqueur and coconut.

Two.

Then she randomly selected four more. All tasted like cherry wine, figs, and chocolate.

Three.

Three fucking Specters.

And she even knew which was which. It was so evident to her now.

Everett was the Specter responsible for designing the

cherry wine shows. They were always flashy and over the top —a large production. The nights when James played the murder victim, he was in charge of the show, and while Dean so rarely put on the show, he still sometimes did.

But they didn't take days off. It wasn't like Everett was the Specter one night, Dean the next, then James. No, they were all the Specter, every night. But they just showed up differently. She saw it all now. She'd known them so well and always found it funny how the Specter communicated so differently in different situations and moments.

It was so obvious now.

James was the shadow and smoke Specter, which fit his methodical and careful personality. Everett was the Specter in mirrors, the one puppeting paintings and objects. He was the flashiest and had the biggest personality.

And Dean?

Dean was the floating voice. He was simple and understated, and he only showed up when people were at their greatest need. He was the helper, and they were the puppet masters, yet he was also the mastermind behind it all. He was the storyteller of the three.

Well, fuck.

An anger like no other burst through Celestine's chest, and she threw the vials against the wall. The glass shattered, painting the room with the liquid. She didn't stop until she had destroyed every single one. She didn't stop until she had eradicated them from her life.

She was fury made manifest.

And in that fury, she devised a plan. She would finally live her life on her terms, outside of the manipulation of Wolfsbane Hall and its wretched inhabitants.

She inhaled sharply and pooled all her energy. Then she

stormed back into the ballroom, James's gun in her hand, checking the bullets. Five.

Perfect.

She kicked her shoes off so that her skin would have direct contact with the floor. She wasn't sure if the house would answer her call because it was a manifestation of the Specters' magic, but she wanted to try.

Trap them.

From the floor, three wooden pillars and snake-like ropes sprang and flew through the room, circling their bodies and tying each of the Specters to their pillar.

Did one of them allow it? Or did the house have its own personality sometimes?

The rest of the Ashbrooks watched on in utter fascination. If they wanted a show, she would give them one.

It didn't matter. Celestine didn't have time to find out.

"Save her." She motioned with the gun at Babette. "You're immortals. Bring her back to life."

"If you answer the riddle correctly, you can save her," Everett said.

But Celestine didn't want to answer the riddle. This was her one act of rebellion. She wouldn't let them win their bets— their death pools. She wouldn't let them get away with their vile games.

The riddle would go unsolved forever, but she would save her friends and family—Babette and Frances.

Celestine cocked her pistol. "I said, save her."

"Cellie, my love, just answer the riddle." James's voice was as soft and to the point.

Celestine shook her head. She pointed the gun at James and pulled the trigger. The bullet tore through his chest.

"We can't die, Celine." Dean's eyebrows drew together, and

he looked at her like he wanted to hold her close and protect her, which she hated.

"No, but I bet that hurt."

"It does," James wheezed, blood dripping from his mouth.

"Save her." Celestine motioned with the gun to Babette once more. "And save Frances, too."

Everett's lips fell into a hard line. "Cece, that's not how this game works."

"Do I look like I care?" She shifted the gun to Everett and pulled the trigger. "This is how *my* game works." Her violent gaze shifted to Dean. "Do you want to get shot, too?"

"No." He sighed, his eyes sparking with sorrow. "If we do this, they will not thank you for it. She will probably hate you for all eternity."

Celestine's nostrils flared. "So be it."

"You'll have to release me."

Celestine swallowed and tilted her head in acknowledgment. "Promise, you'll only save them."

"I promise."

Celestine curled her toes into the floor. "Wolfsbane, release Dean."

Dean got up and moved to Babette. With his eyes locked on Celestine, he asked, "Are you sure?"

"Yes."

Dean cut open his wrist and forced his blood—his undiluted elixir—into Babette's mouth, but when he was finished, the brunette didn't wake up. Her body still had no sign of life or movement. Dean cupped Babette's face and whispered an incantation that Celestine didn't recognize. But Babette still didn't wake.

"What's wrong?" Celestine asked, holding the gun up, readying to shoot Dean, too.

"Nothing." Everett coughed up blood. "It takes time to work. "Death takes time to shift."

Dean left the room and presumably did the same thing to Frances. While Dean was out of the room, she watched as the other two brothers' wounds knit back together in front of her eyes within minutes. It was good to know that she could affect them and cause them pain, but only for minutes.

If she shot them in the head, would it take longer to heal?

She didn't have time to investigate that.

She didn't have time for much else, certainly not enough time to see if Babette and Frances would return to life. She'd just have to go on faith.

Celestine was finally going to value herself above everyone else. She was finally going to do what she wanted, and she wanted to leave and never see another Ashbrook again for the rest of her life. There was no energy left in her body, but she managed to get it to do what she wanted. Without stopping to grab anything, Celestine moved to leave.

She paused in front of James's open wound, pressed her finger into it, and placed the blood into her mouth. She wanted one final confirmation.

It tasted of champagne and raspberries.

Then she left, walking into the Grand Hall and opening the massive double doors at the main entrance. She placed her forehead on the door and rested for a moment.

"Goodbye, Wolfsbane."

Then she squared her shoulders and walked out the door.

Her dress was splattered with blood, and her hair was in disarray. But she was leaving.

For good.

It was the last choice she would make in her short life.

INTERLUDE

Sunday, August 17, 1930
Civic Auditorium - The Opera House
San Francisco, California

Failure tasted like heartbreak, raw and rotten.

Celestine hadn't lost everything after her family's massacre. She had a trust fund and a lecherous male guardian, who had fortunately never managed to touch her thanks to his godsend of a wife. She was gorgeous, glamorous, and protective of young, broken things—probably because she was twenty years younger than her husband. But unfortunately, the wretched husband had lost all their money and Celestine's entire trust on Black Tuesday during the Wall Street crash. Everything was gone in a moment. One small moment changed the fate of their lives and forced them out of their Pacific Heights mansion and onto the treacherous streets of San Francisco. Celestine's guardian lasted a day before blowing his brains out. He couldn't handle being poor.

His wife fared far better, but Celestine lost track of her after three months.

And Celestine...managed. Mostly stealing and hiding. Big

mansions had a lot of empty rooms, and some even had attics that hadn't been opened in years.

But Celestine was sick of hiding, sick of suffering, and worst of all, she was sick of begging. The Opera was supposed to be her ticket out—her way of making money with so few talents.

"Try again next year," the Director said. "You have many of the basics there."

"Thank you." Her voice was soft and hollow. There likely wouldn't be a next year.

Celestine stepped down the stairs, leaving the light, and the darkness slid over her porcelain face, cloaking it and her tears. Slowly, step by step, she moved up the aisle, the next soprano's hopeful song underscoring the devastation coating the chambers of Celestine's heart.

Too consumed by her plight, she completely missed the tall stranger in the top hat who now stood at the end of the aisle, blocking her path.

Her eyes tracked up seconds before crashing into him, and she jolted to a halt, her ankle slightly twisting. Shit. It hurt.

The man reached out, and his firm hands landed on her shoulders, steadying her. A shiver laced through her spine as her eyes tracked his face.

It was veiled in shadows. Entirely in shadows, and Celestine was unsure if she was hallucinating them or if her tears were so consuming she could no longer see straight.

"The Opera directors are fools." The color of his voice was dark, like his shadows. The tone was deep and rich, like a bass singer. "No one should ever let a girl like you slip through their fingers."

"I... What?" Celestine was too dumbfounded to respond.

He cocked his head like a bird of prey. "I have uses for a girl like you. An opportunity far rarer than the Opera."

With a slick, fluid movement, he removed his hands from her shoulders and slid the left one into the inside pocket of his suit jacket. Then he smoothly pulled out an envelope and held it out to her.

Celestine sucked in sharply, her eyes tracing down to what looked like an invitation. The paper was glazed with gold filigree and looping designs.

Hesitantly, she pinched it between her fingers and tilted her head back up to meet his darkness.

She could have sworn he smiled underneath his shadowy veil, but she didn't get to study him more, because he turned on his heel and sauntered out.

But just before the exit, he turned and said, "I hope to see you there, sweet Celine."

She shuddered.

How the fuck did he know her name...or at least a version of it?

Celestine swallowed hard and stared down at the paper.

Slowly, reverently, she peeled open the envelope and slid out the invasion.

Welcome, gorgeous ingénue, to your next adventure.
WOLFSBANE HALL.

Celestine only had three minutes left to live.

She didn't have a plan. What plan was there when one only had minutes to live? The extent of hers was hobbling down the steep San Francisco street with no shoes on and a blood-soaked dress.

If Celestine were going to die, she would do so far away from them. It was her life's curse that she would die on her own with no one to care about her. She'd known this would be her fate since her diagnosis, but it still hurt to know it was true. Perhaps she had manifested it into reality.

She sucked in a tortured breath, her heart beating lethargically. It was finally giving up on her.

But then, it had been giving up on her for years. She had known this day would come.

All Celestine had ever wanted in life was to be loved, to be chosen, and not abandoned. All she wanted was to be wanted. But this dream—for it was only a dream—had caused her to accept terrible circumstances.

She'd been so recklessly loyal that she allowed the Specter and the Phantom to treat her abominably for nine years.

Torturing her, forcing her to murder, making her into a puppet of seduction at the whims of rich, lecherous men, and turning her into a meek little mouse who refused to stand up for herself.

But no longer.

Celestine was choosing herself, even if it meant she'd only live for a few more minutes.

Swallowing, she looked out at the glittering bay. The lights danced down the rolling hills of San Francisco, Coit Tower standing tall on Telegraph Hill, and Alcatraz cutting through the ocean and fog in the distance.

The city was formed from magic, and its beauty was so breathtaking that it was sometimes hard to catch one's breath. With how much time she spent locked in Wolfsbane during the nightly shows, it was sometimes easy to forget the serenity and perfection resting right outside the mansion's sinister doors.

Celestine closed her eyes and let the icy breeze skim her face and stroke her hair, blowing it behind her, the strands twisting and dancing. The wind howled a wicked song, and sailboat rigging clinked against masts, each ding sending a jolt through her. Seagulls cawed at the night sky, flying over the brick-and-mortar shops, searching for food scraps. Sea lions barked at the frigid wind. It all created a symphony of sound that warmed Celestine's soul.

It was a beautiful city in which to die.

"Celine!"

Celestine pinched her eyes tighter closed at the sound of her favorite nickname, uttered by the one she both loved and despised.

Tears prickled at the back of her eyes. She didn't want to care for him, but it was impossible not to. She would never be able to keep him, he also would never be able to keep her, but the nights they spent together talking were the best moments of her life.

She had always been dying.

Celestine always only had limited time with him, and as much as she hated him, she also loved him. He had been her rock, and for the last moments she had left, she would remember him. Her time with him would coat her mind as she took her last steps and last breaths.

And that hurt more than her terminal heart.

"Go away, Dean." It was a broken sob.

"I can't." He caught up to her and clutched her shoulders. "I can't let you die. I won't."

Her lips pinched together, and her cheeks ached from holding back all her emotions. "Tell me why."

"What?" His azure eyes were pleading.

"Why do all of this?" Devastation ate away at her stomach. "Why become the Phantom for one night? Why poison me and torture me on my last night to live?"

He didn't seem to understand her last words, because he ignored them and said, "Because you have to get away. This place, this family, will kill you..." He cupped her face, his fingers sliding through her hair. "I will kill you."

"You already have." Celestine wanted to fall into his touch, but she couldn't. She wouldn't allow it. It hurt too much.

"I am trying to save you from me." The light from the streetlights flickered in his eyes, highlighting the desperation lingering there.

"How noble of you," she spat out. Anger wasn't an emotion she'd felt that often until tonight. She didn't feel like it was a very useful one. Yet it was all she could focus on now. He'd stolen her peace. He'd stolen her peaceful last breaths. "Save me by destroying me?"

"You've met my family. My mother nearly killed you, and

she won't ever stop. She thinks she owns us, and she can't be killed. Ever." His thumb brushed her cheek. "Go to Hollywood, become the star you were always meant to be, and leave this…" He motioned to the city around him and back at Wolfsbane. "Leave me in your rearview mirror."

If only she could do that. But it was as impossible as Dean genuinely loving her. "I can't do that, even if I wanted to."

"Yes, you can." His whiskey-coated voice was hollow with fear. "All you have to do is answer the riddle." Dean knew she'd solved it but refused to say it. "Who is the Specter, Celine?"

"No. I won't say it."

"This isn't a game, Celine. You will stay dead."

"I know."

"And you would commit suicide like that?"

"I am not."

"Yes, you are. Answer the riddle," he begged. "Please."

Celestine shook her head, the movement causing her to feel dizzy, and Dean had to reach out and steady her.

"When, Dean?"

He scrunched his face.

"When? When would you like me to tell you who the Specter is? How about when I am looking into mirrors or talking to an animated painting? That's Everett. Or how about when he's the voice in the darkness or smoke? Then that would be James. And in my bedroom, after it's all over…or when I need the Specter the most, and he shows up as a hovering voice to help me?" Her voice cracked. "That's you, Dean."

Her forehead scrunched, the veins popping out from the anger, tears, and unending sorrow she was holding in her head.

There had been three elixirs. There had always been three Specters.

"There have always been three men who betrayed me," she

seethed. "There is no answer to this riddle, because it is all of you. Congratulations, you made an impossible game and killed your entire cast." She offered a slow, sarcastic clap. "Truly, congratulations."

She felt the poison leave her body, lifting from her like a wave. It was gone, but still destructive. It had already done its damage. It had already ravaged her sickly body.

A proud smile stretched on Dean's face. "It's like your favorite book. I thought you would enjoy the final solution."

He cupped her face again, his eyes measuring her reaction and the effect of the poison leaving her body. But his brow furrowed, because he instinctively understood something was wrong.

"I hate you, Dean." The pain was unbearable now, and hot, thick tears dripped down her face. "But mostly, I hate myself for loving you."

Celestine's knees buckled, and she fell down the street she'd just walked up, and Dean caught her in his arms. Blood trickled from between her blue lips, and she felt the color leaching from her face.

Celestine's secret had finally caught up to her.

The things she had never told anyone else were forcing her to pay up.

And Dean's machinations had sped up the process. The truth was that Celestine Sinclair had always been dying, long before she was ever poisoned.

She'd been dying long before she'd ever met the Specter. Celestine had a broken heart in far more ways than one.

EIGHT MONTHS AGO

The room was cold, bright, and uncomfortable. Celestine sat in her medical gown, waiting for the doctor to come in and update her on her prognosis. She'd been seeing Doctor Levi-Jones for the past eight years since passing out during a Wolfsbane Hall casino night. Dean had rushed her to the hospital, but since she was conscious again, she made sure the medical staff knew Dean wasn't related to her at all and that he didn't have permission to know anything about her medical records.

Celestine was born with a defective heart. She'd known about it for almost as long as she could remember anything. She wasn't allowed to play with the other kids because her parents were afraid that her heart could fail at any minute. They feared that physical activity and too many stressful emotions could kill her.

They tried to stifle her emotions. They tried to make her stoic and broody like Dean. But Celestine wasn't made for hiding anything away. She felt every emotion in a big fashion. She was waves breaking on the shore.

It didn't work, but she never really got to have fun with other kids or be a normal kid. So, she never learned to make friends. Everyone in her life had treated her like a fragile porcelain doll, and the Specter was no exception.

She'd begun to expect it of people.

So when she collapsed, she knew exactly why.

The doctor had given her three years to live back then, but she had made it eight, and possibly she would have made it eight more, but with the frequency of her lightheadedness, she highly doubted it.

She knew she was dying.

It was a matter of when, not if.

So when Doctor Levi-Jones walked in with his clipboard in hand, Celestine immediately asked, "How long?"

"If you're lucky? Six months," he said matter-of-factly.

Celestine tried to not cry in front of the doctor, but she'd never been good at holding it in. Tears spattered onto her hospital gown. It was so much sooner than she'd expected, even knowing since she was little that she would eventually die from her broken heart—her defective heart. She'd hoped she'd make it ten more years.

But that wasn't in her cards.

"What are the symptoms I am going to have?" she asked.

"You will start to experience shortness of breath, persistent coughing with white, pink, and sometimes red mucus, shortness of breath, dizziness and fatigue, nausea, swelling, lack of an appetite, and you may experience confusion and disorientation."

Celestine nodded, unable to give a full reply.

The doctor placed down his clipboard. "Get your affairs in order."

What affairs?

"Yes, sir."

INTERLUDE

Monday, November 5, 1939
St. Mary's Hospital

SIX DAYS AGO

Celestine wrung her hands. She knew the news she was about to receive would be devastating. She was persistently coughing up pink mucus. She liked to pretend it was the night when she had to be a murderer that affected her so much, but it wasn't.

She knew it was the end.

"How long?" she asked, raising her head as the doctor walked in.

"Two weeks at most."

32

Saturday, November 11, 1939
San Francisco Streets

She hated how much dying in Dean's arms meant to her. She hated how much it meant to her that she knew he was *her* Specter—the one she loved. The one she beat at chess and read to.

She hated how much he meant to her.

Celestine nestled her head into his shoulder as he held her limp body on the steep street. She tilted her chin up to see his beautiful and awful as she fell into the depths of death.

"What's wrong?" It was sweet how concerned his eyes were.

Her breaths were short and weak, and she found it incredibly difficult for her even to open her mouth to respond. Her surroundings were blurring together, and it was getting increasingly hard to remember where she was and what was happening.

Her eyes were drooping shut, and the process of trying to keep them open was arduous. "All I ever wanted was for the Specter to be proud of me."

"I am proud, Celine. You're the best player Wolfsbane Hall has ever had."

Her eyes glazed and filled with more tears. "All I've ever

wanted was to be loved and have someone mourn me...to be with me when I die. That all seems so foolish now."

Dean's eyebrows lowered, and darkness pooled into the edges of his eyes. "I don't understand. Why are you not better? You solved the riddle. You saved everyone. You shouldn't be dying."

It was a plea, forged from heartbreak.

"I was always dying." Her breaths rattled. "Will you hold me?" The request came out more as a whimper than words.

Dean pulled her closer into his chest, cradling and cuddling her like it was the last time he would ever touch her. "Celine, I have you," he breathed into her hair. "You're not alone. Never alone."

He had promised her she wouldn't die alone. He'd promised her that he would grieve her death.

She finally believed that might be true.

"At least I got one of my wishes—" Celestine's body went limp, and darkness stole her consciousness.

And her heart played its last beat, never to start up again.

"No, you're not supposed to die. The curse wasn't supposed to affect you, too." The words were only formed from torment. He rocked back and forth with her in his arms.

His voice was far away, like at the end of a long tunnel, and she didn't understand if she was experiencing this moment as a ghost or still in her body.

"No!" It was a wail. "I won't let you die."

He sobbed, distraught, pulling her into his arms and walking her back into the house.

And then there was nothing.

An empty blackness, and she couldn't have told anyone what happened next because she was dead. Truly and fully.

Her heart had failed her.

Sunday, November 12, 1939

Celestine's Bedroom

Death felt much like living. It felt like her cotton sheets, comfortable bed, and goose feather pillows. But death also felt like magic humming through her blood.

Celestine jolted awake, sitting upright like a vampire in a coffin. She swallowed and patted her chest and then her legs. She was flesh. She was alive... Sort of.

Because a vampire wasn't far off from what Celestine had become. A decaying scream crawled out of her throat. The hand she held before her eyes was slightly translucent.

She let out another scream, rolled her legs to the edge of the bed, and swung them onto the floor. A deep numbness settled over her body. And she no longer understood how to feel.

It was too much.

Betrayal.

Death.

Dying.

Resurrecting.

Immortality.

All too much, and she didn't know what to do. She was so confused. She'd never imagined she would be immortal. It wasn't even in the universe of possibilities for her.

So, how did one respond to it?

She didn't know.

But she knew one thing. She meant it when she had said she never wanted to see the Ashbrooks again. They had done too much. They were monsters in human flesh.

But did they even have human flesh? She didn't know.

So she packed. Celestine Sinclair wasn't staying. She couldn't look Dean in the face. After what he'd done, what they had all done, she couldn't look any of them in the face. Before, she was far too afraid to make it on her own. Too scared to leave Wolfsbane Hall, too afraid to abandon her home and her Specter. Or be abandoned by him for leaving.

But she didn't care anymore.

She'd been manipulated far too much and pushed too far.

Celestine was ready to die alone. Ready to leave the men in her rearview mirror.

Being immortal didn't change that.

She'd choose herself.

No one else would.

But just as she was about to leave, Dean appeared in front of her, his ghostly form hardening into flesh.

Celestine sucked in a breath, something inside of her cracking. She didn't want to see him. She just wanted to leave. She was formed from a glass sculpture and was splintering into a thousand small pieces.

He had shattered her.

Celestine didn't even know who she was anymore. She didn't know who she would be without him. He'd become her everything, and in many ways, he shaped her personality, and she was done.

She wanted freedom and to discover who she was without him.

But he was still her greatest weakness. So she dropped her bags and ran to him, jumping into his arms and placing a passionate kiss on his lips. The kiss said everything she couldn't say aloud. It begged him to love her and force her to stay. It punched him and kicked him for betraying her. It clawed at his back and yelled at him. It whispered secrets in his ears and told him how much it meant to her that he had held her in her last moments.

However, it also revealed to him how much she despised him.

Celestine wanted the moment to last forever. She never wanted to pull away, but she forced herself to, because she would never leave him if she didn't.

And he didn't deserve for her to stay.

Her lips left him, and she sucked in one last deep breath, breathing in his scent for one last time.

Oranges and masculinity.

Then she stepped back and said, "Don't come after me." She twisted out of his grasp and picked up her bags.

"The world of immortals is a dangerous place," he said in his dark, liquor tones.

"No more dangerous than you are."

With that, Celestine pushed open the grand double doors of Wolfsbane Hall once more and finally walked out into the sunlight. She closed her eyes for a moment and basked in the warmth. Basked in her freedom.

Without a glance back, she started down the steep hill and toward her future.

She had finally chosen herself.

BONUS CONTENT

Please note: this is a bonus excerpt from SWEET NIGHTMARES which releases on September 17, 2025. This book has not been proofread yet.

PROLOGUE:

Age 29.

Jane was born to die horrifically—just like her parents. So, she wasn't surprised to be looking death in the face. What *did* surprise her was whose face it was—and how much it destroyed her, knowing she had been so cruelly betrayed.

CHAPTER ONE

Age 21.

Jane Whitfield-Klein powdered her face, frantically trying

to fix the smears in her makeup that her *husband* had placed there just moments before.

Only five minutes remained until Jane would debut as the prima ballerina of the Queen's Royalle Ballet. The show was *Lover's Lost*, in which she played the maiden, Isadora, who would eventually fall in love with Death.

Death...

Jane often wished she had married Death. Sure, he was a villain, but he'd do anything for the Maiden: protect her, kill for her, and most importantly, truly love her.

All things Jane's husband would never do. No, he'd rather slap her across the face, ruining her makeup just moments before the biggest performance of her life. Leaving her to fix his mess.

And that was Jane's current task: making beauty from brokenness.

It felt impossible. Her eyes were sunken and purpled from extreme exhaustion and stress, her arms were littered with scratches and discoloration, and her face was hollow. But at the very least—this time—she didn't have black eyes. She hated it when she had to cover black eyes. Because the only thing that could do it successfully was Mirror Cosmetics— cursed makeup that could erase any blemish, at a cost. The wretched stuff came from mirror deals, and everyone knew even the smallest bargain with a Mirror God—also known as Bargainers—was dangerous.

But if cursed makeup would get her on the stage, then so be it.

Jane would accept the consequences, because her dreams were more important than her rotten husband, cursed objects, or gilded, wicked mirrors.

The dressing room door creaked open, and the stage manager peeked his head in. "Five minutes."

"Five minutes," Jane said, trying to keep her voice steady. The hardest part of having an abusive husband, besides the physical and emotional toll, was hiding it from everyone. It was one thing to be a victim. It was another thing entirely for the world to know about it, and Jane would never let the world know. No, she was the perfect, beautiful ballerina, for the world to place on a pedestal and admire.

A puppet on a string for the rich and powerful to prop up and maneuver the way they wanted.

Jane rubbed her face, her elbows on the vanity. Gulping in a large breath of air, she tried to calm herself and salvage the night, which in a matter of moments had gone from a beautiful dream to a decaying nightmare, worse than any Looking Glass nightmare from the most powerful and dangerous Mirror God in the city. This performance was supposed to be the greatest moment of her career, but it was completely soured by her circumstances. Honestly, Jane shouldn't have been surprised. Her life was one tragedy after another and yet, foolishly, she'd believed this night would be different.

It was the night of her dreams. Finally, her life would get better. She'd have the career she'd always wanted, the respect she deserved, the prestige and money that she'd use to file for divorce.

But Jane was a fool.

Her life never went to plan—not a single moment of it. When her parents died, she was forced to move into an orphanage. Then, at sixteen, said orphanage married her off to a *"wealthy"* merchant thirty years her senior.

It was supposed to make her life better.

But *shoulds* and *supposed-tos* were dangerous, and they never quite panned out.

Jane sighed, pushing her middle fingers against the pressure points where her nose met her eyes, then rubbing underneath them and finishing her path by circling her temples. She found this helped calm her anxiety, especially before a show.

With another deep breath, Jane stood up, placed a resolved smile on her face, and cracked her neck before leaving her dressing room and walking to the stage.

The lights dimmed, and a chorus of strings poured out from the orchestra pit, painting the room with sweet enchantment. Jane let the music wash over her as she waited for her cue. The Maiden didn't start off the ballet, so she had some time to acclimate, stretching her feet and getting ready to do her job. But more importantly, she had time to restore her love of dance.

Jane closed her eyes. The music swelled, lighting her core with excitement. Her circumstances didn't matter when the music hit. Nothing mattered. Only dance. Only peace. Only joy. Only the magic of storytelling through movement.

The music reached its crescendo and, like lightning, Jane opened her eyes and hit the stage with a volley of fast bourrée steps to the center. The stage was hers to fill with grace, elegance, and charm. As a ballerina, she was known for her soft, captivating lines and intense artistry. No other dancer in the company could match her acting skills—none could compare to the truth she brought in every movement. When people watched her dance, they lived a little, experiencing every emotion as the character did. They escaped into the story world and lived lives they could only imagine.

Jane breathed life into the story on the stage. She made the audience's soul sing, unlike any other dancer in the company —in the country, possibly even the world. That's just how good she was.

A young prodigy.

No mirror enchantment, no spell, and no false facade could compare.

People traveled from all over the world to watch her perform, and little girls dreamed of one day becoming famous like her.

If only they knew what her life was truly like, they'd never trade places. Because, like mirror deals, her talent and fame came with a hefty price.

Not all that glitters is gold... often, it is rancid at its core.

This ballet began with a difficult variation, followed by an even more challenging pas de deux, and concluded with a quick costume change. Jane had seven costume changes throughout the show, with four people assisting her in changing her headpieces, bodice, and tutu. Often, one of the four had to cut her out of a costume and then sew her into another because the fit had to be that precise.

But Jane loved her first variation because she danced alone in front of the invisible magic mirror at the Queen's Royalle Ballet. There was something so peaceful and calming about it, and every time she danced in front of it, she felt like she was finally home. It rested at the back of the stage, and—to her knowledge—only she could see it. Jane would have thought she was going crazy if she hadn't lived in New Swansea, the country of magic mirrors.

In New Swansea, hundreds of magic mirrors held trapped gods inside, and those gods used their magic through deals, trading information, wealth, prestige, and magic at terrible costs. People negotiated to improve their lives, but the bigger the ask, the bigger the cost and unintended, unknown consequences.

Jane wasn't old enough to have made a bargain yet. Citizens weren't allowed to trade until the age of twenty-three, and then they were required to make at least one deal, called their Mirror Rite. But people could take advantage of others' deals, and there was an entire economy built around them, like Jane's Mirror Cosmetics.

But even though she had never made a deal, the mirrors sang to her soul. They called to her, and sometimes they screamed at her to free them—like she would even know how. The Queen's Royalle Ballet's mirror was no different.

It sang soft melodies of joy and appeared to her when it wouldn't for anyone else, and it was for this precise reason she liked dancing alone to it on the stage. They shared a beautiful synergy.

\#

The show always ended too soon. If she could, she'd stay dancing forever. But her happiness never lasted. No, it was always temporary, and now she had to meet up with her husband, smile for reporters at the gala, and most likely endure *"celebration"* sex which involved her husband rutting on top of her as she pretended to enjoy his small, lackluster penis.

At least when he gave her to one of his debtors for a night, they usually had a bigger package. Jane had to look on the bright side of being a toy for men to use and abuse. It was the only way she survived it. And his debtors weren't *that* cruel to her. None of them cared about her pleasure, but at least most of them didn't hit her—some were even gentle. Her husband was neither kind nor gentle. He seemed to like painting her body with bruises.

The icy midwinter air sliced along her skin as she exited the back of the Ballet and headed first to bathe and then to the gala. Another bitterly cold night in a string of them. It didn't help that the streets of the Gold Quarter were literally made of metal. Not only were they slippery, they were also freezing.

The sweat-soaked strand of hair dangling from her bun hardened into an icicle within moments of being outside.

Not again. Jane groaned.

But her groan was quickly turned into a muffled scream as a man in a balaclava and gloves jumped out at her and covered her mouth with a slightly sweet-tasting rag.

Jane's knees buckled first before her eyes fluttered shut, and darkness enveloped her.

ALSO BY HAZEL ST. LEWIS

OTHER BOOKS IN THE GILDED MIRROR UNIVERSE

WOLFSBANE HALL

COURTING WAR

GILDED WICKED MIRRORS

SWEET NIGHTMARES

AUTHOR'S NOTE

As you may have noticed, I mentioned multiple Agatha
Christie novels in Wolfsbane Hall as a nod to Agatha's brilliance as a mystery writer and crafter of intricate plots and
characters. She was the Queen of Mystery in the 20th century.
Although when viewed from a modern lens, there are many,
many problematic aspects to Agatha's works. I choose to keep
these references in Wolfsbane Hall because my characters exist
in 1939, and if they were to be fans of any mystery writer, then
it would be Agatha.

Novels and Characters Mentioned:

And Then There Were None by Agatha Christie

Death on the Nile by Agatha Christie

Murder on the Orient Express by Agatha Christie

Hercule Poirot, created by Agatha Christie

I also used these books as foreshadowing. I chose every
single one of these books for a reason. I chose *And Then There
Were None* because all of the characters in that novel were ulti-

mately awful, and I'd like to think the same is mostly true of the characters in Wolfsbane.

I chose *Death on the Nile* primarily because of the vibes, but also for the aspects of betrayal laced into the narrative.

And finally, I chose *Murder on the Orient Express* because the answer to that particular riddle was that everyone did it, and it felt fitting considering who the Specter ended up being.

ACKNOWLEDGMENTS

First, I want to thank my readers. I am so beyond thankful I get to share my worlds and stories with you. I wanted to give a special shout-out to my earliest readers. I love you all so much!

Mom and Dad, thank you for everything. I also want to thank my siblings, Jennifer and PJ, and their spouses, Jace and Nichole.

Bacardi, Bella, and Loki, I love you so much it actually hurts me.

Joseph, Carina, and Aylin, thank you for teaching me true friendship and love. I love you much more than words can express, and since I suck at love letters, let me just dedicate Quinn and Giselle's ride-or-die friendship to all three of you!

Michelle, thank you so much for your continued support and love.

Jamye, Brittany, and Amanda, I could not publish without your constant support. I would barely be able to function without you three hiding things from me and lying to me when I am upset, and I love you so much for it! Truly, I am so thankful to have you three in my life.

Tory and Rie, you help me get through this crazy publishing world, and it means so much to me.

Ellie, this book would not exist without your support and guidance. I love you so much.

Giulia F. Wille, thank you so much for being the best artist a girl could ask for! You are so easy to work with, and you make collaborating fun and exciting! I love your work more than words can describe. This cover is beyond STUNNING. It is truly perfect. Cheers to all the future projects we work on together!

Chinelo, Michael, Carrie, Val, Sienna, Kristin, Dianna, Angela, Sarah (SK), Audrey, and Anni, thank you all so, so, so much! I could not make it through this rough industry without you. You all mean so much to me, and I am so lucky to have you in my life!

I couldn't mention everyone here, and I am sorry. I am so blessed because I have so many amazing people in my life (many not mentioned here). Thank you all!

Finally, I want to thank God for being there for me in all things. Thank you for giving me grace and love even when I don't deserve it. I have a beautiful, joyous life, and it's all because of you.

Love, Hazel

ABOUT THE AUTHOR

Hazel St. Lewis is a Northern California-based Fantasy Romance author. Diagnosed with dyslexia at a young age, she struggled to read and write, but fantasy stories inspired her to start storytelling. Unfortunately, now, she is a little too obsessed with Dracula (this will become important soon... wink, wink). When she isn't writing, she can be found playing with her hoard of cats (too many to count...it's a problem), singing songs to said cats—like Cinderella—or painting.

Facebook Group: Shadow Daddy Books, TikTok @hazelstlewis
    Instagram @hazelstlewis
    Email: Info@hazelstlewis.com
    Patreon: patreon.com/HazelStLewis

STAY IN TOUCH!

NEWSLETTER SIGN-UP

Sign up using the link below for Hazel's newsletter to be the first to receive exciting news, updates, and bonus content.
Newsletter Sign-up

FOLLOW ME:

Facebook Group: Shadow Daddy Books, TikTok @hazelstlewis, Instagram @hazelstlewis

JOIN MY PATREON:

Want to read books as I write them? Or see the covers early?
Join my Patreon here: patreon.com/HazelStLewis

PLEASE CONSIDER LEAVING A REVIEW!

If you enjoyed this book, please consider leaving a review. One of the best ways to support authors (especially new ones like me) is to leave a review!